About the author

Gina is a straight-talking Northerner with a penchant for slapstick comedy. She loves to go on adventures with her husband, drink gin with her girlfriends and spend her hard-earned cash on practical things like silver shoes and leopard print kaftans.

Gina's best qualities are laughing too loudly, telling jokes badly and filling awkward silences inappropriately.

Welcome to the family, dear reader. Make yourself comfortable and pour yourself a drink x

Champagne Backpacker

Best wishes,

Gina [illegible]

x

Gina Clock

Champagne Backpacker

Vanguard Press

VANGUARD PAPERBACK

A CIP catalogue record for this title is available from the British Library.

ISBN 978 1 784653 55 2

Vanguard Press is an imprint of
Pegasus Elliot MacKenzie Publishers Ltd.
www.pegasuspublishers.com

First Published in 2018

Vanguard Press
Sheraton House Castle Park
Cambridge England

Printed & Bound in Great Britain

Dedication

For my husband, the original Hot Breakfast Guy, this is for you. For making me the luckiest woman in the world. Without you, I'd have to laugh at my own jokes. I love you more than words can say.

For my parents, thank you, for everything, from the bottom of my heart. I love you.

And finally, for my girls, thank you for the inspiration!

Chapter One
I've Got Something to Tell You

When I told my friends that I was going travelling, I might as well have told them that I was dying.

I had emotional reunions, dinners where people would share their favourite memories of me, photobooks of 'the fun times', letters beginning 'this is the hardest letter I've ever had to write…' And then there was my family. When telling my parents that I had booked a one-way ticket to Australia, my Dad's response was: "You might as well have booked a one-way ticket to the moon; couldn't you have picked somewhere further? Shirley, tell her, this is absurd!"

I must admit, at first the shock value of telling people that I was leaving gave me a real buzz. I was actually doing something with my life. I, Louise Johnson, am going on an adventure. Then, when the reality started to dawn on me that I was travelling to the other side of the world by myself, I, too, joined in with the dying act. I started to savour my rush hour journey to work, relish the way that the cleaner always left my desk sticking out just enough to give me a fresh bruise every day, and became nostalgic about the local sandwich shop getting my regular order wrong every single time.

As far as big decisions go, this was pretty major for me. Allow me to paint you a small picture of myself: I am from a sleepy little village just outside of Manchester. I am an only child, but come from a massive family, you know the type, brassy and northern, all talk at the same time, no spatial awareness and no volume control. My family all have massive hearts but are not massive adventurers. If you trace our family history all the way back to the dark ages, we'd have still been in Manchester waiting for a pie and watching the footie. Telling my family that I was going to Australia by myself was as incomprehensible as telling them that I was learning to play the piano with my toes!

As the time for me to jet off was edging ever closer, I had checklists upon checklists of things to book, cancel or buy. Cancel UK account and open Ozzie account - check. Cancel gym membership - check. Buy flight socks (deep vein thrombosis is just as big a threat as terrorism whilst travelling) - check. Buy backpack (well, it's a case on wheels, I'm really not the type of girl to be carrying heavy things) - check. Pack make-up, heels, sandals, jeans for if it gets a little chilly (the myth that Australia doesn't get cold is exactly that), beach clothes, casual clothes, dressy clothes, toiletries - check, check, check. Captain, I am ready for take-off!

Chapter Two
Fasten Your Seatbelts, It's Going to Be a Bumpy Ride!

The only direct flights to Australia are from London airports, so, the night before take-off, my parents and I check into a hotel in Heathrow to be ready, bright and early, for my flight the following morning. I wasn't about to get a connecting flight from Manchester - guaranteed luggage loss; I'd worked too long and hard on getting the contents of my suitcase exactly right for that to happen!

We arrive at the airport with plenty of time for a good hearty brekky. Although I can hardly eat, I'm a complete bag of nerves. I'd really enjoyed telling people all about the adventure that I was about to embark on. I'd even gone to town embellishing the trip: "I'll probably learn how to surf in a couple of weeks, definitely go into the bush, make my own hut by hand. Probably adopt two or three koalas when I'm there." In reality, I was terrified. Will I even like Australia? Will I make friends? What if it's not for me and I want to come home after a week? I'll be branded a failure!

I manage to hold it together until the final moment that my parents left me at the gate. Being an only child, the bond with my parents is about as tight as you can get, therefore doing this completely alone gave me the distinct feeling of being ripped from the womb with a nurse handing me a bottle, telling me to figure out how to feed myself. Then the tears started to come. At first, they were the stingy tears that don't actually leave your eyes, but the closer I got to the gate, the more they turned from delicate, roll down your face tears to heavy, shoulder-heaving, nose running, sobs.

I was a big, red faced, blotchy mess. What's worse is my red blotchy face clearly made me a target for airport security. Some burly six-foot man strode towards me.

"Excuse me, miss, can you come with me?"

I have always been one of those people that annoying market researchers target on the street or the token weirdo on the bus starts chatting to – I seem to have one of those faces. They pull me to one side and empty the complete contents of my carry on, which includes a cuddly toy (yes, really), spare pants (you never know), aspirin (for the deep vein thrombosis), flight socks, tampons, lippy, roll on deodorant, face wipes, passport, boarding pass and Australian dollars. Whilst feeling up my undies and eyeballing my bear, they order me to step into a self-contained booth to give me an X-ray. After twenty minutes of rummaging around my person and my belongings, security was satisfied that I was neither a terrorist nor a drug mule and send me on my snotty nosed way.

I decide to head straight for my boarding gate. I cannot tell you how many times my name has been called over the airport tannoy whilst sitting in a bar with my girlfriends drinking margaritas, followed by the embarrassing walk down the aisle with everyone tutting at you for holding up their holiday departure. Not this time, this time I am going to be on time and ready for action. Boarding the plane, my phone was going into overdrive with last minute well-wishers sending me their love. One of the last messages I received was from my friend Tom. He told me to keep my eyes and my mind open. This is one piece of advice that I will always carry with me.

When I finally locate my seat, I'm relieved to see that I am sitting next to a girl my age. I had a vision of a fat guy falling asleep with his head on my shoulder. The 'fasten your seatbelt' sign lights up and the air stewards began their safety procedure. At this point, my mind goes completely blank. I am in sheer disbelief that I am actually on a plane travelling to the other side of the world by myself. The engines roar and off we go. I plug in my headphones and listen to 'Big Girls Don't Cry'.

As I am a female, I obviously find out the life history and inside leg measurements of the person sitting next to me within twenty minutes. Her name is Sally, she is twenty and moved to the UK a year ago to live with her boyfriend whom she had met whilst travelling. She wanted to stay in the UK but couldn't get a visa (funny, I thought they handed them out to anyone). We chatted for the majority of the journey, telling stories and sharing funnies. After three hours of sitting, my legs had gone pretty numb so I went for a little wander around the plane, doing the recommended funny leg exercises that make you look like you have to pee. I noticed a hot guy doing the same at the back of the plane, so I crazy-walked my way in his direction.

He's Ozzie and is going home after a few weeks' holiday in the UK. He told me all about his demanding work schedule and that it was the first holiday that he had managed to take in a year. He liked the UK as he could go 'under the radar' without getting recognised too much.

Hold up... Recognised? "For what?" I ask.

"Well, I'm an actor," he replies.

I nod in mutual understanding. "Ah, tough trade. I tried acting when I was in high school, got an A in Drama and thought I'd go all the way to the top, but at college, in the first class of Performing Arts, they asked me to pretend to be a shoe. Not my thing, really, I'm more about buying shoes than pretending to be one."

He nodded along, clearly understanding my struggle. When I took my seat, Sally said to me:

"I can't believe you were just chatting to that guy from Home and Away!"

Chapter Three
I've Arrived!

Thirteen hours of in-flight movies later, I finally arrive at Sydney International Airport. It's eight p.m. and the air is sticky hot. You know, the kind of air that gives you that crazy '80's frizzy hair? I make my way to passport control to get my visa stamped, where they move at the typical Ozzie pace, you know, horizontal. Half an hour later, I finally make it to baggage collection, where, of course, my case is the last to arrive on the carrousel, looking slightly battered and sorry for itself.

Before arriving in Oz, I had made contact with a company that pick you up from the airport, take you to a hostel and introduce you to a group that you spend the first week with. They take you on trips, show you the city and, most importantly, open bank accounts and sort out Medicare for you. All of the grown-up stuff that you know you should attend to yourself, but get side tracked by far more pressing considerations, such as; what colour bikini works best with a tan? The company had arranged for a contact to meet me outside of McDonald's at nine p.m. At 9.20pm a guy in his late twenties arrives. He chucks me and my battered bag into the truck and off we go.

We arrive at the hostel in the midst of a power cut; the place is decorated with remnants of dodgy shaped candles and travellers walking round holding lighters.

He takes me to the reception, where a surfer with matted dreadlocks greets me and checks me in. I drag my bag on wheels up four flights of stairs in the dark and feel my way around the ten-bed dorm, looking for a spare bed and some form of life. Being ten p.m. on a Saturday, everyone is out partying. So I am alone in the dark, on the other side of the world, in a damp smelling hostel. Ten minutes later, I am bordering on hysteria. What have I done? I can't do this, I'm not cut out for this travelling malarkey, I want to go home. After crying for a good thirty minutes, jet lag finally takes hold of me and pulls me into a fitful sleep.

At eight a.m., I am woken up by the sound of someone throwing up in the shared bathroom; must've been a good night. I step out of my bunk bed and introduce myself to the girls in the room.

"Hi, I'm Louise."

"Where are you from?" shouts a girl from the back of the room.

"Manchester," I reply.

"I thought I recognised your accent. I'm from Newcastle; want to come to the beach with us?"

And just like that, I had made friends and was off to the beach.

The girls, along with the sun, sea and sand, made everything feel a hundred times better. We were laughing and joking and comparing boob sizes by midday. We went to a traveller's bar for lunch and did the usual girl thing of finding out everything we needed to know about each other in ten minutes flat:

Hannah is from Newcastle; she has her first month of travelling under her belt and has five more to go. She is loving it, but is conflicted because she has left 'the love of her life' at home.

Danni is Irish and a wild party girl, she has all the war wounds and the stories to prove it. "Jesus, I don't even want to tell ye what happened with me and this fella last night!"

Felicity is, potentially, the poshest person I have ever met. She has come travelling because she has fallen in love with three guys and needed a bit of space to decide which is the one for her. Gin and cigarette in hand, she breathily says, "You know how it is, darling."

Tara and Clara are best friends from London. They are a complete double act and they do everything together, including live together, chain smoke together and "even finish each other's pissing sentences."

Felicity, Tara and Clara have also signed up for the group trips, they invite me to meet them for breakfast before our first trip to the zoo tomorrow.

Chapter Four
Organised Fun

At ten a.m., the girls and I fall into the room, cackling, loud and ready for some fun.

"Christ, we must have the wrong room," said Clara. "It's like a fricking morgue in here. Have we accidently stumbled into an AA meeting?"

She wasn't wrong; our laughter was greeted by twenty patchy sunburned faces looking glumly at us.

"Right," said the leader, whilst clapping his hands in a 'there's fun to be had' gesture. "This is going to be a fun-filled week! [Told you.] We have lots to look forward to: there is a visit to Sydney Zoo… [pause for effect] surf lessons, a trip to the Blue Mountains and we will finish the week with a route sixty-six party bus. It's going to be quite a week, hope you guys are as excited as we are!"

The group manages to muster as much excitement as one would reserve for a smear test.

Shuffling onto the coach, Clara says, "Here, girls, dump your water out of your bottles." She waves a bottle of vodka around. "I think I've found a way to make this week a bit more interesting!"

After getting over that initial paint stripping feeling that straight vodka gives you (who needs internal organs anyway), I've started to feel much chirpier about the group trip. We even manage to get a good old sing song going on the coach. I can't one hundred percent confirm there are other voices outside of the four of ours, but we are certainly having a good time!

Arriving at the zoo, the first image that we are greeted with is a shrine to Steve Irwin, followed by advice on how to avoid a sting from a sting ray. For example: don't attempt to *cuddle* a sting ray, don't try to *feed* it, don't *invade* its personal space and don't make *loud noises* or any *sudden movements*. Scratching off swimming with sting ray from the itinerary, we get the map out and decide which animals to see first. I've always wanted to hold a koala, so I convince the girls to start there.

"It bloody stinks!" said Felicity, doing her best to smile for the camera whilst the koala clawed the sun burned skin off her chest.

Next was Clara. "God. it does as well, it honestly smells like it's taken a giant shit."

As she hands the koala over to me, it does precisely that. Not cute little pellet droppings, oh no, big splodgy shit that goes all the way down the front of my white top! I'm not sure if you have ever covered yourself in shit in thirty-five-degree heat, but the smell starts to travel far and wide at a rapid rate. Of course, the girls find this beyond hilarious and promised to go to the gift shop to get me a new top just as soon as they'd live streamed my humiliation onto social media #koalapoop #poorloulou #lol.

To complete the humiliation the girls buy me the tackiest 'I love Australia Zoo' T-shirt they can find. I run into the loo to change, where a little girl kindly pointed out, "Mummy, that lady smells like poo poo." I quickly throw my top and what was left of my pride in the bin and run out to carry on with this 'fun-filled day'.

Chapter Five
Remain Calm!

Day two. Hungover and ungracefully squeezing ourselves into our wet suits, we are at the beach, learning how to surf.

"This trip has finally started looking up," said Felicity. "Check out the surf instructor!"

Hans, the blonde Swedish instructor sauntered over in our direction. "Hey, ladies, are you here to learn how to surf?"

Cue girly giggles and hair twirling.

"Follow me; we're going to start with you lying on your back on the beach."

"You could at least buy me a drink first!" I giggle to the girls.

We learn the basics; how to paddle lying down and how to jump onto your feet when a wave comes. On sand this seems pretty easy; how much harder can it be in the water?

In short, a lot harder. I got bashed around the head with the stupid board so many times, I'm pretty sure I have concussion.

Flailing around in the ocean. I hear, "Over here!"

I turn to see that Felicity has found a small lagoon where she is lying on her surf board, gently floating around. Ah that's way more my pace! On our boards, we lounge around, soaking in the sun and marking Hans out of ten.

"I'd say seven," said Felicity. "He could do with a bit more meat on his bones, I'd be scared of snapping him in half!"

"I agree, although I'd be more than happy to give it a try. Ha, ha, ha."

"Louise, don't move!" said Felicity as calmly as she could.

"Why, what's wrong?" I say, looking around, panic ridden.

"Stay absolutely still," she repeats calmly.

I look down to see a gigantic, moving black thing beneath us. "Oh my God, oh my God, is that a shark?"

"Don't. Move. An. Inch," she repeats, barely breathing.

"Don't move?" I scream. "It's a pissing shark! Oh God, I've peed myself, I'm peeing myself!"

"What? Stop peeing!" shouts Felicity. "Sharks are drawn to bodily fluids!"

"I can't!" I shout. "I'm scared!"

Felicity starts to signal the guys on the beach by doing a thrusting action for 'big shagging shark' that we were jokingly taught at the start of the session. Once the guys realise that we are not joking, they jump on a speed boat and slowly make their way over to us. By which point I have fluid coming out of every orifice; I'm peeing myself, hysterically crying and sweating so hard that the wetsuit has tightened making it hard to breathe.

"OK, guys," shouts Hans, "to a shark you resemble a seal; all they can see is the board, as the body, and your arms and legs. What you need to do is slowly move your arms and legs onto the board so that nothing is dangling over the edge."

OK, I can do this. Gingerly I pull myself onto the board, shaking and somehow still peeing. It feels like the ground is starting to shake when I realise that the shark is moving. As quick as a flash, the shark shoots below us and does a massive leap into the air, knocking us off our boards and into the water. I scrabble around, grabbing my board and trying to pull myself back up. When I glance up, I see this incredible whale shooting water out of its blowhole and gracefully swimming its way home, totally unaware of the hyperventilating humans it has left in its wake.

Hans pulls us onto the speedboat and whizzes us back to shore. The group runs over to us. "Oh my God, we thought you were goners, you were so brave!"

"I PEED myself!" I irrationally shout.

"It's OK," says Hans, laughing. "Come with me, I have something that will calm your nerves."

Hans hands Felicity and I a shot of whisky each. I knock mine back in one go, still shaking.

"Come on, I'll give you a lift back to the base," says Hans.

The situation is looking up after all! I wave the girls off and jump into the four by four with Hans, where he bombs along the sand dunes and whisks me to safety, like a regular James Bond.

We pull up back at the coach, where Hans leans over to me. "You did really well out there, you were very brave," he said, twirling my hair.

I giggle, but wait, what's that smell? As he gets closer, there's an overpowering musty smell. What is that? I realise, sadly, that it is him, and he is one of the great unwashed. Ah well, crush over. I say thanks for the lift and hop out to the girls, where they are waiting for a full lowdown.

Chapter Six
Do. Not. Run.

Day three of organised fun. The group are starting to loosen up. There are some real characters providing great entertainment.

Des is an East London wide boy, with all of the charm to match. I keep expecting him to open up his jacket with a row of fake Rolexes hanging down the inside.

Then there's Samantha; Sam is full on Girl Interrupted, mysteriously staring into space and deeply reflecting on every experience. We haven't got the heart to tell her that her make-up is channelling more Marilyn Manson than Angelina Jolie.

There's a bunch of girls who all look the same, with similar sounding names. I'm pretty sure they are Tiffany, Stephanie and… Epiphany? Anyway, they came away together and, from what I can tell, do pretty much *everything* together.

There's the token smelly kid who insists on wearing leather at thirty-five degrees. The talker, the whooper and the American who says 'like' and 'totally' every other word.

Next on the agenda is a hike up to the Blue Mountains. The hand-clapping, overexcited leader gathers us all together.

"OK, guys, [he claps his hands] another exciting day [I'm pretty sure he just did jazz hands]! Hope you have your wet wear and your hiking gear. Today is going to be quite the adventure! Before we go anywhere, I need to make you aware of some serious rules. Legislation has just been passed in downtown Sydney that states that you cannot run throughout the town, it is illegal. If you are caught running, you could be fined up to $200."

I turn to the girls. "He's not serious?"

"No, he can't be! Can he?" asked Tara.

"This feels like a bad joke!" scoffed Felicity.

"You run first," said Tara. "If you don't get busted, we'll all follow. Ha, ha, ha."

We clamber onto the bus and make our way up to the Blue Mountains. I'd like to report that the scenery is beautiful and the mountains are idyllic. However, it's pissing it down and the mountains are covered in fog.

"What a disgusting day for a hike!" said Felicity. "I've just had a pedicure done and only brought my flip-flops."

"How long do you think it will take us to get to the top?" asks Tara.

"It shouldn't take too long, hopefully the rain will pass, let's try and make the most of it," I reply, trying to bring some cheer to the situation.

It's safe to say that the rain didn't pass; it's raining so hard that it's turned into that sideways rain that makes you feel like you're getting slapped across the face. We hike for a good two hours, getting wetter and wetter and seeing less and less of the funny side. The chirpy leader didn't let the weather deter him, however. Oh no; he stopped at every strange-looking weed to give us the full, unedited history. God, I was so wet and bored.

"What's that over there?" shouts Clara through sloshy footsteps and crunchy Pac-a-macs.

Squinting, we could see a pub in the distance. Hurrah, we are saved. We shout to the over enthusiastic leader:

"Matt, there's a pub over there. Shall we have a little stop and see if the rain passes?"

Matt and the other equally enthusiastic climbers were clearly not as excited for the warm and dry as we were.

"Think of the view, the feeling of getting to the top…" Blah, blah.

OK, they can pick us up on the way back down.

Entering the pub made me feel strangely euphoric. I peel my soaking wet hair off my forehead, pour the stinky forest water out of my trainers and ask for their largest glass of white wine. Sitting in front of the fire was everything I had dreamed it would be.

Minutes turned to hours and glasses of wine turned to bottles before we realised that it was getting pretty dark outside.

"What time is it?" slurs Felicity.

"Six," hiccupped Tara.

"How long is it going to take them to get back down the mountain? What time did we get here?" I ask.

"Around two p.m.," says Tara.

"Excuse me!" I shout to the bar man. "How long do you think it will take to walk from here to the top of the mountain and back to here again?"

"Oh, a couple of hours, tops," he replies.

Oh God, we've been here for four hours. They must have forgotten us.

"Has anyone got annoying Matt's phone number?"

We all shake our heads at each other.

"We're going to have to navigate our own way back down the mountain!" says Felicity.

In a panic, Tara shouts, "But which way?"

"Well, down, I guess. Come on, girls, we need to go!"

Walking down a mountain in the pouring rain, in the dark, whilst drunk is not an idea I would suggest to anyone. Every shadow looks like an axe murderer. We're all massively jumpy and, apart from shrieking at the occasional branch, thinking it's a snake, no one has said anything in a little while, until Tara suddenly shouts:

"Guys, look! We're nearly at the bottom, there's the coach park sign!"

Cheers all round, we made it!

Then we realise that the coach park is empty.

"They've left us, left us to die at the bottom of a mountain!" shrieks Tara.

"Oh, don't be so dramatic, Tara, we're not going to die. Not yet, anyway. Let's try and find someone," chastises Felicity.

The rain is getting heavier; we can just about see.

"Look, a reception."

We splodge our way in, just as they are locking up.

"Sorry, the mountain is closed; you'll have to come back tomorrow," said a little old lady with her back to us, mopping the floor.

"Excuse me, we came here on an organised trip on the big blue coach that was parked in bay five. They have left without us. Do you have contact details for them?" I ask.

"No, sorry, girls, I don't. You're going to have to get a cab."

"How much is that going to cost?" asks Clara.

"About a hundred bucks," she replies. "To central Sydney anyway, any further will cost you more."

The mood in the cab was sombre.

"I'm going to kill that over-enthusiastic moron!" says Tara. "He's all perky about climbing up the mountain, but can't count how many people he has on his stupid bus!"

We pull into downtown Sydney and try to get our bearings. We ask a lady with a baby how to get back to Coogee.

"You need to jump on the number forty-two, there's one just pulled in over there," she replies.

"Quick, run!" shouts Felicity.

"Don't run! It's illegal, remember?" I shout.

So we quickly power shuffle over to the bus, arriving just in time to see it pull out.

"You should have made a run for it," says an old guy, leaning on his stick.

"We can't, it's illegal to run in central Sydney," I reply.

This set him off into hysterics. When he finally catches his breath, he says, "Flaming tourists."

Chapter Seven
Just Peachy!

You can safely say that the girls and I are not in the mood for any organised fun or hand clapping nonsense today. We want answers. How dare he leave us stranded up a mountain? Tara and I stomp our way over to the office to confront annoying Matt head on.

"Oh hey, girls, how are you?" he asks, annoyingly, as we stomp into the travel centre. "Wasn't yesterday just the best day, aren't you buzzed from all that fresh air?"

"Fresh air, my ass!" shouts Tara. "Where the hell were you? You left us stranded up a mountain."

"I'm sure I don't know what you're talking about," said Matt, looking around sheepishly.

"Maybe this will jog your memory," I said, slamming the $100 cab receipt onto his desk. "We'll take cash reimbursement."

Matt fumbled around, coming up with millions of excuses as to why he couldn't reimburse us. Then we see him clock a guy in a suit in the background.

"Maybe we'll tell your boss about your giant cock up!" I said, shouting loud enough for him to hear.

"No, no, no!" said Matt in hushed tones. "We're all grown-ups here, I'm sure we can come to some sort of arrangement?"

"Yeah, $100 in cash!" Tara responded.

"Well, I'm not sure I can do that," whimpered Matt.

"OK, $150!" I shouted.

"OK, OK, calm down. I'll get the cash."

Tara and I smiled at each other as he scurried off to the back of the office.

Matt arrived back just in time as his boss swanned over. He was all orange skin, gold chain and cheap suit, and he said, "Hey, ladies, how is your trip so far?"

We look over his shoulder to see Matt waving the $100 like a white flag of surrender.

"Just peachy," I said as Tara snatched the cash from Matt's grubby little hands.

"See you tonight!" shouted Matt. "Route sixty-six tour bus party. Yay!"

Chapter Eight
Queuing for the Lift

We spend the rest of the morning relaxing on the beach and starting to see the funny side of the stranded up a mountain experience.

"And then, we got to the bus park and it was completely empty!" recounts Clara.

The girls are finding our misfortune beyond hilarious.

"Anyway," says Danni, "onto important matters: what are you wearing tonight? It's a lumo party so I think we should go and get kitted out into some mega fluro gear. Fancy going shopping?"

There are a surprising amount of shops in Sydney that stock aluminous florescent outfits. I thought it must have been because of the amount of backpackers and full moon parties, but apparently it's the 'fashion' here.

"God, look at the size of my arse!" says Danni. "I'm sure it's multiplied ten times in the three weeks I've been here; must be all that dodgy 'goon' they pass off as wine."

"We're going to have to do some exercise!" I replied, squeezing my fat rolls in the mirror.

"I'm counting that Spanish guy I did last night as exercise!" Danni laughed. "Should have seen the marks on his back this morning; a few vodkas and I think I'm a fricking porn star, ha, ha, ha!"

Back at the hostel the girls had the dorm set up ready for a good night.

"Right girls, pre-game drinks are lined up over there," says Clara. "Every time anyone says 'lumo' or 'fat arse', they have to down two fingers."

It's safe to say that by the time we left two hours later, no one could remember what day it was or where we were going.

Boarding the bus, Danni spots one of the promo guys and, drunk, whispers, "Girls, check him out, I definitely would!"

Embarrassingly, he heard and struts his way over. "Evening, ladies, ready for a night you'll never forget?" He says this with a little wink in Danni's direction. "Vodka shots are at the back, here are your lumo head bands, wrist bands and whistles. Let's get the party started!"

The bus is decked out like a 70s porn star's boudoir. The seats are covered in crushed velvet animal print, there are day-glow beads hanging down separating off the back 'fun section', a stripper pole in the centre and a rotating DJ booth at the back. But hey, there was free booze flowing and cheesy tunes pumping!

The bus stops at ten bars and we have to do that horrible challenge where you drink your drinks in alphabetical order from A-Z. . Some people started with absinth; I chickened out and started with an Appletini. The night is going really well until we have our first man down at eleven p.m. Tara has somehow found herself having a little lie down on the back of the rotating DJ booth, projectile vomiting as she spins.

"Oh God, she's spraying everyone's ankles!" says Clara. "I'd better take her home. Have a good night, girls; see you tomorrow."

At three a.m., the rest of us stagger off the bus and stumble into the hostel.

"Oh my God, I am seriously going to die!" hiccups Felicity. "Why is the room spinning so bad?"

We were hammered; you know that kind of drunk where you have to hold onto the floor because it won't stop spinning?

"Oh God, I'm going to be sick!" I just about make it to the bathroom and projectile vomit for about fifteen minutes straight.

Felicity came and lay next to me for solidarity when I started to do that stupid drunk crying. "Why did I get so druuuuunnnnkkk? [sob] I'm so spinney, it's horribbbblllеее [sob]."

"It's OK, darling," says Felicity, holding onto the floor. "You'll feel much better once it's all out."

Ugh, another big wretch.

"Good girl, get it all out." Felicity carries me back to bed, tucks me in and hands me a bottle of water. I have never been so grateful for a friend in my whole life.

Just as I fall into a drunken slumber, the most piercing sound I have ever heard penetrates my ear drums.

"What the hell is going on?" shouts Tara over the loudest siren in the world. 'What time is it?"

"Four a.m.," says Hannah, squinting at her phone with one eye. "It's the fire alarm. Come on, we need to get out!"

The piercing sound of the alarm against my fragile drunk head is enough to make me want to jump out of the window.

Luckily, Felicity has sprung into organise mode. "Come on, girls, get up! We have to go!" She runs over to the safe and pulls out the essentials; passports, hair straighteners and fags.

Of course, we are on the top floor of the hostel, which means that we have to make our way down ten flights of stairs with the piercing alarm drilling tiny holes into my brain. Tara is the first out - she flings the door open and lies down on the pavement.

I stagger out behind her, rubbing my head I realise that I still have three pieces of clip in extensions in my hair and a set of fake eyelashes stuck to my cheek. Tara has big black eyes from rubbing her mascara and lipstick smudged across her face. Felicity looks like she's invited a bunch of hornets to live in her hair, Hannah is still in her fluro dress, with the headband now around her neck, and Clara is clutching onto her fags with a blanket around her, looking like she'd escaped a mental hospital.

The fire engines come speeding around the corner and a bunch of firemen fit for a Diet Coke advert jump out and approach the hostel... after they'd stopped for a quick laugh at the state of us.

"Don't worry, ladies, we'll get you back in to complete your beauty sleep in no time."

Kitted up with their hoses at the ready, they line up and make their way into the hostel. We peer around the door to see what was happening.

"You have got to be kidding me!" laughed Tara.

"What?" we all shouted.

"Look!" She points inside where the firemen were.

Wait! No, they can't be?

"They are actually queuing for the lift! The fire brigade is queuing for the lift… in a fire!" said Tara.

This was enough to make us scream with laughter.

"Only in Australia!"

Chapter Nine
Right Airport, Wrong Plane

Coming to the end of the first week, our 'organised fun' is finally over. The girls and I have decided to continue travelling together up the east coast; we want to do the entire coast, so we're planning to head south to Melbourne and then working our way back up north to Cairns.

Our bags are packed… well, as packed as they are can be. Our clothes have turned into a communal wardrobe, so all of our belongings are haphazardly stored in each other's cases. We seem to have managed to lose underwear and gain additional hair straighteners.

"OK, everyone, ready to go?" I said.

"What time is the flight?" asks Tara.

"Eleven a.m.," replied Felicity.

"Have I got time to have another nap before we go?" sighed Tara.

"No, you can nap on the plane!" said Felicity. "Come on, we need to get a wiggle on."

We all bundle into a cab when Tara shouts, "Shit, I've left my passport behind reception."

"The meter is running, girls!" said the taxi driver helpfully.

"Ugh, I'll meet you at the airport. Go ahead without me, I'll only be ten minutes behind!" said Tara.

"Are you sure? We'll get out and wait," Hannah replied.

"No, go, I'll be right behind you," said Tara.

The doors slam shut and off we go.

"One of us should have stayed with her, you know what a liability she is," said Hannah.

"She'll be fine," said Danni. "All she has to do is get to the airport, she can't go that wrong."

We arrive at the airport with half an hour to spare; we speed through check in, run through security and get to the boarding gate just in time to bundle onto the plane.

"Where is she?" said Felicity. "She's going to miss the bloody plane."

"I've just called her," said Clara. "She said she's on the plane!"

"Really? How did she manage that?" Felicity replied.

"No idea," said Clara. "Let's just get on."

We make our way down the aisle, banging our luggage on poor unsuspecting passengers as we go, take our seats and look around. Tara definitely isn't on the plane.

"Call her again!" I said.

On speaker, I can hear Tara. "I'm on the plane, on row twenty-seven, next to the horizontally challenged guy with the bald head."

"Tara!" shouts Felicity. "You can't say that."

"What? I didn't say fat!" she retorted.

We look to row twenty-seven. Not only is there no 'horizontally challenged' man, there is also no Tara.

"She's on the wrong bloody plane!" said Danni, shaking her head.

"Told you we shouldn't have left her!" Hannah replied. "Let's get an air steward. Excuse me, our friend has somehow boarded the wrong plane; we need to get her before we take off."

"Ladies, please take your seats, we're about to take off," said the stewardess, who was wearing way too much make-up.

"Oh crap, give me the phone. Tara, you're on the wrong plane, you need to get off and get the next plane to Melbourne."

"How do you know you're not on the wrong plane?" replied Tara helpfully.

The air stewardess said, "Ladies, please switch your phone off and take your seats, the plane is about to take off."

"Tara, get off the plane..." is all I managed to say before the steward snatched the phone out of my hand.

An hour later, we arrive in Melbourne. Tara texts to say that she managed to get off the plane that was going to Perth and is now boarding the next flight to Melbourne. I feel like telling her to hold hands with a sensible adult to make sure that she gets here. She's only going to be a couple of hours behind us, so we grab our cases and arrange to meet her at the hostel.

"Hello, ladies, and welcome to Melbourne!" says the very charismatic manager. "Once you have deposited your bags, pop back down for your complimentary glass of goon and I'll tell you all about the events that we have coming up over the next week."

"Goon?" said Danni. "Do we look like goon drinkers to you? Make it a glass of champagne and we'll be back!"

"Ah, champagne backpackers, I see!" replied the manager. "I'll see what I can do."

The hostel is actually really nice. It's brand new and hasn't got that lost soul feel about it like the hostel in

Sydney. It's full of energy and, even at two in the afternoon, it is buzzing. We open the door to our room (one of the perks of travelling in a group is that you don't have to share with strangers).

"Wow, it's so clean!" said Hannah. "Wish we'd gotten here sooner, bet there's no bed bugs here!"

It was lovely. Fresh white linen and comfy beds, the stuff dreams are made of. We all pick a bed, have a quick outfit change and make our way back down.

"Ladies, this way to the bar," said the welcoming guy. "Here you go, a glass of champagne for each of you."

Impressed, we all gratefully took a sip.

"This week, we have a live band on Tuesday and ladies night on Wednesday - ladies drink for free! Movie night is on Thursday, a pool party on Friday and BBQ on Saturday. We hope that you enjoy your stay. Anything that I can do for you, just give me a shout. My name is Todd."

"Ah, he was lovely," said Danni. "Dibs, ha, ha."

We're starving so head out to St Kilda high street to find some lunch. The town is very cool; it's a rustic surfer town, very relaxed and full of backpackers.

"That looks nice!" said Clara, pointing at a restaurant across the street. "Fancying trying it out?"

The restaurant is a full on, military style attack on your senses. There are scented candles, clashing incense sticks, floaty rain music and someone swishing a brush around what looks like a giant pan, making a 'hoooommmmm' sound. We are shown to our table... well, I use the world 'table' loosely. It's a Moroccan picnic style blanket and we are invited to sit with our legs crossed on the floor 'to be closer to nature'.

"Nice one, Clara!" said Hannah. "You've bought us to a fricking hippie commune. Feel like they're going to ask us to take our clothes off in a minute!"

"I love it!" laughed Danni. "This is so funny, I'm going to take a selfie of me and that guy in his pants."

"I don't care where I eat as long as the food is good," Felicity said. "My stomach is growling; I need some meat!"

Well, that was actually the only thing that wasn't on the menu; we had wandered into a Vegan café.

"You have got to be kidding me!" said Felicity.

"Let's give it a go. It's pretty busy in here, it must be good," replied Hannah, trying to ease the tension.

"What I don't understand," pondered Danni, "is that, if they hate meat so much, why do they make all of their food resemble meat? Look at this: veggie nuggets, veggie sausages, veggie burger… I mean, if you're going to be a veggie, I think you should commit and just chomp on your sticks of broccoli. It's like lesbians using a strap-on; just get a fella, ha, ha, ha."

"God, my stomach is so bloated, the only vegetable I've had in about a month is potato and that was in my vodka!" said Danni as we strolled back to the hostel to meet Tara. She was waiting outside in some random get up.

"What happened to you?" Clara shouted as we crossed the street.

"They didn't get my luggage off the plane that I accidentally boarded. I only realised when I got to baggage claim, and so I went to the airport shop and bought this!"

She was wearing a sombrero so that 'we couldn't lose her again', a Timmy Mallet style yellow polka dot bikini, an inflatable rubber ring, two books (one on online dating, the other on fifteen-minute meal ideas), condoms, bug repellent and four kaftans.

"Well, we certainly won't lose you in this get up!" said Danni. "Come on, let's get you a drink."

Chapter Ten
Jesus?

According to our traveller guide book, if you are in Melbourne, you have to drive along the Great Ocean Road. It's 240km of beautiful scenery that spans the south coast of Victoria. We packed an overnight bag, rocked up to the rental shop, hired a mini-van, inserted the 'driving music' CD and Thelma and Louise'd it towards the coast.

After driving for a few hours, everyone is getting a bit niggly in the car, so we pull over at a local surf joint to grab some food.

"G'day, ladies, what can we get ya? How about some shrimp on the barbie?" said surf dude number one.

"And a nice cold beer to wash it down?" said surf dude number two, living up to all Ozzie stereotypes in two sentences.

"Right, girls," says Felicity in organisation mode, "we need to decide where we're going to stay tonight. If we drive for a few more hours, we'll make it to Lorne; it looks like there's loads of places to stay there. Are you all OK to keep going for a few more hours?"

We all nod in agreement.

Driving along the coast , Felicity points to what looks like, an abandoned B&B up in the hills in the middle of the woods. I'm sure I've seen this movie and it equates to murderers with chainsaws hiding in the bushes! There is no way that I am staying here.

Felicity pulls the car up in front of the house and jumps out. "It's a bit creepy girls, don't you think?" I say, with a little quiver in my voice.

"Oh, don't be such a wimp, this is so cool!" Felicity says, opening the door and letting herself in.

"You can't just walk in. Where are the owners?" asks Tara, clutching onto my arm.

Felicity seems to have put her big girl pants on today and starts to venture down the corridor in the haunted house.

"Seriously, Felicity, this place is giving me the willies!" said Clara. "There are definitely dead people in the walls!"

This place had a touch of the Bates Motel about it: the walls were covered in dark stained floral wallpaper, there was old wooden furniture smattered around the place (clearly haunted with trapped spirits), dark sticky carpet and unsettling large grandfather clocks everywhere.

"Bong!" All of the grandfather clocks chimed at the same time, rattling the entire house.

"Shit the bed!" shouts Hannah "Nearly gave me a fricking heart attack!"

Felicity isn't looking as brave now. "You're right," she said, making a swift U-turn back towards the front door. "We shouldn't have come in uninvited."

We all scurry along behind her, desperate to get out.

"Jesus!" said Tara.

"What?" we all shout.

"Look, it's Jesus, he's outside!" she said, pointing through the window.

We look outside to see a man with long, silvery hair standing with his arms spread in the middle of the garden, like Jesus. However, unlike Jesus, he was wearing a tie die T-shirt and baggy surfer shorts.

"That must be the owner," said Felicity.

"Or Jesus" replied Tara.

"I really don't want to stay here, girls. It's making the hairs stand up on the back of my neck," I said to the group, with Hannah and Clara nodding in agreement.

"Oh, where's your sense of adventure? You only live once!" said Felicity.

"Yeah, and let's hope that doesn't end tonight!" whispered Clara.

Felicity could not be deterred. She strode outside and shouted to the Jesus man, "Excuse me, is this your place? We'd like to stay the night if that's OK?"

"Not all who travel are lost," Jesus mysteriously replied.

"Okaaaaay, how much does it cost per night?" asked Felicity, ensuring that she sees this crazy idea through.

"What is money when I am already rich?" he replied.

"Well, that's cleared that right up," I said. "Come on, girls, let's go."

We all turn to walk towards the car when he theatrically announces, "You do not choose a room, the room chooses you!"

I look at Felicity and whisper, "You cannot be serious; this guy is bat shit crazy!"

"Come on, girls, we have to stay for at least one night, think of what an adventure it will be!" Felicity said, pulling our bags out of the car.

"Yeah, when Casper and his mates keep us up all night!" replied Clara.

"OK, let's vote. Who is for staying?" asked Felicity.

Felicity, Tara and Danni raise their hands.

"And who's for going?"

Clara, Hannah and I raise our hands.

"We have a tie, let's flip a coin," I say.

I flip the coin and shout heads for the leaving group. Of course, it lands on tails.

"Yippee! Come on, girls!" Felicity shouts as she runs inside.

Chapter Eleven
Did You Say Pirates?

We wander through the upstairs corridor, looking at the rooms.

"So, how does the room choose us exactly?" asks Danni.

"God knows. I'm going for the least creepy," I reply. I open a door to my right and see a nice big room, with a large king-sized bed and fresh, white linen. "This room has chosen me!" I shout mockingly. "I'm not staying on my own, though, anyone want to share with me?"

"I will!" shouts Hannah.

"Don't you think it's weird that we appear to be the only guests in a ten-bedroom B&B?" I ask Hannah.

"It's because of the dead bodies in the walls," she replies, hugging a pillow in the middle of the bed.

"There aren't any dead bodies!" laughs Danni as she walks in. "Just a crazy, harmless hippy!"

We were really tired from all the driving, so decide to stay in, watch TV and read some magazines. We make our way into the lounge, past the tenth grandfather clock that I've seen, when Tara points at the rustic 60s box TV that goes further back that it does sideways.

"How are we going to watch Enders on that?" Danni says, feeling her way around the antique TV.

"You don't, mostly because it's a pile of shit!" said some unknown voice from the doorway. We all turn around to see four guys smiling at us.

Of course Danni is the first to jump up.

"Oh hi! I'm Danni, this is Louise, Felicity, Tara, Clara and Hannah."

"I'm Scott, this is Rob, Chuck and Ben," he replied.

The guys come into the living room and sit with us.

"So," says Scott, "where are you all from?"

We do the usual pleasantries of general background stories, what we've done in Oz so far, plans for the next few months etc., when I fade out of the conversation until I hear the word 'pirates'.

"I'm sorry, did you just say pirates?" I ask.

"Oh yeah," says Rob. "Haven't you heard? This area is completely haunted by old pirates. Rumour has it that they are stuck here with the shipwrecks all along the Great Ocean Road."

"Oh, stop it!" Hannah said, hiding behind a pillow. "This place is creepy enough!"

"What a load of crap!" scoffed Felicity.

"Well," started Chuck, "you'll soon see tonight! They start their evening walk at midnight, when they check the beds of every building along the Great Ocean Road, looking for maidens!"

This makes me laugh. However, the girls are not laughing - they all look terrified. "Oh, come on, girls, they're just winding you up! I promise you that no pirates will be waking you up tonight. Maybe Jesus will, but no pirates."

Now that we are totally creeped out, we all go upstairs to our bedrooms. Getting into our bed Hannah says, "Do you want to be the big spoon or the little spoon?"

"I don't want to be any spoon. Get off!" I reply.

"But the pirates!" Hannah protests.

"Look, Han, there are no ghost pirates, I promise you. Go to sleep."

Around midnight I am abruptly woken by Hannah jumping on top of me and screaming that there is a ghost in the wardrobe.

"I promise, Louise, I'm not lying, I saw the door open and close! Please check!"

I stagger out of bed, using my phone for light.

"Get a weapon, just in case!" Hannah whispers.

"What weapon do you suggest works on a ghost pirate?" I whisper back, but pick up my hairspray just in case. Carefully, I tip toe over to the creepiest looking wardrobe I have ever seen and, for reasons unknown, knock on the door.

"What are you doing?" said Hannah. "Do you expect them to knock back?"

"Well I don't know, do I?"

On tenterhooks, we both stand staring at the wardrobe… and then, it knocks back! We both scream and leg it out of the room, bolting into Felicity and Danni's room and incoherently shouting about the ghost knocking on the wardrobe door.

"Oh for goodness sake!" said Felicity. "You woke us up because a ghost is playing knock knock!"

"Come on, you have to come with us!" Hannah pleads with Felicity.

"Christ! Come on, Danni!" Felicity says, poking her to wake up.

I throw a hairbush at Danni and a shoe to Felicity.

"Weapons!" I say.

We walk into our room, turn on the light and make our way to the wardrobe.

"Are you ready?" says Felicity.

"Ready!" we all reply, weapons poised.

Felicity swings open the door and… there's nothing there!

"What? That's not possible," I say. "It knocked back, I heard it."

"You two are going mad," said Felicity. "We're going back to bed."

As Danni and Felicity are walking towards the door, something grabs Felicity on the ankle from under the bed. She screams an almighty scream. We see something reaching out, I spray my hairspray, Danni throws her shoe and Felicity lobs her hairbrush.

"Jesus Christ!" shouts the voice. "Are you trying to pissing blind me, it was just a joke!"

Scott pulls himself from under the bed, rolling around on the floor with swollen eyes and a sore head.

"What's going on?" says Jesus, popping up behind us.

This makes us all scream and I accidentally spray him in the face with hairspray!.

"Oh God, I'm so sorry, you made me jump!" I said, trying to rub his eyes.

Tara and Clara come running in to witness two men rolling round on the floor.

"Jeez!" said Tara. "What kind of party was this? And where was our invite?"

Chapter Twelve
Awkward

Needless to say, breakfast the following morning was a tad awkward. Scott's eyes were red and inflamed and he was sporting quite a bump on his head. I wasn't sure if that was from the shoe or the hairbrush.

"It serves you right! Don't sit there looking sorry for yourself. If you creep up on a bunch of girls, this is what happens; you get your arse whooped!" laughed Danni.

"It was only supposed to be a joke, didn't think you'd all go Jackie Chan on me!" sulked Scott, much to our amusement.

"Has anyone seen Jesus today?" asked Tara. "I felt really bad when you sprayed him in the eyes, Louise."

"He crept up behind me!" I protested. "With the light from the TV in the room behind, he had a white glow around him. I was convinced he was a ghost!"

"So you blitzed him with your ghost busting hairspray, did you?" laughed Felicity.

"I really should find him and say sorry, I feel awful," I say to the group.

As I wandered around the haunted house, I realised that I didn't know Jesus's real name, I was knocking on every door trying to think of a plan as to what I'd address him as when he opened it. I came to the fourth door when I heard a noise inside; this must be it. I knock on the door and hear a big, booming, East London accent.

"Here, Doris, someone is at the door, be a lamb and see who it is."

Clearly not Jesus's door. I was ready to apologise and walk away when a slender old lady opened the door and I could see Jesus in the background with a big old shiny bald head!

"Er, hello," I say awkwardly. This has thrown me off guard. "I came to apologise to…" Crap, what's his name? "... the owner." Nailed it!

"What for, my love?" said the nice old lady.

"Well, I accidentally sprayed him in the eyes with my hairspray last night because I thought that he was a ghost!" I mumble, embarrassingly.

"A ghost?" she laughs. "That's a new one! Hold on a second, love."

She shouts to Jesus, who incidentally is called John, a pretty average name for the Messiah, and I see him quickly shove his wig on as he runs to the door. Awkwardly, his wig is not sitting quite right on his head and it's given him a bit of a fringe with a side ponytail.

"Er, hello," I say. "I'm so sorry for last night. Some stupid boy hid under our bed, it gave us such a fright, and then you popped up behind me so I sprayed you in the face with my hairspray, because that was my weapon, you see!"

John is looking very confused. I'm not sure if it's because his wig isn't on straight and all of his mystical powers are off.

"That's OK, my dear, let the truth set you free!" he replies in his fake wispy voice.

I want to tell him that I heard him bellowing in his East London accent, but that would be awkward for both of us.

"We'll see you again on the road less travelled!" he finished.

"Great. Well, it's been, erm… enlightening, thank you for having us and have a great day," I reply.

As I start to walk away, I hear him shout, "Did you hear her, Doris, and her ghost story? What a bell end!"

Chapter Thirteen
Twelve Large Rocks

"So, what exactly are the Twelve Apostles? Isn't it something to do with aliens?" asked Tara.

"No, that's Stonehenge," replied Danni, slurping on an ice pop.

"None of them have anything to do with aliens!" said Felicity. "Did you two even go to school?"

"OK, Miss Know-It-All," said Danni, "how did those big rocks get there if it wasn't aliens?"

"It's due to erosion," replied Felicity. "The limestone eroded to become caves in the cliffs, which in time split the cliffs to essentially become separate chunks of rock."

"Well, look who swallowed a dictionary!" said Tara sarcastically.

"Ugh," said Felicity, slapping her head. "I would have swallowed an encyclopaedia, not a dictionary. I can't cope with this conversation!"

"I still say it's aliens!" said Danni, followed by Felicity shaking her head and rolling her eyes.

"OK, the Twelve Apostles should be coming up on the right. We should see a car park any second now, so keep your eye out, girls," I say to the group as chief navigator.

"It's there, behind the big tree!" shouts Hannah as Felicity starts to turn. "Not that tree, the other one!" she yells, nearly causing Felicity to crash into a log.

As we make our way over to the viewing platform, we can hear passers-by murmuring 'Wow', 'Incredible' and 'Amazing'. Excitedly, we all grin at each other and run over to see this natural phenomenon. There was approximately three minutes of staring, until Danni breaks the silence.

"Is that it?"

To be fair, she said what we were all thinking.

Hannah, being ever the optimist, said, "Well, it is a bit of a miracle if you think about it. Mother Nature did this all by herself."

We all turn to look at her.

"If you squint your eyes, some of the rocks kind of look like faces!"

We all turn back towards the rocks, feeling that we owe these chunks of limestone some more of our time. After a good seven minutes of rock staring, we give up and head back to the car.

"Are we so uncultured that we can't appreciate a work of natural art?" moaned Felicity.

"It would have been better if there was some information on the aliens," replied Danni.

"For the last time, there weren't any... oh, forget it!" replied an exasperated Felicity.

"Girls, look over there!" shouted Clara. "Our first shipwreck on the shipwreck coast!"

It was a very small part of the ship that remained, but it was slightly more exciting than the big rocks. We ran down to the beach to have a dip in the ocean and examine the part of the ship that was left behind.

"Maybe this is one of the parts that is haunted by the ghost pirates," said Tara.

"Or the pleb that was hiding under your bed!" laughs Danni.

When we get down to the beach, there are approximately one billion starving mosquitos ready for dinner. Within seconds of our toes hitting the sand we get bitten, literally, all over our bodies.

"Aaaah, one of those little bastards has just bitten my foof!" shouted Tara.

"Why is your foof even out?" Danni shouts, ferociously swatting the mozzies away.

"Well, I've been really itchy in my front bottom lately and my mum said that I should give it some air. I thought, how am I going to do that without getting arrested? Then I had a eureka moment and decided that I just won't wear pants!" replied Tara, jiggling from one foot to the other.

"Generally speaking, in life, if you find yourself with your foof exposed, you have taken the wrong path!" shouts Danni as she runs back towards the car. "You need to seriously evaluate your life choices!"

We all leg it back up the hill in 35°C heat back to air con safety. When we arrive back at the car we look like we've just escaped some kind of scientific experiment.

"Oh God, look at the state of us!" said Clara, panting. "Has anyone got any of that mozzie ointment?"

Standing in a public car park, we all lather ourselves in soothing ointment.

"What am I going to do about my foof?" said Tara, trying to inconspicuously scratch.

"I read in a magazine that natural yoghurt is really good for anything to do with the front bottom area," said Hannah. "We could stop at a shop and pick you some up."

Three convenience stores later we finally find one with natural yoghurt.

"I haven't got a spoon though," said Tara.

"You don't need one; you can just pour it into your pants," Hannah casually replied, taking in our shocked faces. "You put it into your pants and the good bacteria will work its magic at the source. You'll feel better in no time."

"At no point did you mention that this would go into my pants!" stated Tara, verging on hysteria.

"Oh, stop being such a sissy. Grab a pair of pants, go to the bathroom and pour it in!"

Five minutes later, Tara left the bathroom, walking like John Wayne.

"Hey, Tara, where's your donkey?" laughed Danni.

"Ha, ha, very funny! How long do I have to leave this in? Feels like I'm wearing a nappy! Although it is quite soothing."

"Told you!" shouted Hannah.

Chapter Fourteen
Hot Breakfast Guy

After a week on the road it was good to get back to the backpackers in Melbourne with a change of clothes and the same bed for a short time. Now that we were back in one place, we decided to do some exercise. Our midriffs were getting a little too splodgy with way too many hot guys around.

"I'm going to pop and get something to eat first," I say to the girls. "I'm way too hungry to even think about working out."

"I'll join you!" said Hannah

"Me too!" added Felicity.

Whipping up a culinary feast in the kitchen (aka pouring milk onto my cereal), I hear a voice next to me, "Seasoned chef, I see?"

I turn around to see this beautiful guy looking at me. He had big, surfer-style, shaggy hair, piercing blue eyes and a dazzling smile. Of course, I don't act even slightly cool and manage to somehow send my bowl of cereal flying, covering both of us in soggy cornflakes.

"Oh God, I'm so sorry! That's really embarrassing!" I mutter.

"Don't worry, no harm done," he replies, peeling off his soaked T-shirt, revealing a six-pack and big, muscly shoulders.

"Jeez!" I realise I have just said this out loud.

Laughing, he says, "Can I get you another bowl?"

I manage to mumble something along the lines of "sure." He effortlessly pours me a new bowl and walks it over to a table. Sneaking a look at the girls, they wave me along and mouth, "Go, go!"

"I'm Zack," said the six-pack.

"I'm Louise," I reply, sucking in my non-six-pack.

"So, how long have you been in Melbourne?" he asks with his perfect pearly whites dazzling me. Seriously, this guy looks fricking Photoshopped.

"Er, only a couple of days." Play it cool, Louise. "We've just been down the Great Ocean Road for a week, we got back yesterday."

"Oh really? I'd love to do that, was it good?" he asks.

"Yeah, it was great, apart from my friend getting bitten on her foof because she wasn't wearing pants."

Oh my God, why did I just say that out loud? Why, why?

Laughing, he nearly spat his healthy low carb breakfast out. "Wow, OK, so you're a sharer?" he said, still chuckling.

"Oh God, not usually, I've no idea why I said that; my friend is going to kill me!"

This is too much; this is beyond embarrassing! Stumbling over a chair, I tell him I have to go as my friends will be waiting for me. As I'm running out of the breakfast room in horror, he shouts, "Hey, Louise, it's ladies night tonight. Meet me there?"

Again with the dazzling smile. God, I'm going to have to wear sunglasses.

"Er, sure, see you there!" I reply as I run head on into the door frame, nearly giving myself a concussion. This really couldn't get much worse. I turn around to see him laughing to himself.

I collapse into a heap around the corner as Felicity and Hannah run round to meet me.

"Nice touch, chucking the bowl of cereal at him!" said Felicity. "I wanted to see what was underneath!"

"I didn't do it on purpose!" I whine. "God, I'm such a mess, that was horrendous!"

"Oh, it can't have been that bad," said Hannah, reassuringly. "What did you say to him?"

"I told him about Tara's foof!" I moan with my head in my hands.

"Why on earth would you say that?" said Felicity, hysterically laughing.

"I don't know, he asked me about the Great Ocean Road and it somehow just came up!"

This made the girls scream.

"You seriously need to work on your game," said Felicity. "This is hilarious!"

"Well, he asked me to meet him at ladies night tonight, so it can't have been that bad!" I say sulkily.

"Really? Louise, this is major! We have to decide what you're going to wear! Right after we tell Tara that the hot breakfast guy knows about her foof!" laughed Felicity.

Back in the room, Tara was less than amused that I was sharing her foof woes.

"What if he has a really fit mate and he warns him off me because of my foof incident?" she shouts at me.

"I didn't say which friend it was, I'll just point at Felicity!" I reply, laughing.

"I'm excited to see what talent is on offer tonight after seeing HBG!" Felicity says dreamily.

"HBG?" asked Danni.

"Hot Breakfast Guy!" Felicity replied.

"Well, as much as I'm convinced that he is referring to me as Hot Breakfast Girl, I need to get my arse in the gym – stat!" I say.

"You girls go on," said Danni, lounging on the bed. "I'm going to stick with my gripper knickers!"

Walking along the beach to the gym, Felicity suddenly shouts, "He's there, he's there!"

"Who's where?" I say as Felicity drags me behind a bush.

"HBG. He's on the beach, it looks like he's a surfing instructor."

"Where? I can't see him?" I reply looking through the cracks in the bush.

"In between that big throng of girls!" Felicity shares helpfully.

"Of course he is! What's he doing chatting me up when he can have the pick of the bunch with them?" I whine.

"Right, Louise, I'm not having this! You are beautiful and intelligent. We just need to hide the part that is slightly scatty, accident prone and falls over all the time."

"But as you said, that's all the time; I'm a complete disaster!"

"Look, you're not going to marry the guy, just relax and have some fun," she said, holding onto my shoulders.

"You're right, thanks for the team talk. Could have left the scatty part out though and just stuck with beautiful."

"I'm nothing if not a realist," Felicity replied.

After the gym, I'd like to say that we were sporting a post-workout glow; however, we're so dishevelled we look as if we have dived headfirst into a swamp and wrestled the biggest alligator there.

"Jesus, I knew there was a reason I don't work out," said Felicity.

"I'm sure it'll get easier over time," I say. "Oh sod it, glass of fizz?"

"Thought you'd never ask!" said Felicity.

Chapter Fifteen
Ladies Night

Getting ready for ladies night, there are gripper knickers all over the bedroom. The girls are more than a little bit excited about who I can introduce them to, now that I am 'well in there' with HBG. I keep reminding them that it was a disastrous ten-minute conversation, but they will not be deterred.

"So on a scale of one to ten, how ridey was Hot Breakfast Guy?" asked Danni, squeezing herself into a tiny pair of really short shorts.

"Depends," I say. "What does ridey mean?"

"It's Irish for how shaggable," she says, wriggling on the bed, trying desperately to get into the shorts.

"Oh then, very ridey!" I reply, laughing "You really need to not get your hopes up, though. Honestly, I was a total disaster: I told him about Tara's foof!"

Tara rolls her eyes.

"Still sorry about that Tara! Spilled my cereal all over him and ran into a door! He's hardly looking at me as a catch. You saw those girls all over him on the beach; he probably won't even turn up!"

Two hours and two bottles of champagne later, we are ready. We head straight to the bar, collect our free drinks and start to shake it. I try to act completely cool and composed, like I'm not really looking in every nook and cranny for HBG. Oh God, he's there… wearing a dress? OK, play it cool Louise, don't make a scene.

"He's there!" shrieks Felicity. Too late, scene made. "He looks better in a dress than you do, Louise!" she giggled. "Go over and say hi."

"No way!" I reply. "If he wants to talk to me, he can come to me."

"You're so stubborn, Louise!" said Danni. "If you don't go over I will!"

"I'm not going to be one of those girls throwing myself at him!" I reply. "I'm going to casually dance over here and catch his eye; then he can come over to me."

I am having such a good time with the girls that for a second I actually forget about HBG. Danni has pulled some Irish guy; they are having the time of their lives quoting Irish sayings at each other that no one else can understand. Felicity is snogging the face off the welcoming guy, Tara and Clara are dancing on the pole and Hannah is… actually, where is Hannah?

"Where's Hannah?" I shout up to Tara.

"On her phone again!" she shouts back, rolling her eyes.

This can't be good; every time Hannah sneaks off on her phone she comes back with a heavy heart and wants to go home. You see, Hannah's boyfriend is still at home. He was fully on board with her travelling and following her dreams, but they miss each other like crazy.

"I'm going to find her!" I shout to the girls.

As I push my way through the throngs of withering bodies, someone grabs my arm. I turn and realise that it's HBG, in the flesh.

"You're not leaving, are you?" he asks, with that dazzling smile.

"Actually, no," I reply, quickly fixing my hair. "I was just going to check on my friend, she's outside on her own."

"Fancy some company?" he asked.

"Sure." I smile back.

I turn to see Danni doing her 'ridey' signal.

As we make our way outside, I laughingly say, "I like your dress!"

"Girls drink for free, so I thought, I've got the big hair and the pink watch, just need a dress to complete the look!"

So he has a personality as well! We turn the corner and there's Hannah, sitting on a step, crying.

"I should go and make sure she's OK," I say to HBG.

"I'll have a drink waiting inside with your name on it," he said, and kissed me on the cheek.

I wander over to Hannah. "I think I'm in love!" I sigh.

"That's not love, babe," she sobbed. "You're thinking with your lady parts!"

She probably had a point as we'd only exchanged roughly thirty words. Anyway, back to the situation at hand.

"What's wrong, Han?" I ask, putting my arm around her.

"I miss him so much, it's so hard being this far away."

"Do you really want to do this, Han? You've had an amazing time; no-one would judge you if you went home."

"I can't go home, I really do want this adventure and I love spending time with you girls!" she said, wiping her nose on her sleeve.

"Well, in that case, this really is a once in a lifetime opportunity. We have to grab it by the horns and make the most of it," I reply, trying to bring some positivity to the situation. All I needed to do was swash buckle to make it complete.

"Do you think it would be weird if I asked him if he wanted to come and visit for a couple of weeks?" she asked, looking longingly into my face.

"Of course not, I think that's a great idea! In fact, why don't you do it now?" I say, swept up in the moment.

"OK," she said, wiping the tears from her eyes. "Will you stay here with me while I call him?"

"Of course!"

"He said yes!" The world is back to spinning on its axis and Hannah has a smile back on her face.

"Come on, let's go back and have a boogie!" I grab her hand, wipe the mascara from under her eyes and pull her inside.

As promised, Zack has a drink in his hand and tilts his head at me as I walk in. I tell the girls I'll be back soon and make my way over.

"Is your friend OK?" he asks.

"She's fine, thanks for asking."

Gorgeous and cares about my friends – yep, definitely in love!

"No worries, here you go," he said, passing me a drink.

We got to talking. To be honest, I can't really remember what was said; I was too busy checking out his insane body. He must live in the gym; I wonder how many cows he eats a day? As my mind is wandering to weird and wonderful places, he kisses me and I stare at him in shock.

"I'm sorry, was that not OK? I thought I was getting the signals?" he apologised.

"No, it's fine, you were, you just shocked me! After I told you about my friend's foof I wasn't sure what you made of me, then I walked into a door..."

Oh God, Louise, stop rambling! Laughing, he cupped my face and kissed me again. It was one of those earth shattering ones that make your knees go all wobbly.

Grabbing my hand, he said, "Come on, let's dance!"

My legs are not entirely working, but he manages to pull me behind him onto the dance floor.

It took the girls approximately ten seconds to swarm over and introduce themselves.

"Hi, HBG, I'm Felicity. I've been dying to meet you!"

Oh God, this is cringey.

"HBG?" he asks.

Before I can jump in and change the subject, Felicity says, "'Hot Breakfast Guy'; it's what we've been calling you!"

"Really?" he laughs, looking at me.

In response, I make a weird noise and wriggle about nervously. Then Tara bowls on over - oh, this is going to be bad.

"All right, HBG, got any hot mates you can hook me up with? I'm not the one with the manky foof, that's someone else... err, she's not here!"

By this point, he is crying with laughter.

"I'm sure my mates would love to meet you. Want me to introduce you?"

Tara, Clara and Felicity all but pounce on him as he leads us over to his friends.

"Guys, this is Louise and these are her mates."

"Louise, hey?" one of them says. "Do you know, he's been talking about you all day?"

"Really?" I say, surprised. Oh my God, he talked about me; this really is love at first sight.

"Yeah, you're the girl that threw cereal on him and then ran into a door, aren't you?" he said, laughing. "Oh, and the story about your mate's… err, what did you call it? Oh yeah; foof! We've been dying laughing all day! I couldn't wait to meet you!"

I make a weird high pitched sound in response, trying to act unbothered but failing miserably. "Yep that's me!" I reply. "The hot mess!"

"Hot, definitely. I'm not sure about mess!" Zack says whilst giving my waist a squeeze and winking at me.

Oh God, my legs are going to go again!

Hours of dancing later, HBG offers to walk me back to my room. He plants another knee-buckling kiss onto my lips and it takes every ounce of will power I have to say, "See you in the morning." He smiles at me and says goodnight.

Chapter Sixteen
The Morning After the Night Before.

The girls are awake bright and early, going over the antics of the night before.

"Ugh, what time is it?" I mumble.

"She's awake!" Tara shouts.

"Oh my God, tell us everything!" she says. "We were so jel of you and HBG, you were SO cute together!"

I manage to pull myself up onto my elbows. "There's not much to tell, really, you saw it all."

"Oh stop it, Louise! We know you are screaming inside!" shouted Hannah from the corner.

"OK, it was incredible!" I shout to the girls, laughing. "He is so nice and not just hot; his personality is amazing."

"Really?" said Felicity. "What did you talk about exactly?"

"Oh, you know, this and that…" I trail off.

The girls start laughing raucously.

"You weren't paying any attention to what he was saying, we saw you!" screamed Tara.

"Someone's at the door!" said Hannah.

"Who knocks on the door at this time in the morning? Tell them to feck off!" said Danni.

"Erm, Louise, it's for you!" said Hannah with a little smile.

"What? Please tell me it's not HBG?" I mouth to Tara as I desperately try to tie my hair up. Oh God! It *is* HBG! What the hell is he doing here?

"Bad time?" he says, with that million-dollar smile.

"No, no not at all, I've been up for ages!"

"HA!" I hear from the background.

Stepping outside, I pull the door shut behind me.

"What are you doing here?" I ask.

"I had such a good time last night, I was wondering if I could take you to breakfast?" he replied.

I was suddenly very aware that I was standing in the corridor in my pyjamas, with crazy hair and morning breath.

"Can you give me half an hour and I'll meet you downstairs?" I say as casually as possible.

"Sure," he replies in his cool but casual way. "Don't keep me waiting too long."

And with that, he gives me a wink and saunters off.

Opening the door, I nearly knock all of the girls over as they all have their ears pressed to the door

"Subtle," I say.

"Ahh, Louise has a *breakfast* date with Hot *Breakfast* Guy. What are you going to wear?" says Felicity, way too excitably for this time in the morning.

"Can we come?" asks Danni.

"No, you can't fricking come! I need a shower!"

Outfit number twenty-seven was a winner! I was trying to go for the effortlessly cool, thrown together, yet stylish, look, but this was not something that I was good at in thirty minutes. I had decided on a black silky vest top with denim shorts, hair casually thrown up, light natural make-up, flip-flops and sunnies.

"Beautiful," says Tara.

"Well, it's as good as it's going to get on four hours of sleep and a hangover!" I say.

"Text us where you are at all times," says Hannah. "He could be a rapist."

"Oh God!" Felicity sighs.

"Well, you don't know!" protests Hannah. "He could be!"

"OK, Mum, I'll be sure to text you!" I say, laughing.

I walk through the reception, trying to locate him, when I spot him in the middle of about ten girls. This was a bad idea, what was I thinking? I was just about to turn to go back to the room when I hear him shout:

"Louise! Hey, over here!"

I act as though I've just seen him, whilst dodging daggers from every girl in the vicinity. He parts the crowd and makes his way over to me.

"Ready?" he says, holding his arm out for me.

"Ready!" I reply, latching on.

"So, I'm not sure what your favourite breakfast food is, but there's this amazing place that does a bit of everything. I thought we could start there," he says.

Start? Things are looking up. HBG and I will be married with babies in no time, I can feel it!

"Here we are!" he says, pointing at a really cool, surf shack-style venue.

"It's perfect!" I reply, gushing. Reel it in, Louise!

Tucking into our breakfast, we chat about everything; where we're from, family, siblings, friends… "Out here, I'm working as a kite surfing instructor. You should come down to the beach one day, I'll give you some free lessons."

"Thanks for the offer, but I'm not that great in the water after my last experience of learning to surf!" I reply.

"Well, that sounds intriguing!" he said. "Please, go on."

"Well, it involves a whale and a lot of pee! Definitely a story for another time. Maybe a time with copious amounts of wine!"

"I'll definitely hold you to that!" he says. "Anyway, I came to pick you up so early because I have work today. Can I see you tonight?"

Again with the smile! God, I am melting over here.

"That would be nice!" In my head, I'm singing, *"Going to the chapel and we're gonna get married."*

I walk to meet the girls with a spring in my step.

"So, how was it?" asked Felicity.

"Did his mate ask about me?" shouted Danni from behind.

"It was amazing! Sorry, Danni, I didn't ask about his mate; I was too busy dodging the reflection from his sparkling gnashers! That guy is like something out of a magazine! He's asked if he could see me tonight. I said yes, is that too keen?"

"It's not too keen," replied Felicity.

I could sense there was a 'but' coming.

"But [there it is] you do need to remember that we're only here for another week and a half, Louise. Enjoy this for the fleeting romance that it is, but don't get too attached, OK?"

She had a point; it was something that I didn't want to think about, really. I'd only spent approximately five hours with the guy. I am hardly in love, I just need to pace myself; yes, that's what I need to do.

Chapter Seventeen
Head vs Lady Parts

Throughout the week, Zack and I have been near enough inseparable. Whenever he's not working, he's with me. I've met his friends, he's met mine, we've laughed together, been to dinner, walked along the beach.. Taking Felicity's words of warning into account, I think I may have blown it. I know that I'm far too attached for something that, for all intents and purposes, is supposed to be a holiday romance. So why does it feel like so much more? My taste in men varies from the ridiculous to the horrendous, so to have a guy show an interest in me who looks like he's walked straight off the cover of Men's Health with a personality to boot, I'm just not ready to let go of that. I need to talk this out with someone. I need my mum.

Whenever I call home my parents put me 'on conference', which basically means that they put me on speaker so that I don't have to repeat myself, but what it mostly means is that they talk at the same time and don't listen to anything the other one has said. Today was no exception. After fifteen minutes of listening to concerns over the stolen marrow from the local vegetable fete, how little Jimmy had cheated because his dad worked at some pharmaceutical company and he injected the potato with something 'dodgy' to win, and the crazy neighbour who had been cleaning her car at three a.m.

in her nighty with a mop again, I couldn't take it anymore.

"OK, Mum, Dad, I need to talk to you about something!"

"I haven't told you about my hair appointment yet!" Dad whines.

"Oh, it's a corker!" said Mum. "You'll laugh your ass off at this one!"

"One more story, then I really need to talk to you about something, OK?" I plead.

"OK. Off you go, Frank," said Mum.

"Well, it was Thursday morning…" he starts.

God, this is going to be a long one, I can feel it.

"Dad, don't worry about setting the scene, I've got it, you're in the hairdressers, go from there!" I plead.

"Spoil sport!" Dad huffs. "OK, I'm in the hairdressers," he says theatrically, "I've just had my hair washed and the lady tells me to take a seat in the other room…"

"So what does he do?" Mum jumps in.

"Who's telling this story, Shirley, me or you?"

And then of course they get into a ten minute argument about who's telling the story.

"Dad! Just tell me what happened."

"OK, OK," he says. "So she says—"

"Yeah, I know: 'take a seat in the other room'. Then what?"

God, this is painful.

"Then he lifts up a bloody chair and walks it into the other room!" shouts Mum, wetting herself laughing.

"Shirley, I was supposed to be telling the bloody story! Now you've flipping ruined it!"

"Oh Dad, you didn't really take a chair into the other room, did you?" I asked.

"Well, the instruction wasn't clear!" he protested.

My mum is still laughing and repeating the story over and over again.

"Mum, Dad, I need to talk to you about something. Can you pay attention for five minutes?" I plead.

"Talk to your mum, love, I'm going to the loo," said Dad, trailing off.

"That should buy us half an hour!" laughed Mum. "What's up, love?"

"Do you remember the guy I told you I met?" I asked.

"Oh yes, Hot Baguette Guy," she replied.

"It's Hot Breakfast Guy! Anyway, doesn't matter, I really like him, Mum, and I don't know what to do. I have so much travelling left to do, but I feel like I want to stay here and see where this goes."

"Well," started Mum, "what was the advice that you gave to Hannah when she was upset the other day? You said to her that this is a once in a lifetime experience, and I really believe that to be the case, love. Everything looks better with a bit of sun and sand. I think you should stick to your travel plan and keep in touch, you never know, you may meet up again down the line. But don't throw your dream trip away for a guy that you've spent a week with, no matter how good he looks in a dress!"

Mum was right, this was my once in a lifetime trip. I need to stick to my guns and stay with the original plan. I'm going to talk to Zack about it when I see him at the St Kilda Festival tomorrow.

Chapter Eighteen
Just Feed Me to the Alsatians!

"Do you think it even needs discussing, Louise?" asked Danni, sticking her tongue out whilst sticking diamantes onto her face. "Isn't it a given that it's a fling as you're both travelling?"

"That's the thing," I say. "I'm not sure that I want it to be a fling, but I'm not sure what the options are, either."

"OK, just don't come across as Mrs Needy!"

She had a point. Maybe I'm thinking about this way too deeply. I definitely need some Dutch courage for this conversation!

Faces painted, drinks in hand, we were dancing away to the live music. St Kilda had really gone to town for this festival; there were thousands of people all the way through the town and dancing on the beach.

"This is what travelling is all about!" shouted Hannah. "This is amazing!"

"Louise!" shouted Clara. "There's HBG!" She pointed into the crowd.

He stopped and greeted all the girls individually. He always remembered exactly what was going on with them and gave his take, from a 'male perspective'. The girls loved him and I had a feeling they were not alone.

"Hey, babe." He greeted me with a big smooch.

"Hey, I got you a drink and meat!" I replied.

"Ah, key to my heart!" he said, tucking into the pulled pork.

It was so hot in the afternoon sun that I was melting.

"Fancy coming back to mine for a bit? Get some shade?" he asked.

"Sure! Girls, I'm heading off for a bit, will call you later."

His flat was simple but nice, very beachy, literally, he had sand everywhere. Snuggled up in his room, I had to broach the subject.

"Zack, I need to discuss something with you."

"Oh boy, this sounds serious!" He laughed. "Are you trading me in for a younger model?"

"Maybe, I haven't decided yet," I joke, which causes him to grab me and tickle me.

"I'm being serious!" I squeak. "We need to talk!"

"OK, I will put on my serious face and give you my full attention. Wish I wore glasses; I could look extra serious! Oh, hang on!" he said, jumping off the bed. "How about this?" He was standing completely starkers in a pair of sunglasses. "I know it's more of a bodyguard look, but it's the best I can do at short notice!"

Laughing, I pull the glasses off his face and ask him to sit next to me.

"I was going to try and play this cool," I say, "but I think the sun, mixed with beer, has given me heat stroke, so I'm just going to go for it!"

"OK," he says, looking dubious.

I clear my throat and start. "I know that I'm supposed to see this as a holiday fling and I shouldn't get attached, but the truth of the matter is, I'm attached and there's nothing I can do about it."

"Louise..." he interrupts.

"No, let me finish!" I say. "I need to get this out. As I was saying, I know this is supposed to be a fling, but the truth is I don't want it to be. I don't know how this is going to work, because I am going to travel the east coast for six months and you are going to Fiji. It may just be a pipe dream, but I'm throwing it out there that I would like to try and keep this going!"

I'm looking at his face, trying to see some glimmer of what he is thinking. He looks confused and sad. Oh God, maybe he thinks I'm crazy. I shouldn't have said anything. Louise, why don't you shut up?

"Can I speak now?" he asks with a smile.

"You may!" I reply.

"I was trying to think of the right way to package this in my head."

Oh God, he's going to tell me to man up and get over myself. This is beyond awkward: I'm going to end up being heartbroken over a two-week fling. How embarrassing.

"But," he continued, "I'm just going to say it."

Bloody hell, I haven't got any nails left. Just say it, will you?

"I feel the same!"

Oh thank God!

"I don't know what it is about you, Louise. You're clumsy, crazy and not my usual type at all."

OK, this is not as flattering as he thinks it is.

"Despite all of that, you're the coolest chick I've ever met and I'm big time falling for you!"

"You are?" I say.

Oh my God, this is real, I knew it was! Maybe I'll look at rings tomorrow... OK, slow your role, Louise. Get back in the room.

"The thing is, Louise, we've both come out here for our own adventures and I would never want to stop you chasing your dream. I hope that you feel that way for me, too?"

This has taken a bit of a U-turn. "What are you saying?" I ask.

"I'm saying that I think we should both stick to our original travelling plans, but speak as often as we can. We can call, Skype, email, do all we can to keep in touch. Then leave it in the hands of the gods to decide our fate?"

I smile at him and snuggle back into him, hoping that he doesn't notice the tears in my eyes.

Snapping us out of our bubble, it sounds like there is someone walking through the front door.

"Who's that?" I ask. "Is it your flat mate?"

"Ah shit!" he says. "I didn't think she'd be back yet, stay here and be quiet."

"Why am I being quiet?" I ask, scrabbling around, looking for an answer to this situation in my head.

"Shhh," he says and, with that, hobbles out the door, pulling his shorts on.

I knew this was too good to be true. He's got a fricking girlfriend, the scumbag! How can I not have seen this? I grab my things and start to get dressed when I hear her screaming like a wild banshee.

"Who is in there, Zack?"

This isn't good.

"I've told you, don't bring your hoes back here!"

Who's she calling a hoe? Also, she seems very open about him having other women, just not in the flat... how progressive!

She's going mental. I can hear things being thrown around in the kitchen. I look out of the window and see that I am only one story up; if I jump just right I can land on the garage roof below. As I'm straddled halfway out of the window, my phone rings.

"Shhh," I tell my phone. It's Danni.

"Hey, will you two stop bumping nasties and come out, you're missing an amazing party!" she says, sounding half pissed.

"Danni, I'm in trouble!" I whisper.

"It's Louise!" she shouts really loudly. "She's in trouble!"

Ten seconds later, I can hear the girls racing over.

"Louise, it's Felicity. What's wrong?"

"Zack has a girlfriend," I say, close to tears. "She's here, in his flat, going crazy. I'm halfway out of the window, I'm going to jump!"

"Louise, no!" shouts Hannah. "I know it seems bad now, but this isn't the answer! You will get over him and find someone new. Granted, maybe not with his model good looks, but you will find someone!"

"I'm not going to kill myself, Hannah!" I whisper. "I'm trying to get out of the flat. I can't use the front door because she's in the kitchen, going crazy and throwing things at him!"

"Oh thank feck!" shouts Danni. "She's not killing herself, she's hotfooting it away from a psycho!"

This couldn't get any more ridiculous if I tried, until I hear another voice on the phone.

"Louise, this is PC Davenport with the St Kilda police."

You have got to be shitting me.

"Your friends have reported domestic abuse to me here at the festival. Can you please give us the address that you are at and we will come and get you?"

Jesus.

"Everything is fine, officer," I say, hanging out of the window. "My friends are getting a bit carried away. Can you give the phone to the sensible one, please?"

"Which one's that?" he rightly asked.

"The posh one!" I say.

Felicity is back on the phone.

"Fliss, I don't need the police, I need you. I'm literally just off the main street. Can you come get me?"

"On my way, darling!" she replied. "Don't fear, I will be there in a jiff."

Now I just need to angle myself slightly to the right, then I can land on that roof. One, two… bang! Phew, I made it, just in time for a pack of hungry Alsatians to run in my direction.

Luckily, I had some kangaroo jerky in my bag. "Hope you like this!" I shout as I throw the jerky at the dogs.

This calms them down so that I can jump down off the garage roof and onto the road, just in time to see Felicity running round the corner with a glass of gin.

"Here you go, sweetie, thought you would need it!"

Chapter Nineteen
It's His Washboard Abs!

The girls have rallied together to meet me and find out what has happened.

"I'm going to kill him!" said Danni. "How dare he come into our lives and treat us like mugs!" She thought about what she had just said as we all stared at her. "*You*... I mean treat *you* like a mug. It's not on," she said indignantly.

"I feel like such an idiot!" I sob to the girls. "Of course he's got a girlfriend! I mean, look at him!"

"It's his washboard abs" Tara added dreamily.

"Well, screw him!" said Danni. "Give me your phone so that you can't call the tosser and let's have a bloody good night!"

Maybe this was a blessing in disguise. There's no point me getting hung up on someone that I'm not even going to see for six months at best. I just feel so stupid; how did I not see the signs? Maybe because there weren't any. He's good, I'll give him that. Danni's right, he is a tosser.

Around seven p.m., we're all starving.

"I could murder a pizza," said Clara.

"Me too," I reply. "Come on, let's get some food and come back."

Walking down the high street, someone was shouting my name.

"Louise!" I turn to see HBG running down the street. "I've been looking everywhere for you! I've called you about a hundred times. Why didn't you answer your phone?"

"Why do you think?" shouted Danni. "Thinking you can take us all on a walk down the garden path with your nice hair and your good teeth! Well, now your dirty secret's out. We know about your minger of a girlfriend!"

To be fair, I didn't see what she looked like, but was happy that Danni had my back, even if she was addressing us as the royal 'we'.

"Come on, Louise, let's go!" said Felicity, throwing HBG a dirty look as the other girls formed a line across the street so he couldn't get to me.

"She's not my girlfriend!" he shouted.

That stopped me in my tracks.

"Don't fall for it, Louise!" said Danni. "He's a dirty dog!"

I can't help it; I have to know.

"Why would someone who lives with you get so upset about you having 'hoes' in your room if she's not your girlfriend?" I shout over the girls.

"OK, I realise I'm not completely innocent in all of this," he said, looking genuinely sorry about the situation. "I was seeing her a little while ago. A few months after we broke up, I needed a place to stay; she had a room to rent and offered it to me. I didn't realise she was using this as a gateway for more."

"Well, no shit, Sherlock!" said Tara. "So you move in with an ex, thinking that she didn't want more! Good job you're pretty!" she scoffed.

"It's the truth, Louise, I promise you!" he pleaded. "Look, I meant everything I said to you today, and I'm so sorry about the afternoon ending with you jumping out of a window!" He produced that winning smile.

"I don't know. Girls, what do you think?" I ask the panel.

Danni walks straight up to him and stares into his eyes.

"If you hurt her, I'll chop your nob off and post it to your mum!"

"Good to know!" said Zack, looking mildly terrified.

"For what it's worth, I think he's telling the truth," said Felicity.

I look at the girls, who all independently give me the nod.

"Want to come for pizza?" I ask. "All of the shimmying down drainpipes I've done today has made me hungry!"

"I'd love to," he replied.

And with that, he was back in the fold.

Chapter Twenty
Cocktails with the Queen

The time had come to say goodbye. I was putting on my brave face and HBG was doing his best to assure me that we would talk all the time and nothing would change, apart from that big blue wet thing and the thousands of miles that were going to be in between us.

"I promise I will call you every day, morning and night, so you won't have chance to forget me!" he said, whilst giving me the biggest bear hug.

"Make the most of your adventure," I say, snuggling into his hair, "because when we go home and get married and have babies, life is going to be really boring. Enjoy your freedom!"

"I'll hold you to it!" he said, giving me a final goodbye kiss.

On the coach travelling back to Sydney, I had a little cry. Our parting felt so final, yet I had so much hope. I was going to miss HBG, that much was certain, but we had made a promise to each other to make the most of our adventure and I planned on doing just that.

"Ooh, that would be lovely… Are you sure there is room for all of us? I'm sure they would love to… Thank you so much for the offer, we'll see you soon."

Felicity hung up and turned to us.

"Girls, I have the best news! My auntie has a place just outside Sydney and has said we can stay with her!"

"All six of us?" Tara asked. "How is she going to fit us in?"

"Don't worry about that, darling," she replied. "Louise, this will be just what you need to cheer you up; a little luxury always does the trick!"

With our luggage in tow, we stood staring at a massive set of wrought iron gates. Through them, I could see a sweeping driveway with a fountain in the centre and the world's largest house behind it. Felicity wasn't wrong, it was more than 'a little luxury' – this place was a fricking mansion!

"Are you sure we're OK here, Felicity?" asked Tara. "I didn't realise we were having tea with the Queen! I feel well underdressed."

"Oh hush, darling, we'll be fine," Felicity replied, ringing the bell.

"Hall residence," a posh voice said from the telecom.

"Oh hi, it's Fliss, Auntie Cassandra is expecting us."

The gates open and what appears to be a beach buggy comes hurtling towards us.

"Good afternoon, ladies," said a lovely old man with white gloves and suit tails. "May I take your bags?"

He piled our travelling backpacks and cases onto the buggy and drove us to the front door. This was surreal. Backpackers one second, a mansion the next; I felt like my brain was going to explode from the contrast.

"Darling!" shouted a lady in a ball gown, running down the steps to meet us.

"Auntie Cassandra!" Felicity replied. "Thank you so much for having us all, we're so very grateful."

We all nod dutifully. I'm not sure if we should curtsy.

"Girls, the pleasure is all mine, I get so bored rattling around this big old house. It will be great to have some girly company! Come; let us have some cocktails by the pool. I wasn't sure what you would all like, so I had a mixologist come in. Tell him whatever flavours are your favourite and he'll mix the most divine cocktail for you. He's simply the best!"

I overhear Danni saying she is going to ask for a hotdog flavoured cocktail!

The house is incredible; we all have our own room, all six of us. It's unbelievable! Each room has a magnificent four-poster bed, a chaise longue and a private bathroom. This really is how the other half live! In my room, I shut the door and dare to take my first glance at my phone. True to his word, Zack had called; this gave my heart a little flutter. I got comfy on the bed and called him back.

"Hey, you," he answered. "I miss you!"

"I miss you too!" I replied. "So where are you up to on your adventure?"

"I've just made it to Fiji," he said. "It's a slice of heaven. I'm staying in a little shack right on the beach. There's no one around, it's beautiful. The only thing that is missing is you!"

This made my stomach do a little flip.

"Where are you?" he asked.

"Well, believe it or not, I'm in a mansion overlooking a tennis court! Felicity's auntie invited us all to stay. It's unreal!"

"Slightly different paths we have taken then!" he laughed.

"Slightly!" I laugh back.

"Well, I have to go. Have an amazing time and say hi to the girls for me."

I tell him that I will and ring off.

There is a little tap on the door and Hannah walks in.

"Can you believe this place, Louise? It's unreal, isn't it?"

"It sure is!" I reply.

"I've honestly never been anywhere like this before; it's quite intimidating, isn't it?" she says.

"There's no need to be intimidated," I tell her. "We all put our trousers on the same when it comes down to it!"

She nods. "Have you heard from HBG?"

"I just spoke to him, it felt really weird. We're the same, but different, if you know what I mean?"

Hannah squints and looks at me.

"What I mean is, the conversation is still the same but knowing that we're not going to see each other soon is really strange."

"You really never know what the future holds, Louise. I've seen the way you two look at each other, people would kill for that! Be patient, I think you can make it work, and when you do, you will have so much respect for each other, doing your own thing and coming back to each other. It feels like Romeo and Juliet!"

"You know they both died at the end, right?" I laugh.

"Well, you know what I mean. I think you can make it work."

"Thanks, Han."

We have a big hug and meet the girls downstairs for 'dinner service'.

Dinner service is something to behold. We are invited to sit at a ginormous dining table where waiters are standing two paces back from every seat. I go to sit down when a waiter jumps and pulls the chair out for me. God, this is full on; I didn't get much training for this where I'm from! I reach for the wine. I need to steady my nerves, I feel like a fish out of water. The waiter all but bats my hand away and pours a glass for me. I feel so uncultured. Looking around the table, I can see that the girls feel the same.

"A toast!" says Cassandra, raising her glass. "To the good times, the bad times and all of the times in-between."

We all glance at each other and take a sip.

"Tomorrow, I thought we could all go out on the yacht," Cassandra says, shrieking with delight. "What do you think, girls? Champers on the yacht! You can tell all your friends about it!"

"Wow, I've never been on a yacht before!" said Clara.

"Me neither, here's to a new first!" I say, clinking glasses.

The dinner consisted of five courses. I'm going to be the size of a house by the time we leave. We say goodnight and go back to our rooms. I check my phone one last time and HBG has text:

"Night, gorgeous, hope you're having fun in the fancy house while I am in my shack! Speak tomorrow. HBG ☺ x."

Chapter Twenty-One
Just the Help!

We all receive an individual wakeup call at seven thirty a.m. sharp. Ugh, there really is no rest for the wicked! I walk over to the tray of freshly squeezed orange juice that has been left by the window and see that there is a note:

Morning ladies,

We will assemble at eight thirty am sharp for breakfast on the terrace, followed by carriages at nine thirty to the yacht for a day of fun.

Lady Hall

Carriages? Why do I feel like I'm going to turn into a pumpkin! Walking into the shower, I hear my phone buzzing. I run over to see that it's Zack. Wow, he really is keeping his promises.

"Good morning! What are you doing up so early?"

"I couldn't sleep," he responds whilst yawning.

I can imagine him stretching sexily. God, I wish I was in bed with him.

"What about you? You're never up this early, did you shit the bed?" he laughs.

"Actually, one will be venturing out on a yacht today!" I reply in my best posh voice.

"La de dah!" he says. "Well, have the best time, I'm just doing my twice a day call so that you don't forget me!"

"I'll never be able to forget you!" I say, smiling. "I'll talk to you later, OK?"

"OK, talk later."

After breakfast, we are escorted, via a black limo, to the yacht.

"I feel like a VIP," said Clara.

"Cassandra, do you think you could introduce me to a rich bloke so that I can be a lady of leisure with a big house like you?" said Danni.

We all roll our eyes at her.

"What? You know you were all thinking it!"

The yacht is like something you would see on a music video. I'm expecting P Diddy to jump onto the deck at any moment.

"All aboard, ladies!" Cassandra shouts as we all follow with open mouths.

On the long sofa that curves inside the front of the yacht (I'd love to say port or starboard, but I haven't got a clue which is which), there are six individually folded towels, bottles of sun lotion and pairs of flip-flops.. Zack was right; la de dah, indeed!

We cruise around Sydney, stopping at the harbour and various beaches; we are going to 'anchor down' in the middle of the ocean so that we can have a quick dip. I have to say, I'm looking forward to this as the deck is a sun trap and it is about a billion degrees.

"What about the sharks?" Hannah asks Lady Muck.

"Oh, don't worry, darling, there is a net. We're far enough in that they won't be able to get through that."

"A net!" Danni shouts. "Have you seen the size of their teeth? We need a fricking iron wall, not a net! I'm not going in, that's for certain!"

"Oh, don't be such a spoil sport!" said Felicity, diving in. "The water is divine; come on, jump in!"

It's like jumping into a bath; the water is so warm. I'm having a great time splashing around, attempting to snorkel, when Danni starts throwing pieces of bread at me, encouraging a load of little fish to start nibbling on my body like I am the last supper!

"Stop it, Danni!" I shout, freaking out.

It's like tiny little plungers all over my body, sucking the life out of me. Of course, this encourages Danni to keep going.

"Danni! I'm serious, stop it!" I protest.

As she's about to throw the last of the bread, Tara pops up behind her and pushes her in!

"Ha, ha, ha! Karma's a bitch!"

Back on the yacht, I assess the damage. I have got approximately one hundred little bite marks all over my body.

"Looks like you've got loads of hickeys… or scabies," Tara comments with a mouth full of croissant.

Brilliant, just what I need. I need to get some ice on these bumps so that they don't swell any more.

As I walk around the yacht, a man jumps down from what I assume is the roof and lands right in front of me. I scream and start to do what can only be described as a cross between a karate chop and a fly swotting action, shouting, "Hi-ya!"

The girls come running round to see me standing on one leg, karate kid style, ready to lay my deadly kick, when Cassandra shouts, "Stop! Stop! Louise, what on earth are you doing?"

"This man jumped down from the roof; he was clearly going to kidnap us, so I Mr Miyagi'd his ass!"

This is clearly too much for the kidnapper. He drops to the floor, hysterically laughing. In a Mexican accent, he recounts his version of the story:

"Lady Hall, I come to serve drinks, so I drop down from top deck. This lady assume I am bad man and starts to scream at me." By this point, tears are streaming down his face as he laughs. "I didn't have time to speak before she starts swotting at me like fly!"

He is now officially on the floor, howling with laughter along with everyone else. Well, this is embarrassing.

"How was I supposed to know other people were on this thing?" I say sulkily to the girls.

"Oh, don't fret, darling, he's just the help!" said Cassandra.

I roll my eyes and bend down to help the guy up who is wiping the tears from his eyes still laughing. 'Just the help'? Jesus, how rich is this lady? If I had a team of people on my yacht, I would at least consider mentioning it.

"Anyway, if he was 'a bad man', at least we can count on you to go full Lord of the Flies on him!" Danni creases up laughing.

"Sod off, you lot!"

"At least you gave everyone a good laugh!" said Hannah kindly. "It's a bit stuffy on here, I needed a giggle."

"Glad I could have been of service!" I say, squeezing her hand.

"Right ladies!" shouts Queen B. "Next stop, Bondi Beach. Assuming none of you have been before, it's one of Sydney's most famous beaches. We should be there in twenty minutes; in the meantime, soak up the sun and enjoy a cocktail."

"I could definitely get used to this," Danni said, eyeing up 'the help'.

Bondi Beach was a little disappointing. I'd heard so many stories about the place. I'm not sure what I was expecting, but this wasn't it.

"What a shit hole!" You can always trust Danni to eloquently put words to emotions.

"What's that over there?" shouts Clara. "Looks like they are filming something! Come on, let's try and get on camera."

There is a massive production crew following a tanned guy holding a puppy.

"The camera is angled to the right, so we need to get in the sea in that far corner and splash around in the background," said Danni.

"Thought you were scared of the sharks!" laughed Tara.

"Screw the sharks; this could be my ticket to fame! Come on, Louise!" Dragging me through the water, Danni kept making me fake laugh as 'there was more chance of getting in the cut'. Spoken like a true Director. We're shoulder high in the water, pulling ridiculous smiles and splashing 'like we're having fun', when Hannah shouts:

"Girls! Behind you!"

I turn to see that we are underneath the biggest crest of a wave I have ever seen!

"Oh God, Danni, look!" I scream.

"Hold your nose!" she shouts.

We get pulled into this washing machine style wave and I haven't got a clue which way is up. I'm getting chucked all over the place and I can't even see Danni. Just as I'm about to really freak out, the wave spits us out. We grab each other and, coughing and spluttering, make a run for it, out of the water.

"Louise, where's your top?" Danni says.

I look down and see that my baps are on full display. Scurrying around in the water, a big, fat, hairy man comes up to me with a pervy smile, holding my bikini top. Yuk!

Chapter Twenty-Two
Do I Know You?

The next morning, the girls head off to the beach again; I have decided that it would be safer on land, so I am going shopping instead. Hannah and Danni have decided that they need a day out of the sun, too, so are coming with me.

"This shopping centre is massive!" Danni said in awe. "You don't get anything like this in Ireland! Ooh, can we pop into that lingerie shop? I'm too embarrassed to give my pants to Lady H's cleaner to wash, I'm going to keep buying new pairs instead!"

Inside the store, I see a girl from the other side of the room smile at me. I rack my brain, trying to place her face. As I get closer, she smiles again. I must have met her in the hostel in Sydney the first time round.

"Hi, how are you?" I ask her.

Smiling, she replies, "I'm very well, thank you. How are you?"

"I'm so sorry, I just can't place how we know each other!" I reply, scanning her face for clues.

"Err, Louise..." interrupts Danni.

"Did we meet in the hostel in Coogee?" I ask.

Laughing, she replies, "I've never stayed in a hostel."

"Louise!" hissed Danni.

"In a minute! I'm trying to figure out how I know this lady. What's your name?" I ask.

At that question, Danni turns and walks away. Wonder what's up her arse?

"Elle Macpherson," she replied, smiling.

"Elle Macpherson, Elle Macpherson… I know that name."

Then the penny drops.

"Oh God, that's so embarrassing, I'm so sorry! Please ignore me. Of course I know who you are, I thought I must have met you somewhere before, but clearly I just saw you on TV!" I mumble away.

Ahh, ground, swallow me up!

Gracefully, she replies, "No worries at all, it could happen to anyone." With that, she walks away.

"I am such a muppet! Why didn't you stop me?" I whine to Danni.

"Seriously! I bloody tried, you told me to shut up! God, you're so embarrassing," Danni says, shaking her head.

"What did she say?" asks Hannah.

"She handled the situation far more gracefully than I did, that's for sure! She looked incredible, did you see her skin?"

Still laughing, we head out to the main street to grab a bite to eat. As we take our seats, we hear someone shouting to Danni; it turns out it's one of her friends from home. She pulls up a chair and joins us.

"Stacey, this is Louise and Hannah."

We all say hi and introduce ourselves. We catch up on where we have been on our travels and Stacey mentions that she has just left Fiji.

"A guy I'm seeing has recently gone to Fiji," I say to her.

"I hope he wasn't a kite surfing instructor," she laughs. "That guy was so fit, everyone on the island was trying to get with him!"

She sees my face. "Oh God, it wasn't, was it?"

Danni stares at her and does a little 'shut up' face.

"No, it's OK," I say, trying to hide that horrible sinking feeling. "We're not exactly seeing each other, it's... well, it's complicated."

"Well, if it makes you feel any better, he didn't go near anyone; he said he had a girlfriend."

"Really?" I say with a massive smile on my face.

Laughing, she says, "Really! He seemed genuinely swept off his feet, Louise."

OK, my appetite is back, I just need to figure out how to chew with this massive grin on my face!

After lunch and a bit more shopping, we are handed a leaflet for a tour around a 'haunted' prison.

"We should do this tonight!" said Danni. "It will be so much fun!"

"I'm in!" I say.

"I'm not!" said Hannah, shaking her head vigorously. "You shouldn't mess with things like that, what if it's really haunted? A scary prison ghost could follow us home!"

"We've dealt with pirate ghosts; prison ghosts are the next logical step if you think about it!" I laugh.

Danni calls and books seven tickets. "No backing out now!"

Back at the palace, we tell the girls that we have booked tickets. "Fabulous! What fun!" screeches Cassandra.

She really is bored!

"We need to leave at seven p.m. to get the bus at the end of the road to the prison," says Danni.

"A bus? Nonsense!" says Cassandra. "My driver will take us in the limo."

Danni turned and winked at us. She's such a schemer!

At seven p.m., we're ready to go, apart from the small fact that Cassandra seems to be wearing a ball gown. We all look at Felicity. She clears her throat.

"Ah-hem. Auntie Cassandra, we're going to a dirty old prison. Don't you think maybe you should wear something a little more appropriate, that you don't mind getting dirty?"

"Yeah, people will think you're a right nob if you turn up in that!" Danni added as we all cringe.

"Oh, I see. Sorry, girls, I didn't mean to let the side down," she replies.

Ah, now I feel really bad.

"You know what? Wear whatever you're comfortable in," I say, which makes all the girls stare at me.

"Great, let's go!" Cassandra replies excitedly.

This is going to be interesting.

At the prison, the tour guide looks us up and down.

"Where did you lot meet? Keys in the bowl situation??" He laughed.

"Here are our tickets; move out of the way, chuckles," Danni retorts whilst barging past him.

This place is beyond creepy; the cell windows are brick surround with no glass and have bars in-between so we keep getting a draft as we walk past each cell. It feels like someone is breathing down your neck.

"Did anyone bring spare pants?" Felicity asks, clutching my arm.

The tour guide does the old girl guide trick and tells the story of the haunted prison with a torch underneath his chin; the place is near enough pitch black. Felicity was right, spare pants would have been a good idea.

He walks us through, telling the story of heinous crimes that the inmates committed, and how their spirits are trapped here today. On the top floor, we stop at a viewing platform where people used to watch hanging executions.

"I can't believe that people used to volunteer to watch," said Hannah.

"There would be queues around the side of the prison back in the early 1900s. People were desperate to come in and watch," the guide explained. "It was considered a social event, and warmer than their homes."

"That's horrible," Felicity replied, shaking her head.

"The spirit trapped here is the spirit of Billy Bob Jones," the guide continued. "Billy Bob was here under several counts of murder and assault. He was a mean man and had to be moved around the prison strapped in a straitjacket as he posed too great a threat to other inmates." He pauses for effect. "It was at this exact point that Billy met his demise by hanging. People say that they still hear the screams today."

Just as he finished his sentence, a body dropped down from above us with a rope around its neck, letting out the most petrifying scream.

We scream and grab each other making a run for it out of the prison.

Except, we can't get out! He has locked the doors and is laughing hysterically.

"Oh my God, we're stuck in this old prison with a psychopath!" Clara cried.

Whilst Tara and I are kicking the door, desperately trying to open it, the guide shouts, "Girls, girls, calm down. It's OK, it's a dummy, look!"

I have to peel Felicity off me before I can glance back and see that it was a joke.

Danni walks up to him and shouts in his face, "I nearly shit my pants!"

Chapter Twenty-Three
A-maze-ing

A few days in a touch of luxury was definitely what the girls and I needed. It was such a treat to be fed and watered around the clock. If only we could take this place with us on our travels. Next on the agenda was Byron Bay. Bags packed, we said our goodbyes to Cassandra and 'the help' and made our way to the bus station; alas, the luxury travel was over. It was good while it lasted!

We settled onto the coach with our books and music, ready for an eight-hour journey. I'm quite enjoying travelling around by coach, the scenery is incredible and you see something new every ten minutes. Our half way pit stop was in Port Macquarie. As the coach pulled into the car park, the driver advised us that he had a family emergency and had to go back to Sydney. Another driver is en route, but we need to keep ourselves occupied for six hours.

"Great, a six hour delay! What are we supposed to do for six hours?" huffed Danni.

"Well, according to my guide book, there is a wine tasting venue with a maze!" suggested Felicity. "They start you off with various samples and then you have to hunt the next glass down via the clues. It's only half an hour away from here; we could easily go and come back again within six hours."

"Let's do it!"

We are greeted at the vineyard by a guy that looks like Santa Claus with a tan.

"Hey there, ladies! Are you here to try out our delicious wine?"

"We certainly are!" replied Felicity. "However, we only have around four hours; is that enough time?"

"As long as you don't get lost in the maze, you'll be fine!" he chuckled.

Hmm, that sounds ominous!

"OK, ladies, gather round," tanned Santa shouts. "This game works best if you split into teams. As there are six of you, I suggest three and three. One team starts on this side of the maze, the other team starts from the other side. The first team to the centre wins a bottle of champagne! This is Sheila; she will take three of you to the south side of the maze. When you hear the bottle pop, it's time to start."

We split up; Danni, Tara and I go to the south side with Sheila while Clara, Hannah and Felicity stay with Santa.

"On your marks, get set…" Pop goes the bottle!

"What's the first clue?" screams Tara, getting way too excitable.

"It says: 'Where in Australia is Steve Irwin from? Turn right for Sydney or left for Melbourne'."

"It has to be Sydney," says Danni. "There was memorabilia all over Sydney Zoo!"

"Just because there's memorabilia in a zoo doesn't mean he's from there!" snapped Tara.

"I'm ninety-nine percent certain that he's from Melbourne," I say to the girls. "I'm sure I read it at the zoo."

"OK, Louise, it's on you; left it is!" said Tara.

We race to our left where we are met with a glass of rosé each and our next clue.

"Wahoo, we did it!" we cheer. "Quick, down the drink and onto the next clue."

My head is slightly fuzzier now, but my determination is kicking in.

"When was Australia colonised?" Tara read.

"How the feck should we know?" shouted Danni exasperatedly.

"What are the options, Tara?" I ask.

"Right for 1788 or left for 1800."

We all stare at each other blankly.

"OK, on three, shout which direction you think. Majority rules. One, two, three…"

There are two lefts and a right.

"Left it is!" We run to the left for what feels like ages and run into a dead end.

"Ugh, it's the wrong way! Turn around, we need to run back."

We run back to where clue number one was, and it is gone.

"Someone's moved it! We're never going to get out of here alive!" Tara cried.

"Oh, don't be so dramatic, Tara!" Danni shouted. "Look, on the floor, the cork is still there. We were definitely here, which means we need to go that way."

We run around the corner to see a glass of red and our next clue. Yes!

In the distance, we can hear the girls cheering.

"Come on, knock it back, we have to hurry," shouts Danni.

"OK, clue number three," I read. "What does Ozzie rules relate to? Turn right for rugby or left for football."

"It's football!" shouts Danni. "Quick, run right!"

As we run, hurtling round the corner, we can hear the other girls getting closer. Our competitive natures kick in at warp speed. "Next clue, hurry!" I shout.

Knocking back our third drink, white wine, my head is more than a little squify.

"Read it, Tara, read it!" shouts Danni.

"What famous TV series was made in Sydney? Left for Neighbours, right for Home and Away."

"They both were, weren't they?" said Danni.

"Neighbours was definitely Melbourne, because I went on the tour with Zack. It has to be right!" I say.

"Loser!" Danni shouts. "Come on, let's go."

This passage takes us down a tunnel and into a cellar.

"Why do we keep ending up in creepy places?" said Tara, hiding behind me.

"Look, the next drink is there. Ugh, this is going to come back up again soon!" I say as I knock back the fourth glass of wine.

"For your final round, the team has to split up and follow their own course of wine based questions. The winning team will need to have all members at the final post before the opposing team. Use the head torches provided and follow your clue into the deep, dark cellar. Good luck!"

"I can't do this on my own, it's too creepy and I'm half drunk!" protests Tara.

"We'll open up the clues together, and make sure that we all head in the right direction, OK? Now put your head torches on!" I order the girls.

"Clue number one: 'You will find me at room temperature; the older I am, the better I taste'."

"Has to be red wine!" shouts Danni.

We look around and see 'the red corridor' written above one of the passages.

"OK, Danni, you take that one. Next question: 'I am a traditional accompaniment to chicken and fish'."

"What does accompaniment mean?" shouts Danni.

"It means pairing; must be white wine. Where's the white passageway?" All of the passageways are looking a tad blurry now.

"It's around here," shouts Danni.

"OK, Tara, you take that one. Last clue: 'The newest vintage is the freshest in this category'."

"It has to be rosé;, where's the rosé tunnel?" asks Tara, swaying around.

"It goes further underground. Louise, I know you hate small spaces; I'll take that, you take mine!" shouts Danni, in military mode.

"Thanks Danni, you're the best! OK, girls, see you on the flip side! Hurry!"

We all take off in our separate directions. I'm so glad that Danni took the underground option, I would have definitely freaked out. Where does this passage lead? All I can see is tunnel. My heartbeat is pounding in my ears with every step. I think I can see light; I push myself to keep running when I hear voices. I see an exit light on a set of stairs and start to climb up. Damn it, Felicity is already there!

"Yes! I'm first! Ha, ha, we beat you!" shouts Felicity, basking in her glory.

"Actually, the entire team has to be here for you to win!" I say, sticking my tongue out.

"Damn it, come on, girls!" she starts shouting. "You can do it!"

I join in. "Come on, Danni and Tara, we've got this!"

Laughing, Felicity passes me a glass of champagne. "This was fun."

"It really was a great shout by you. Ooh, I can hear someone." Pushing up a piece of grass, Danni comes climbing out of a hole. "Wahoo, we're in the lead! Tara, where are you?" I shout.

Next is Clara.

"Two for two, it's getting close!" said Danni. "Come on, Tara!"

"Shush, shush! Listen," I whisper to the girls. "I can hear someone shouting in the distance."

"Oh for God's sake, look up!"

We turn and see Tara has somehow managed to get on top of the roof of the visitor centre. Just as we are shouting at her to come down, Hannah comes running around the corner.

"Victory is ours!" shouts Felicity.

"Bloody Tara, never should have had her on our team!" sulks Danni.

Santa walks straight to the centre of the maze from a side door, which is rather disappointing after all our efforts. "Well done to the North Team," he says. "Here you go, a magnum of champagne!"

"Wahoo!" we hear from the top of the visitor centre.

"I have to say, no one has ever ended up in there before," said Santa.

"I can believe it!" I reply, laughing. "Come on, let's go and get her."

We manage to make it back to the bus just in time, steaming drunk. At least the rest of the journey goes quickly. After a good long nap, we all get woken up four hours later in Byron Bay.

Chapter Twenty-Four
Now Is Not the Time for Hysterics

"That smells amazing!" said Danni sleepily. "Must follow food smell."

We drag ourselves out of bed and head towards the communal kitchen.

"Good morning, ladies! Welcome to the Sunshine Hostel. Please take a seat. Here is your welcome breakfast: freshly cooked pancakes and fresh orange juice. Just a little welcome from the management team."

"Wow, this is amazing! Thank you," said Felicity.

"My pleasure. Anything we can do for you, just pop by the front desk and we'll be happy to help."

"What a nice guy, I don't think we've ever had such a warm welcome!" said Felicity.

"Yeah, it's not like we've just stayed in a palace. About time we had some luxury!" Danni laughed. "Shall we scoff this lot then head into town?"

Byron is a quaint little surf town with all of the soul to match. Everyone that lives here is a 'surfer dude' with a laid back style that comes from years of not taking life too seriously. I'd describe it as more of a hippy commune than a town. There are wind chimes in every window, all the women are wearing floaty skirts with bandanas and every guy had dreads. The town's motto might as well be 'peace and love'. I like its quirky charm. There is such a feeling of calm here that you can't help but let it rub off on you. It was a little too much for some of the girls, though.

"We should get our hair braided while we're here!" said Hannah.

"Ooh, and henna!" added Clara.

"I want some of those baggy fisherman trousers!" Tara piped in.

"Yeah, and later on we can all go and smoke weed and say 'peace, man' to everyone!" Felicity said sarcastically.

"Well, we could if we wanted!" Tara replied.

We manage to talk the girls out of morphing into complete hippies within five minutes of being here and head to the beach.

"I'm still a little hungover from the maze; I'm going to go to sleep for a bit," I tell the girls. There's nothing better than having a nap with the sun on your skin.

An hour later I can feel one of the girls messing with my arm, trying to wake me up.

"Leave me alone! I'm knackered and want to sleep," I moan, brushing them off.

They do it again.

"Ugh, why are you so annoying?"

I take off my shades and look around. All of the girls are in the sea. Huh, then who touched me? I feel it again, look down and see a ginormous spider on my arm. I scream and start trying to hit it off, but it's clinging on tightly and not letting go.

"Help, help, spider!" I scream at the top of my lungs.

The girls leg it out of the ocean and stop short as they see it. I see the colour drain from their faces. This thing is the size of my hand!

"Get it off!" I scream.

Felicity throws her bag at me and Danni throws a flip flop, neither of which go anywhere near the spider!

"Oh my God, it's bitten me…"

My eyes are stinging and my mouth is dry. There's a blinding strip light that's hurting my eyes. Oh, my head hurts, where am I? I'm so confused. OK, Louise, think; what's the last thing you remember? I was on the beach and… oh God, I was bitten by a spider. Am I dead? I hear a male voice in the distance.

"Louise," said the voice.

"God?" I reply.

"No, not God, Louise, I'm Dr Harrington. You have been bitten by a spider and had a nasty shock. You're in Byron Hospital."

"What? Hospital? How did I get here? Why can't I remember anything?" I panic.

"It's OK, there is nothing to worry about; luckily it wasn't a poisonous spider so there is no venom in your blood."

My eyes are starting to come into focus. I look around the room and the girls are there with blotchy eyes.

"Oh thank God!" shouts Danni. "We thought you were dead!"

"Now is not the time for hysterics, ladies!" said the doctor, chastising them. "Please give us a moment."

The girls all hug me one by one as they leave the room.

"We'll be right outside. If he touches you, just scream!" says Danni, staring at him. "I'll kick his ass!"

"Doctor, why can't I remember getting here?" I ask.

"Even though the spider wasn't poisonous, when it bit you it pumped a little infection into you that made you temporarily lose consciousness. Your friends did a remarkable job of getting you here ten minutes after the event. They ran in, carrying you by your arms and legs. I'm afraid that's why you are still a little woozy; they banged your head on the door frame as they were racing into the hospital. You have a little bump."

I lifted my arm to touch my head; it had a big bandage around it.

I look down to my other arm. "Jesus Christ!" My arm was about TEN times its usual size; the spider must have laid about a hundred eggs in it!

"Louise, you need to stay calm. You have a serious mixture of drugs in your system, it could make you—"

Before he finished the sentence, I projectile vomited all over him and his nice white lab coat. Ugh this day has quickly gone from bad to worse!

Three hours later, the doctor said that I should be OK to go back to the hostel. I wasn't so sure. The way that they had bandaged the egg on my head left a massive tuft of hair sticking out of the top like a scarecrow, I had managed to bite my lip when I threw up and my arm was ten times its usual size. I was doing a really good Nutty Professor impersonation.

The girls were doing a great job trying to reassure me: "No one will notice... you look absolutely fine... we'll get you a bandana..."

I was draped over Felicity and Danni's shoulders as they carried me back into the hostel. The lovely owner ran over.

"Oh my goodness, what happened? Have you been in a car accident?" he asked with a face full of concern.

"Oh, she doesn't look that bad, stop fussing!" said Danni.

"It's OK, Danni, he's only being nice. I was bitten by a spider," I tell him.

"Oh gosh! Did it crawl all over you?" he replies.

"No, the head injury is this lot's handiwork. It actually bit my arm," I say, laughing.

"Oh, you poor thing! Rest in the hammock and we'll look after you," he said, rushing to get me some tea.

"Zack called a few times, Louise; we didn't know what to say. I think you should call him back, though; he'll be worried. Here you go, I'll dial him for you."

"Thanks, Han."

"Oh my God! Louise, are you OK? What the hell happened?"

Oh no! She'd video called him, just how I wanted him to see me!

"Sorry, I thought this was a call." My rational answer should calm him down.

"What? Louise, what happened? Have you been in an accident?" His eyes are nearly popped out of his head with worry.

"I'm OK, don't worry. I got bitten by a spider," I reply.

"On your head?" he asks.

"No, here!" I point the phone at the huge lump on my arm.

"Jesus! That looks so painful. If you got bitten on your arm, what happened to your head?"

Laughing, I say, "This lot smacked my head into the hospital door frame trying to get me to a doctor on time."

"You look like death!" he says.

"Stop flattering me, it's embarrassing!" I laugh.

"Sorry," he laughed. "Are you sure you're OK?"

"I've had better days, but honestly, I'm fine. I really didn't want you to see me looking like this, can we talk tomorrow?"

"No way! Get comfy, I'll chat to you until you fall asleep."

He did just that. A few hours later, I woke up to the phone on my chest and drool on my chin. Ugh, I hope he didn't see that.

I quickly became the talk of the town. Walking down the street, people pointed and stared at me like I was Quasimodo. Others showed kindness via their offering of fruit. I had so many grapes given to me on a daily basis we had to keep going back to the hostel.

The tablets that I was on were strong, to say the least. I constantly felt that I was walking on marshmallows, and I'm pretty sure that I'd had one or two conversations with inanimate objects. At least I was in the right place for it; the hippies accepted me with open arms and advised me to 'go with it, man', and explore my inner self.

By day three, I could remove the bandage on my head and wash my hair. What a treat! The water on my head felt divine. The swelling on my arm was also going down; I was starting to look and feel normal again. Much to the dismay of the town, they had lost their local tourist attraction. The grapes dried up and I was ousted from the hippies. Apparently inner peace is harder to find when you shower.

To say that I was ready to leave was an understatement. The girls kept saying that we should stay a few more days as I'd missed so much of beautiful Byron. I was sad about that, but honestly that spider was haunting my dreams. When I woke up in the middle of the night, swatting Danni with my flip flop, I knew I had to go.

Chapter Twenty-Five
Blackpool on Steroids

Felicity had taken it upon herself to become my nurse. She had even set an alarm on her phone for every four hours to make sure that I took my pills. At one point, I'm pretty sure she was making aeroplane noises and flying the pills into my mouth, although I can't be one hundred percent sure as I was completely off my head on meds at the time.

On the coach (in front of everyone), she shouted, "Louise, time for your meds!" followed by sniggers all round. Great, I'd just escaped being the village idiot in one place and now my reputation was preceding me before we'd even managed to get to Surfers.

Surfers Paradise was only an hour and a half away from Byron. Even though the distance is small, the contrast is huge. From the relaxed, natural surroundings of Byron, we were thrust into a garish, unapologetic Vegas of Australia. After four days in bed, I was ready to have some fun and where better to have it?

I started planning our evening before we'd even had the chance to check into the new hostel.

"Right, girls, tonight I need you all on form! The tablets are officially finished, I no longer look like an Oompa Loompa and I am ready to have some fun!"

"Are you sure, Louise?" said Felicity filled with concern. "You have literally only just finished your tablets, maybe we should just have a nice dinner tonight and hit the town tomorrow?"

"No way! The beast is unleashed and I am ready to paaartay," I say, doing a little dance walk.

"I'm in!" said Danni. "You've been right boring these last few days, let's get you hammered!"

"YES, Danni, let's do this!" Danni and I high five as the rest of the girls look to each other nervously.

"I saw that!" I say, busting them. "Don't worry, I promise I'm fine."

The hostel was... well, it was a place to sleep. It wasn't going to win any awards, but it was cheap and it was central. Dropping our bags off, we headed into town to get to the centre of the action.

This place is like Blackpool Pleasure Beach on steroids. If you swapped the Brits with bulldog tattoos for hot people, you wouldn't be too far off. There was a haunted house on every corner, arcades, ice-cream shops, candy floss and girls in gold bikinis with cowboy hats.

"Why are all of those girls dressed the same?" asked Tara, pointing at the group of scantily clad, golden bikini girls.

"I've got no idea," replied Danni. "Although, if I looked like them, I'd probably parade around in next to nothing as well... bitches!"

"Look! They're taking money off those guys. Are they hookers?" said Clara, standing on her tip toes to see.

"I doubt they'd be openly taking money in the middle of the day if they were hookers!" said Tara, rolling her eyes.

"What do their sashes say? I can't see," said Danni, trying to climb onto my back to get some height.

"It says 'meter maid'," said Clara. "What's a meter maid when it's at home?"

"I have no idea," replied Danni, "but it's making me think we should have a salad for lunch. Can't have the skinny bitches stealing all of the action tonight!"

Drinking games started at around five p.m. To start the merriment, we played 'Never Have I Ever'. If you have done the deed that was being asked, you had to knock back a shot.

"Never have I ever had a one-night stand," says Danni, eyeing the group dubiously.

She, Tara and Felicity downed their drinks.

"What a surprise!" laughed Hannah, followed by Felicity throwing a pillow at her.

"OK, me next!" said Clara. "Never have I ever cheated on someone."

Only Danni that time.

"Danni!" we all shout, throwing things at her.

"What? It was a long time ago… and he asked for it!" she said, laughing.

"OK, never have I ever kissed a girl," said Felicity.

I glance around and knock mine back.

"Louise!" the girls gasp.

"What? It was in college. I thought everyone was doing it!" I laugh.

The game went on for a couple of hours, by which point we were raring to go. Look out, Surfers, we're coming to get you!

We bar hopped for a few hours in the kind of bars that you stand around looking cool in, not the type you actually have fun in.

"We need to find somewhere we can cut some shapes," slurred Danni. "Let's ask the gold bitches." She staggered towards the meter maids. "Oi, minute maids!" she shouted across the room.

Cringe!

"It's 'meter' maid, not 'minute' maid," bikini number one answered.

"What's a minute maid?" laughed bikini number two.

"I don't know! What the feck's a meter maid?" asked Danni, swaying around.

"We put money into the meters... you know, where people park their cars? They can keep drinking and we make sure they don't get a ticket!" said a very polite bikini number three.

"That's an actual job?" hiccupped Danni. "That's hilarious!"

"Sorry about our friend," Clara apologised. "She's a little drunk."

"So, do you need money in your meter or not?" said an agitated bikini number one.

"No, we don't," Clara replied. "We're actually looking for recommendations for a club, if you have one?"

"What do we look like, tourist information? Piss off!" said number two.

And that was the end of that.

A few streets over, we see an entrance to a club with a massive queue all the way down the side of the building.

"Anyone got any ideas on how we VIP our way in? I really don't fancy queuing in that for an hour!" I ask the girls, propping myself up on a lamppost.

As we are crossing the street, three large black SUVs pull up and a bunch of very large men jump out.

"They'd give HBG a run for his money, Louise!" laughed Clara.

"Who are they?" I ask. "They have to be famous." We hear people chanting. "What are they saying, I can't make it out?"

"I think they're saying Gay FL?" said Hannah.

As we wet ourselves laughing, Felicity says, "I think it's NFL, Han, but close enough!"

"Come on, this is our window!" says Tara as she runs across the street. "Hi, guys, fancy escorting a group of ladies into the club?" she shouts.

"That is some pair of balls she's got on her!" laughed Danni.

"We're British!" she shouts. "You know the Brits know how to party!"

"You've got some front, lady, I'll give you that!" one of them replied. "Come on then!"

The bouncer opened up the rope for us and we followed the Americans in.

"Good work, Tara! I never in a million years thought they would say yes to that!"

"As my mum always says, you don't know unless you ask!"

Not only did they get us in, but we had somehow blagged our way into the VIP area.

"How cool is this?" I shout to Felicity over the music. "Come on, let's dance!"

Shots are flowing; we're dancing our pants off having such a blast when I hear a commotion behind us. I turn round to see Danni shouting in one of the players' faces. Oh Danni! I run up to the booth and hear her shouting, "NFL? More like Gay FL!" Finding herself hilarious, she's falling about laughing.

"Danni, shut up!" I whisper.

"Who plays NFL? Pussies, that's who!" she shouts in a second guy's face.

The bouncer looks at us and points to the door.

Grabbing Danni, I say, "We'll show ourselves out."

As soon as the fresh air hits, Danni starts to chuck up everywhere.

"We need to get her some food," Hannah says, holding her hair back.

"There's a pizza place over there." Felicity pointed.

"We'll go. Come on, Tara." I grab Tara's hand and walk across the street.

In the pizza place, there are a bunch of rowdy people getting increasingly agitated that they are not being served.

"Where are the servers?" I ask one of the guys.

"God knows; we've been waiting for ages!" he replies.

"Tara, look, those pizzas are nearly done, we just need to pull them out of the oven," I whisper.

We look at each other. Tara is the first to break. "Ah sod it, come on!"

We jump behind the counter. "Who wants pizza?" we shout, laughing. The crowd goes wild! This must be what Beyoncé feels like!

We're pulling them out of the oven, slicing and dicing, handing pizza out to the masses.

"I feel like Jesus when he fed the five thousand," shouted Tara over the rabble.

"Someone's coming!" a guy shouted from the back.

"Tara, quick, grab a couple of boxes!" I shout.

I slide over the counter, Tara chucks the boxes at me and I make a run for it. Bombing out of the shop, we shout "Run!" to the girls.

"Oh shit!" shouts Felicity, seeing two guys running behind us. "Clara, Hannah, grab Danni! I'll hold them off!"

As we are bombing down the street, I turn to see Felicity throwing her shoes as if they were a pair of grenades!

"That was hilarious!" said Clara as we collapse back into the hostel.

"Well, if we get stuck for money, we could always work in a pizza place!" Tara laughed.

"Sure those nice men would give us a reference."

Chapter Twenty-Six
That's a Big House!

Our time in Surfers continued in a similar vein. We mostly abused the meter maids, got steaming drunk and spent way too much money in haunted houses. After a week of pickling our livers, we were ready to move on to a calmer setting. I was well and truly over my spider bite and had more than made up for the four days in bed in Byron.

Our next stop is Brisbane. One of Tara's friends from school has a house there and has invited us to stay. We are a man down as Hannah's boyfriend is arriving tomorrow, so she is flying back to Sydney to travel with him for a few weeks; we'll pick her back up when we get to Airlie Beach.

"Have the best time, Han! We're going to miss you so much!" I say through a big mop of hair. "Get your fix and then get back to girly time, OK? It's not going to be the same without you."

"Oh, I'm going to miss you all so much!" she cried. We all pile in for a group hug and see her off to the station.

"Right, no other fecker is leaving!" said Danni. "I can't take it; it's like the Spice Girls breaking up. We've basically lost Scary Spice!"

"You've definitely got the Scary Spice title!" laughed Felicity.

"Why the feck am I Scary Spice?" Danni replied.

"No idea!" we all replied, laughing.

"Stevie says we need to take the train to Brisbane town centre and then change to a place that sounds like a kangaroo with a broken jump," said Tara, rummaging around in her bag.

"What are you talking about?" asked Felicity with her head in her hands.

"I wrote the name of the place down on a piece of paper and put it in my bag - now I can't find it. I remember thinking that it sounded like a kangaroo with a dodgy jump, though, so let's look for a station that sounds like that!"

Felicity snatches the map off Tara exasperatedly. "There's nothing here that sounds like a kangaroo! There's Moorooka, Indooroopilly, Toowong, Sherwood..."

"That's it: Toowong!" shouted Tara

"How the hell does that sound like a kangaroo with a dodgy jump?" I ask, shaking my head.

"Think about it!" says Tara, like I'm the crazy one. "Imagine a kangaroo jumping, but it doesn't jump straight up; it jumps slightly crooked. You could imagine it making a 'Toowong' sound."

"It's too early for this level of crazy!" said Danni, lying on her bag. "Can someone with a brain navigate?"

"I'll navigate," said Felicity, taking control.

We actually made it to Toowong disaster free, which, seeing as though this was a Tara plan, was a first. At the station, Tara is on the phone to her friend, who is giving her directions. Felicity takes the phone from her hand.

"Hello, Stevie? This is Felicity, I can assure you that it would be much quicker if you give me the relevant directions and I will lead, mostly because Tara is an idiot," she informed him matter-of-factly. We heard him laughing on the other end. "OK, roger that, we'll be with you shortly. Come on, girls, this way!" she said, strutting down the street.

"You didn't need to call me an idiot to one of my oldest mates," sulked Tara.

"If he's one of your oldest friends, he's well aware, darling!" replied Felicity curtly, which made us all roll around laughing.

Felicity tells us that we are nearly there and points to house number twenty-one.

"That's a big house!" said Clara. Unfortunately, with her South London accent it sounded like she said 'big ass' right behind a rather large lady.

"What did you just say to me?" the lady said, turning round, marching towards Clara.

"I said that's a big house," Clara repeated. Again, it sounded like 'ass'.

"No, no, no!" Danni and I jump in the middle. "It's her accent. She's saying 'house', it just unfortunately sounds like 'ass'," we say, trying to defuse the situation.

"Yeah, I would never say you had a big ass to your face," said Tara helpfully.

I managed to move my head just in time to see this massive arm fly past my face and bust Tara straight in the nose.

"You need to learn some bloody manners!" said the big ass as it strutted off.

Stevie stepped outside of his house just in time to see the commotion and Tara's broken face.

"Tara! What the hell happened?" he shouted, running down the street in bare feet.

"She thought I said she had a big arse, but I was saying big house!" she sobbed. "I told her I'd never say that she had a big arse to her face and she hit me!"

"Let's assess the damage." I run my finger down her nose, and although it's very swollen, it's not broken. "You just need some ice on it for a bit and you'll be fine."

As we walk towards the house, the other two lads who live there come running out.

"Jesus, what happened to your face?" said the first one.

"You should see the other guy!" laughed Stevie. "Girls, this is Tommy and Bernie."

"This is Danni, Felicity, Louise and Clara." Tara introduces us. "Can I please get some ice?"

"Of course, of course, come in!" said Tommy. "Can't believe you picked a fight within five minutes of being here."

"Glad you find it funny, my face is killing me!" said Tara through the towel on her face.

"Pop your head back, you'll feel fine in no time," said Stevie kindly. "Whilst the ice is doing its thing, I'll give you guys a tour."

This place was like something a famous rapper would live in. There was a swimming pool, a pool table in the centre of a room of mirrors, six bedrooms, a bar and a jetty that lead straight onto a lake at the back of the house.

"Are you lot drug dealers?" asked Danni. "I'm not against it, I'd just rather know in case the Popo come and I have to pop a cap in someone's ass."

"Good to know!" laughed Stevie. "Sadly, nothing as exciting as that. We work at the local Wooly's... you know, the grocery store? We're all in management there.

The cost of living is so much lower here, so, if you come slightly out of the way like we have, and there's a bunch of you, you can get a massive house. I've got an ex that could do with getting popped with a cap in her ass if you're offering, though?"

"Not going to lie, I was kind of hoping you were drug dealers, we could use a bit of excitement!" Danni sulked.

"Excitement! Tara just got punched in the face," I said shaking my head.

"Oh yeah! You're right, that was funny." She laughed and walked away.

"Honestly, I have no idea what I'm going to do with that girl," I say to Stevie.

"I'm sure we can find some mischief to get up to, to keep her occupied!" He said following her down the stairs.

The guys were really welcoming and set us up on the terrace with a barbecue and a load of beers. It was lovely looking over onto the jetty. I picked a moment that everyone was occupied and snuck off to my room to Skype Zack.

After fifteen minutes of making sure that my hair and make-up looked 'naturally beautiful', I called him.

"Hey, stranger!" he answered. "I was starting to think that you forgot about me."

"Like that would ever happen! How are you? What's new in Fiji?" I asked.

"Well, it's all go here!" he replied, laughing. "The fast pace is something that I'm going to have to get used to! I went fishing this morning; it was so cool, Louise, you'd love it. Out in the ocean when no one is around, it's so peaceful. Then this afternoon I did some surf lessons down at the beach. We're heading out to a bar tonight as there are a load of new arrivals."

"New arrivals?" I ask. That means new girls; I don't want him around new girls!

"Yeah, a big old group just arrived from Oz, should be a blast!"

"Yeah, should be!" I reply, trying to keep my voice neutral.

"How about you, where are you now?" he asked.

Just as I was about to reply, Bernie walked in. "There you are, I was wondering where you got to. Are you coming for a drink?"

"I'll be down in a bit!" I say.

"OK, don't be too long; your mates can put some booze away, we're nearly out!" he said, walking from the room.

I turn to look at HBG. His face had fallen.

"I'm sorry, I didn't realise that you had company," he said. "I should go and leave you to it."

"No, Zack, it's not what it looks like!" I say, panicking.

"It looks like you're lying on a bed and a guy just walked in asking if you wanted a drink. I don't need to be a genius to figure that one out, Louise!"

"OK, that part is accurate. He's nothing to do with me though…" I try to explain.

"You don't have to explain, Louise, we never said we were exclusive. I just thought that went without saying."

"We are!" I stutter. "I haven't been near anyone else; all I think about is you!" I'm close to tears now; I need to clear this up and quickly.

"Have a good night, Louise. Talk soon."

"Zack, no!" I shout.

He hung up.

No, no, no! He can't think this of me. I need to speak to him.

I dial back again; it rings for what feels like eternity, but there is no answer.

OK, I'll have to text:

Babe, please talk to me. We are staying with Tara's school friends. I am sharing a room with Fliss. I promise you nothing has happened. Please call. X

I sit looking at my phone for way too long.

Nothing.

Felicity comes in through the door. "Louise, are you OK?"

"No!" I sob.

"What happened?" she asks, jumping on the bed next to me.

"I was on Skype with Zack and Bernie walked in, he got the wrong idea and hung up on me. He said that there was a load of new arrivals from Oz today. Oh Fliss, what if he does something with another girl because he thinks I'm with someone else? I'd be devastated."

"Oh, Louise, this is what I was talking about getting too attached," she said, stroking my hair on her knee. "It was a beautiful holiday romance - God knows we all fancied him a bit - but that's all it was. I really think that you need to pull back from him now. It's not healthy sitting around crying about someone that you don't really know."

"But that's the thing, I do know him!" I say, pulling myself up off her knee. "I've never felt this way about anyone before, Fliss. I know that it sounds ridiculous, as we've only known each other for a short space of time, but I can feel it. He's the one."

Felicity looks at me for a short time. I can see her taking all of this in, trying to measure up whether I am crazy or right.

"OK," she says.

"OK, what?" I reply, wiping my nose on my sleeve.

"What's his number? Let's call him off my phone, hopefully he'll pick up," she says, smiling. "If he's 'the one', then we need to fight for him!"

"Oh, thanks, Fliss," I say, giving her a big hug.

Using Felicity's phone, we call HBG.

"Hello?"

It's a female voice; I look to Felicity with wide-eyed panic. Putting her hand up to me, she mouths to me to stay quiet.

"To whom am I speaking?" Felicity asks.

"This is Sandra, who is this?" she asks back.

"What kind of a name is *Sandra*?" I mock whisper, pulling a face in the background.

"Is HBG… er, Zack there, please? It's imperative that I speak with him," Felicity says in her best angry teacher voice.

"He's a bit busy at the moment, can I take a message?"

"It's really important that I speak with him!" said Felicity whilst wrestling with me to keep the phone away. "Can I ask where he is?"

"He's in the shower," said the lady.

This is too much for me. How can he have moved on this quickly? We argued literally ten minutes ago!

"Listen here, Sandra, if that's even your *real* name!" I inexplicably shout. "Up until ten minutes ago, Zack and I were in a long distance relationship. We had a little misunderstanding that, yes, was my fault, but I didn't think he'd move on with a tramp like you in the meantime. Stay away from him or I will march over to Fiji and kick your ass!" By this point, I am all but foaming at the mouth.

Danni comes running in, taking in the situation. "What's happening?" she asks, running over to me.

"Zack's got another girl, she answered the bloody phone!" I cry.

"She's on the phone now?" said Danni.

"No, no, no!" mouthed Felicity, shaking her head.

Too late, Danni grabbed the phone. "Listen here, slut face, Zack is Louise's. Go and get your own toy!" she shouts down the phone. "Where the hell is he? I want to speak to him now!"

"Ladies, ladies," said the voice, "I've told you he's in the shower. If he wants to speak to you, I'm sure he'll call you back as soon as he can."

I'm in full blown hysterics now.

This is too much for Danni. "Get Zack onto the fudging phone now!" she bellows down the phone.

The line went dead.

"Oh God, this is so much worse than I was expecting!" I cry to the girls. "How could he do this to me so quickly? I thought we were solid; I know it's hard with the distance." Then the penny dropped. "To move on that quickly, he must have had her on the side already…"

The girls don't say anything; they were clearly thinking the same thing.

"Look, Louise, we did all we could. If he's going to move on that quickly, then he's not worth it," said Danni. "Come on, let's sort your face out and get you a drink."

Chapter Twenty-Seven
Up the Proverbial Creek

Ugh, my head hurts. I consumed a lot of gin last night to try and push the images of HBG and Sandra out of my head. I bet she's all skinny and hot, and got her shit together! Where is my phone? Rummaging around in my bed, I finally find it by my feet. I pull it up to my face, hoping that I didn't do any drunk dialling. There are fifteen missed calls off HBG! He called me back!

"Felicity, wake up!" I say, shaking her.

"Ugh, I'm so hung over, I might actually die!" she moaned.

"It's HBG; he called fifteen times last night! He obviously feels horrible about what he did and was calling to apologise! I'm going to sort my face out and Skype him."

This puts a spring in my step. I run into the bathroom, splash some water onto my face and brush my teeth. He must be feeling awful. Hmm, how shall I play it? Shall I be the woman scorned or the martyr? I decide on keeping my face cool and neutral, and to let him do the talking.

Dragging herself to a vertical position, Felicity sits with me.

"Go on then!" she says.

The dialling tone has started. God, why do I feel so nervous?

He's there! He answered!

"Hi," I say as neutrally as I can.

"What the hell, Louise?" he says very angrily.

Hold on, how can he be angry at me? He's the one who cheated. I'm just about to vocalise this when he interrupts my thoughts.

"Are you trying to get me fired?" he all but spits at the phone.

"Fired? What are you talking about? We gave your bit on the side a bit of a talking to, if that's what you're referring to! Wait, are you shagging your boss?" This thought makes me sick; I didn't think he was that guy at all.

"Louise, I'm not shagging anyone!" He shakes his head exasperatedly. "My boss answered my phone and said that you were rude to her! I mean, what the hell, Louise? You cheat on me and then get the other fricking Musketeers to scream at my boss. Seriously, what is wrong with you?"

"Your boss?" I repeat, in a bit of a daze. I look to Felicity and see the realisation spreading over her face.

Sandra is not the other woman; she is his boss.

Shit.

"OK, this has been a massive misunderstanding!" I start.

"I'm all ears!" he said, looking severely annoyed.

"OK, from the top. We are staying with Tara's mates, who happen to be boys. I'm sharing a room with Felicity... look," I say, pointing the camera at a dishevelled Felicity.

"Hi," she smiles meekly.

"Tara got punched in the face by a fat chick. Then you jumped to conclusions thinking that I was with another guy, which in turn made me crazy and scream at Sandra who I have just learned is your boss! So in a nutshell, it's a giant cock up and I hope that you don't run out and buy a Louise-shaped voodoo doll!"

He doesn't say anything for a good twenty seconds. My dad always taught me that the key to negotiation is to wait; the first person to speak is the first to break. So I hold my tongue and patiently wait.

"What a mess!" he says, shaking his head. "Although, it is kind of funny if you think about it!"

Yes! I am forgiven!

"Look, Louise, to save any doubt, I want you to know that there is no one else. If ever a woman answers my phone, it will be for a reason!" he explains.

"Don't go thinking you can use the boss excuse every time!" I laugh. "For the record, there is only you for me too."

"We'll make this work, Louise, I'm sure of it. In fact, I was thinking, after my contract has finished up here, why don't I come back to Oz to meet up with you? We can see how things go when we're in the same area code and make a plan from there," he said with that winning smile.

"That would be incredible!" I say, with the biggest, goofiest smile. Clearly not playing it cool at all.

"I have another two months here," he says. "Let's keep in touch and, closer to the time, I'll book a flight and come and meet you. OK?"

"OK," I say with the biggest grin.

Just as we are about to ring off, Danni comes barging in.

"Is that the cheating scumbag on the phone?" Oh no.

"Danni, it's fine, it was all a big misunderstanding."

Too late, she has grabbed the phone. "Listen here, mister!" Oh God! "We all knew you'd be a hard dog to keep on the porch, but at least have a little dignity and cheat with someone with a cool name like, I don't know, Madonna or something, not frickin' Sandra. I mean, does she do your knitting? Is that what the appeal is? She can knit you a pair of long johns!"

"Danni, give me the phone!" I plead, wrestling with her to get the phone back.

"No, Louise, he's a dirty dog! You need to stay away from him!" she says, holding my phone whilst gripping me in a headlock.

"Danni, she was his boss!" I shout through her armpit.

"He's shagging his boss? You really are a walking cliché, aren't you?" she shouts at him.

"His boss answered his phone, that's all! They're not shagging, she was just a nice lady that we tore to pieces." I manage to muffle whilst my face is being shoved into the duvet.

"What?" Danni said, looking really confused. She turned to the phone and asks Zack directly, "Is this true, HBG?"

He replies, "Yes, Danni, you lot went to town on a sweet old lady who owns this place!"

"Oh God, that's bad. Is Sandra OK?" she asked, looking the most concerned I've ever seen her look.

Walking outside, he says, "Why don't you ask her?" He pointed the phone at a lovely old lady who was pinning the washing up onto the line. Ugh, this is awful.

We bunch in together so that she can see all of us.

"Hi Sandra, I'm Louise, commonly known as Chief Crazy!" She laughs at this. "I am so sorry for what my friends and I said to you last night, it was unacceptable. I hope that you can accept our apology, we feel terrible." The girls nod in agreement.

"From what Zack has told me about you, you are a spirited young lady," she said, smiling. "That definitely came through on the phone call last night!" She laughed. "I believe you should fight for love and, from what I heard, you were doing just that. No harm done here, my love."

"Thank you and sorry again," we all mutter.

Zack comes back onto the screen. "I'm going to go and run off with Sandra for a bit" he said, laughing. We heard Sandra giggle with delight in the background. "I'll call you later, OK?"

"OK, and sorry again, Zack," I say, squirming.

"Cringe. That was the worst ever," said Danni. "Are we psychos?"

"Potentially," Felicity and I both said in agreement.

Chapter Twenty-Eight
One Broken Chakra

We suggested to the guys that maybe it was time for us to make our way on to our next destination. The way that they leaped out of their seats, called a cab and carried our bags out made me think that we may have slightly overstayed our welcome. The fact that Danni slept with two of them and refused to talk to them during the day probably didn't help.

Next on the list was Noosa. I was really excited to go there as the guidebook said that it was a hotspot for dolphins. I've always wanted to swim with dolphins; it would be a major tick off the old bucket list.

The coach dropped us in the centre of the high street. We were surrounded by boutique shops and sun-kissed fashionistas. It was the epitome of beach chic. We stuck out like Donald Trump in a gay pride parade.

"We need to ask someone where the hostel is," said Clara.

"I'm not asking this lot!" replied Danni. "They've all got their drivers waiting outside the shops and we're going to ask where the hostel is!"

"Surely they must be used to travellers," said Clara. "It's on the East Coast trail, loads must pass though."

Felicity had the map out in the middle of the street to ensure that we really looked like tourists.

"The hostel is just over the hill that way." A lady with a giant, floppy hat and a perfectly manicured hand pointed.

"Oh, thank you," said Felicity. "How did you know we were looking for the hostel?"

Looking us up and down, she said, "Lucky guess!" She laughed to her friend as they walked off.

"Bitches," Danni muttered.

The hostel was the definition of chilled. There were hammocks, fire pits for the evenings and people sitting around playing guitars.

"Celebs should check themselves in here instead of rehab!" said Danni. "They'd be all 'zenned out' in no time."

"It does have the budget retreat feel to it, I agree," replied Felicity, running her finger Mary Poppins-style along the reception desk.

"Ladies! Welcome to paradise!" said a surfer guy behind the counter. Spreading his arms wide, he said, "This is my church - use the Earth's natural elements to re-centre your chakras."

"How do you know if your chakra is off centre?" Danni asked.

"Excellent question!" he replied. "Wait here."

"Nice one, Danni, he's probably gone to get his crystal ball!" said Tara.

"Or a big stick!" said Clara.

"A what... oh God, he actually has a big stick!" said Felicity, staring in disbelief.

"Step forward, young lady," he said, beckoning to Danni.

I can only describe what he did next as a drunken dad dance whilst singing something that sounded strangely like Hakuna Matata. After his big finish, which sadly did not include jazz hands, he informed Danni that her chakra was, in fact, broken.

"Ah bollocks, really?" asked Danni.

"Really! But don't fear, Mother Nature is here to repair you," he replied.

"Are you saying that you're Mother Nature?" asked Danni suspiciously.

"No, I'm not," he replied, "but I can help."

"Sorry to break this intervention, or whatever it is," said Felicity, "but would it be possible for us to drop our bags off into our room?"

"Of course, of course, here is your key. You are third door on the left," he replied.

"I'm going to stay here and get my whatsit fixed!" said Danni. "It's probably the reason I've been so constipated."

The room was interesting. There were three beds and two hammocks.

"Bagsie a bed," shouted Felicity.

"Me too," said Tara.

"Me three," shouted Clara.

"Unlucky, Louise, you get the hammock."

Ah crap.

Sliding my bag under my hammock, I looked around the room. There were Buddhas staring at me from every angle.

"We've got to behave ourselves here, girls, I can't take the accusing eyes of the Buddhas."

I quickly learned that trying to get into a hammock was like trying to pat your head and rub your stomach at the same time. The only way to do it was to stick your tongue out and do slow, gentle, non-jerky movements.

"I'm in, I'm in! Ah, shit, I'm on the floor!"

"Oh, for the love of God!" says Tara, shaking her head.

"What?" I ask from the floor, mangled in the stupid hammock.

"Look at her!" she says, pointing to the door.

I turn around to see Danni completely naked, bar a dirty old Aladdin style rug wrapped around her with some form of basket on her head.

"Danni? What the hell are you doing?" asked Clara.

"I'm getting tuned in with Mother Nature," she replies, jiggling around, trying to balance the basket on her head.

"And that entails dressing like a gypsy, does it?" Felicity asks.

"I am not dressed like a gypsy, thank you!" she replies. "I am wearing the cloth of nature to bring me closer to the elements. This is going to fix my chakra and hopefully help me take a shit. Honestly, I'm so blocked up, I'll try anything."

"I have no words!" said Tara.

"Why are you on the floor, Louise? You look like a right weirdo!" said Danni, still jiggling.

"Low blow coming from the hobo!" I laugh. "I fell off this stupid hammock. Me and you got the short straw, we're staying on the hammocks for a few days."

"Really? That's amazing!" She chucks the basket off her head and makes a leap for her hammock. Needless to say, the rug comes off and she ends up doing some form of naked handstand, fully exposed for the world to see.

"Yes, my child!" said the creepy surfer guy, who happened to walk in at that moment. "Shred your shackles and be free!"

"OK, that's quite enough from you!" said Felicity, pushing him out and shutting the door in his face. "Danni, put your clothes on, you can be at one with the dolphins."

There is a 'Love Bus' that leaves the hostel every thirty minutes to go to Rainbow Beach where the dolphins are. We typically just missed the last one, so we have to wait another thirty minutes for the next. We go and sit in the main courtyard and soak up the sun while we wait.

"Louise!" Tara whispers to me, nodding her head to the left.

I turn around to see a guy with a fully tattooed face sitting right next to me and staring intently at me.

"Er, hi," I manage, feeling very uncomfortable.

"You smell good," he replies, taking a big long sniff of my hair.

"Erm, thanks, it's… shampoo," I manage to mutter.

"Ah," he replies, nodding his head. "Would you like me to read your palm?"

Felicity is ferociously shaking her head behind him.

Ah, what the hell; when in Rome… "Sure" I reply.

He takes my hand and makes lots of 'ooh' and 'ah' noises. Eventually, he says, "Well, the good news is you are going to marry a handsome stranger and have a long and happy life together."

"Really? Ah, that's nice!" I reply.

"Yeah, it also shows that he'll have tattoos on his face!" he says seriously.

"Oh," I reply, acutely aware that he has a firm grip on my hand and is still giving me that intense stare.

"I'm only messing with you!" he says, rolling around laughing. "Unless you're up for it? Then I'm totally serious."

I laugh this time, but his face doesn't change.

"Oh, I, erm, actually have a, erm, boyfriend," I mumble.

"Ah, lucky guy," he says, letting go of my hand. "Sorry if I scared you, I can be pretty intense."

"Oh, no worries," I say, looking to the girls, who are all staring at me with wide eyes.

"People tend to misjudge me, you know? Like, everywhere I go, they just stare at me," he says, looking genuinely upset.

"It's probably because you've got tattoos all over your face!" said Tara with as much subtlety as a sledgehammer.

"And what's wrong with that?" he asks. "Why can't I express myself?"

"You can do whatever you want, just don't act shocked when people stare at you. Surely that's the point!" she says, clearly unaware of the mounting tension.

"That is not the point!" he says, slowly standing up.

I'm giving Felicity the 'we need to go' look and praying that she gets it.

"I think I hear the bus!" she shouts. "Come on, girls, let's go."

"It was lovely to meet you," I say to the face tattoo man, grabbing Tara by the arm and steering her away.

"The point is self-expression!" He is near enough shouting now. "Why can society not accept me for who I am?"

"You're putting that image of yourself out there, so you have to accept it!" Tara responds.

"Shut up, Tara!" Felicity says, getting worried now.

"No, why should I shut up? If you go around with your face tattooed and sniff people like a weirdo, people are going to think you're a weirdo!"

This makes him stop in his tracks. He bends over… oh God, what is he doing? Standing up, he lets out this deep grumbling belly laugh.

"She's hilarious!" he shouts, slapping his leg with glee.

"Yeah, she's a riot!" Danni mutters, pushing Tara out of the square.

"Tara, you really need to learn how to shut the hell up some times!" said Felicity.

"It was his fault!" she sulked.

"Just get on the bus," I say, shoving her on.

I was expecting some sort of dolphin sanctuary, but we are dropped at a secluded lagoon, just off the main beach, where apparently the dolphins swim right up to you. There's a couple called Jonathan and Judy who care for the dolphins and manage their routine around meal times to ensure that people have a chance to interact with them. Armed with buckets of fish, we wade out into the water at waist height and wait for the dolphins to come for some grub. Standing still in the water was a bit nippy, but you have to make as little movement as possible or you will scare them off.

"Here we go!" says Jonathan. "The stars of the show are making their way over."

"This is so exciting; I've been wanting to do this forever!" I say to the girls.

"I think something is wrong, Jonathan!" Judy shouts climbing up onto the lifeguard's chair to see more clearly.

"He's injured, everyone out, he won't come in until he sees it's safe. I'll run and get my kit. Jonathan, I think you'll need to go out to him."

We wade out of the water to give Jonathan space to do his thing.

"I can't see anything, can you?" I say to the girls.

"No," Felicity replied.

Jonathan swims quite a way out. He is there for a little while and we are all getting a bit worried.

"Is he OK?" we ask Judy.

"He's fine," she replies. "He needs to get the male dolphin's trust before he will come closer in with him; he's quite badly hurt, this may take some time."

Fifteen minutes later, Jonathan swims back to shore. He is holding onto the dolphin's fin, who is bleeding really badly. Judy very gently approaches the dolphin with her kit.

His poor fin had a massive chunk missing out of it and his skin is severely punctured. We sit on the beach about three meters away from him, holding our breath in anticipation. Every time Judy goes to put some medicine on him, he makes a terrible pain a shrieking sound. It was gut-wrenching.

"What's that over there?" Danni whispers.

Taking the binoculars, I look out to the spot. "There's another dolphin!" I shout to Judy.

"Which direction? East?" Jonathan asks.

We all look at each other; none of us have any idea.

"That way!" I point.

"OK, I need you to stand," he shouts to me, "and hold your arm in the direction of the dolphin. I need you to do this sign" – he waves his arm up and down – "when I am getting close. OK?"

I climb up to the lifeguard's chair and focus my binoculars. Standing, I hold my arm out in the direction of the dolphin. Jonathan swims in that direction, every now and again looking back to me for guidance.

"I need help!" Judy shouts.

"What do you need?" Felicity asks.

"Come into the water, I need you to hold the kit. Walk very, very slowly; I don't want you to scare him."

Felicity carefully makes her way into the water, pausing every other step so as not to scare the dolphin. When she gets there, Judy passes Felicity the kit as she continues to patch him up.

I look across to Jonathan; he is about a meter away from the other dolphin. He is doing a strange little splash, gently tapping the top of the water; it must be a way to communicate. Slowly but surely the second dolphin moves closer to him and lets him hold onto its fin.

"He's got the other dolphin!" I shout to the group.

As Jonathan brings the second dolphin closer to the shore, he tells us that she is the girlfriend of the injured dolphin. As she didn't have a scratch on her, he tells us that the male dolphin must have protected her, most likely from a shark attack.

The girl dolphin swims straight up to the male, making a high-pitched sound. He replies with the same noise.

The male dolphin, now patched up and fed, is looking much happier. Judy and Jonathan apologise for us not having the opportunity to touch them today. We tell them that we completely understand and say we will come back tomorrow. We stand on the shore, waving the dolphins off, but they don't move. They both remain where they are, close to the shore. Judy and Jonathan tell us that they have never seen this before.

Judy went back into the water and they immediately swim over, nuzzling into her. She invites us in one by one to gently stroke them and say our goodbyes. They hung around for a good half an hour, clearly enjoying the attention. Then the male dolphin did his high-pitched cry, indicating that it was time for them to go, and they swam off into the ocean.

It was one of the most incredible experiences I have ever had. I will never forget it.

Chapter Twenty-Nine
Trespassers Will Be Prosecuted

The following day, we go for a walk around the Noosa headland. For wildlife spotting, it is incredible. There are koalas in the trees, the odd kangaroo and even a snake. The only downside is that it is about forty-five degrees and we are absolutely melting. The old adage of 'only mad dogs and Englishmen go out in the midday sun' was particularly apt today, as we were the only people around for miles. What was worse is that the headland is so high above the water, there was no way we could jump into the sea for a dip.

"Do you reckon we'd die if we jumped from here?" asked Danni, slumping against a tree.

"At this point, I'm willing to risk it!" said Tara, wiping the sweat from her top lip.

"I bet we can get closer to the sea if we keep walking a little further," Felicity says, reading the map. "Just around that bend the path dips quite a bit, we could probably jump from there."

"OK, let's keep going!" Danni said, pulling us up one by one from the shade.

As we drag ourselves around the bend, dreaming of a breeze, we see a man-made rough path down to the ocean. We are clearly not the only people who have been caught short.

"We either swim or have a three hour walk back," says Felicity. "I reckon it's a good forty-five -minute to an hour's swim; are you all strong enough swimmers to do that?"

Looking around at each other, we all nod.

"What about our shorts and flip-flops? We'll be soaked through!" said Tara.

"Don't know about you, but I'm already soaked with sweat! I'd choose sea water over that," said Danni. "Just stick your shorts on your head if you don't want them to get wet and put your flip-flops on your hands, like hand flippers!" She, did a little demonstration.

As I slid into the water my skin sizzled; it was like running a hot frying pan under cold water. We put our shorts on our heads like chef hats and stuck our flip-flops onto our hands, as Danni had suggested, and started to swim towards the beach.

"I hope no one sees us," said Tara. "We look ridiculous!"

"There's no one around, we'll be fine!" said Felicity, leading the way.

"Let's aim for that patch of beach there!" Felicity shouts.

Following along behind her, we are about a hundred metres from the shore when we see what looks like a wedding precession making its way onto the beach.

"Oh no, look at all those people!" said Tara. "We can't swim in looking like this!"

"There's nowhere for us to go!" said Felicity. "Unless we try and swim back towards the cliff? I don't think we can climb back up from the sea."

"How long can you hold your breath?" said Tara. "We're going to have to go under!"

"Not for an hour of wedding photos, that's for sure!" replied Clara.

"How about we tread water here for as long as possible? They can't make out what, or who, we are from there; we can just stay here," said Tara.

"My legs are killing; I can't tread water for that long!" Clara whined.

"Look, they haven't noticed us, let's just aim for the far corner and sneak around the back, OK?" I say.

The girls nod in agreement. We've all stopped talking, clearly in stealth mode. We make it to the far corner of the beach and clamber out without anyone seeing.

"Yes! We made it!" high fives all round.

"Now we need to figure out how to get off this beach. It looks as though it's fenced off around that massive building," Felicity said, looking around.

"Oh no, look at the sign!" Tara said, pointing.

Private Property
Trespassers will be prosecuted

"Is this someone's house?" I ask.

"It can't be. It must be a restaurant," said Tara.

"We need to find a way out without disturbing the wedding." said Felicity.

We shimmy along the fence towards the side of the building.

"Can you hear that?" Tara says. "It sounds like a kitchen; I bet we could sneak through there."

"How are we going to explain the fact that we're soaking wet! ?" Danni hissed.

"I don't know! Have you got any better ideas?" said Tara, pulling a face.

"No," Danni sulked, "I'm just saying!"

"It's probably our best option. Come on, let's go." Peering through the door, I see another door that looks like it leads towards the front of the house. "We need to wait for a lull, then run through that door there."

I hold my arm up and make a fist like they do in army movies. The kitchen staff leave with trays of food.

"Move, move, move!" I whisper to the girls, pushing them past me whilst keeping look out from the rear. I'm loving this. I feel like GI Jane... minus the muscles and skill.

The pot washers stare at us, but they don't say anything so we keep on going.

Tara abruptly comes to a halt. "Crap, it's an office," she whispers back to us, as we all pile up behind her.

"Is there anyone in there?" Felicity asks.

"Not that I can see," she replies.

"We need to keep moving, go in!" said Felicity.

The office is very decadent, all gold furnishings and mahogany woodwork with thick luscious curtains. You just know that whoever owns this regularly sits with their feet on the desk, smoking cigars and bellowing orders at people. I should investigate what kind of job that is; I could see myself doing it!

"There's someone coming! Hide!" whispers Felicity.

After running around in circles for a few seconds, Felicity and I jump behind the curtains, Danni dives under the desk, and Tara and Clara hide behind the couch. Danni is actually covering her eyes.

The door swings open and we hear two sets of footsteps walk in.

"Is it not enough that I am paying for this goddamn sham of a wedding? Now you want me to offer that ridiculous man a job as well! I think I've done quite enough, don't you?" said the male voice.

Felicity and I pull an 'oh dear' face.

"You have done so much, my darling, and I appreciate all of it. I just know it would mean the world to Cindy if you offered him a position at the firm. You know, keep it in the family?" the female voice replied.

"He is not my family!" the male voice boomed.

It went quiet for a second and then the door slammed. I popped my head around the curtain to see that the lady was still there and that she was crying.

"Prick," she muttered under her breath. She dusted herself off and walked out.

"That was intense, wasn't it?" said Danni, crawling out from under the desk. "I reckon we should stay and see what happens. This is better than Enders!"

"I think we should get out sharpish," said Felicity. "Imagine how mad he'd be if he found us in his house!"

"Try the door, Felicity!" I say, nudging her.

"Why me?" she replies.

"You're the most sensible out of the lot of us, I think you should do it," I tell her.

"I'll do it!" says Danni.

"No!" we all shout.

"Jesus, keep your hair on!"

Felicity carefully opens the door, just a slit.

"What can you see?" I whisper.

"The front door is over to the left; we'll have to run through a pretty large reception area. I don't know how we're going to do it without getting caught," she said, biting her nails. "We're going to have to go one at a time; if one gets caught, they can at least cause a distraction for the others."

"No way I am going out there on my own!" said Clara. "You heard how angry that man was, he'll eat me for breakfast!"

"She's right, Felicity, safety in numbers," I add.

"OK, we need to cause a distraction," said Felicity. Any ideas?"

Just as she said that, someone shouted for everyone to go to the beach for photos.

"This is our opportunity, everyone get ready!" Felicity says, peering through the crack in the door. "OK, looks like the coast is clear, let's go!" She creeps out of the door.

Felicity is first; she points to her left and creeps around the corner. Clara is next, closely followed by Tara. Danni turns to me and grabs my hand. I smile at her and nod to go.

Felicity, Tara and Clara have made it through the front door. We're close behind when I hear a male voice shout:

"I just need to grab my hanky, darling."

Shit, shit, shit. I grab Danni and pull her up the staircase. We try the first handle that we come to. It's a bathroom, we run inside and close the door behind us. We can hear footsteps running up the stairs and they're getting closer.

"He's coming in here!" Danni mouths to me.

Quietly, we hop into the shower and pull the curtain closed in front of us. We stand still, completely frozen staring at each other. How the hell are we going to explain this if we get caught? Holding each other's hand tightly, we hear the door slowly open and quietly close.

A man walks over to the sink and turns on the tap. We can hear him splashing himself with water.

"Come on, Charles, nearly there, just push through," we hear him say.

"Who is he talking to?" Danni mouths to me.

"Well, not us!" I mouth back.

There are more footsteps outside. The door handle rattles. There's a female voice.

"Darling, what are you doing? Everyone is waiting!" she says.

Danni and I stare at each other; her grip on my hand is tightening.

"I won't be a minute!" he replies.

She rattles the handle again.

"Why is the door locked? Can I come in?" she asks.

"No! Just go away, I'll be there in a minute," he says.

"Charles, open the door this minute!" she shouts.

"Cindy, please leave me alone for five minutes." He sounds close to tears.

"Charles, I agreed to this," she whispers through the door, "but we have to at least look like we are on the same team."

There is a rustling sound.

"What is he doing?" I mouth to Danni.

She carefully looks around the shower curtain and looks back at me with wide eyes.

"What?" I mouth.

"He's getting undressed," she mouths back.

Oh.

"I just need to cool down, I think I've got a bit of heatstroke," he says. "I'm going to have a quick shower and then I'll be down in ten. OK, sweetheart?"

"OK, darling, but please hurry; our guests are waiting."

We hear her walk away.

I've got my eyes closed and I'm gripping Danni's hand. He whips the curtain across and lets out an almighty scream… I guess he's seen us!

I open my eyes to see that he is completely starkers with his member standing to attention, clutching a bottle of baby oil

"Jesus!" Danni says, covering her eyes.

We hear footsteps running back.

"Darling, what is it?" The woman is back. "Please open the door. Are you OK?"

I put my finger to my lips, telling him to hush, and point at his predicament.

"Er, I, er, stubbed my toe on the bath. I'm OK, don't worry, be down in a jiff!" he says, holding eye contact with me.

I nod at him: well done, naked guy.

The footsteps are gone.

"Who the hell are you?" he hisses at us. "And what are you doing in our shower?"

"Not what you were about to do, that's for sure!" laughed Danni.

"Look, it's a long story!" I say, looking anywhere but down.

"I'm listening," he says with his hands on his hips. I wish he'd get a towel.

"OK, long story short, we swam back from the headland and ended up on your beach. We were trying to get out without interrupting your wedding, or, er, anything else." I reaching round and throw a towel at him.

"God, this day has gone from the sublime to the ridiculous!" he says with his head in his hands. "I don't know what I'm doing, I shouldn't be here!" he sobbed.

"Then why are you?" Danni asked.

"That's really none of our business!" I say, giving Danni the 'shut up' stare.

"Well, you've seen me naked, I think we're pretty well acquainted now," he laughs. "The thing is… well, the real thing is… OK, this is hard…."

"For the love of God, spit it out, man!" Danni sighs.

"I'm gay," he replies.

"Ah, and I'm guessing the bride doesn't know?" I ask gently.

"Oh, she knows, all right!" he replies. Danni and I glance at each other. "I know it sounds bad, but we're best friends and we thought it would be better for each other if we did this. She's gay, too, you see."

"Well, this is quite the pickle, isn't it?" said Danni.

He looks distraught.

"How in this day and age is it not OK to be who you are?" I ask.

"You clearly haven't met our families."

"Are you officially married now?" I ask.

"Not yet. We are supposed to be doing our vows on the beach in half an hour," he replies, looking forlorn.

"Then it's not too late!" I say. "Take a minute and think this through. Marriage is supposed to be forever and it is supposed to be with someone you love."

He grabs me and gives me a big bear hug. Awkwardly, his towel drops to the floor.

"Well, whoever you end up with is going to be very lucky!" I say, making us laugh with a mixture of anxiety and concern for this poor guy.

"Come on, let me get you out of here," he says. "There's a fire escape outside one of the guest bedrooms, no one will see you."

"Thank you so much! And remember, it's not too late!" I say, giving him a parting hug.

The girls were waiting around the corner as we run around.

"What the hell happened?" asked Felicity. "We were devising a breakout plan!"

"We were trapped in the shower with a gay guy. It's a long story!" Danni laughed.

As we are walking down the street, we hear, "Son of a bitch!"

"Looks like he's told them!" says Danni.

"Good for him!" I reply.

Chapter Thirty
Sisters Before Misters

After a week in Noosa, we were relaxed and 'at one' with the world. Danni's chakra had been fixed; we know because she shouted 'eureka' when she went to the toilet the following morning. We'd patched up our differences with the face tattoo guy (real name Phil), and called in at the dolphin centre to find that the male dolphin was healing well and was back to his usual pattern. I'd even figured the hammock out, and I have to say it wasn't half bad. I could have quite easily stayed for a little while longer, but we had agreed to meet Hannah at Airlie Beach in two weeks' time, so we needed to keep moving.

The bus journey from Noosa to Hervey Bay is only two and a half hours. From what I understand, there's not much to do in Hervey Bay itself; most people only stay there as a base to explore Fraser Island. Fraser Island is a massive island off the coast of Australia that travellers flock to as a rite of passage. There is a company that you can hire four-by-fours and camping gear from, and they let you loose on the island for four days.

As we chat to a group of girls on the coach, they mention that they had to book their equipment and camping gear a month in advance for the island as it is so busy at this time of year. Typically, we haven't booked anything, so start to panic.

"I told you we should have booked!" sighed Danni.

"At what point did you ever mention booking anything?" shouted Felicity.

"OK, girls, chill out!" I say, pushing them apart. "I'm sure that there is a solution. Let's try and call them now."

"I'll call them," said Danni.

"No you won't!" replied Felicity snippily. "I'll call them. You'll end up booking some naked hippy retreat or something equally as ridiculous if you do it!"

"There was no need for that!" stropped Danni.

"Sorry, Danni," said Felicity, reaching out to her. "It's just the last time we left you unsupervised, you actually came back naked with a basket on your head."

"Fair point," Danni conceded.

Felicity moved to two vacant seats and called the adventure company.

"They've just had a cancellation; we can go tomorrow, but we have to pay now and no refund," Felicity whispered, covering the phone.

"Fine with me!" I say, looking around at the girls; they all agree.

"OK, I'll put it on my credit card; you can all pay me back. We have to go, though, whatever happens, or else I lose one hundred dollars a head," Felicity says, shooting us all a warning look.

"Don't worry, we'll be there. Nothing's going to pop up between now and tomorrow, is it?" I say, laughing.

We arrive at the hostel and check into our room. Think military chic, aka army camp beds, khaki green furnishings and rough blankets. We're a long way from Cassandra's mansion!

"I'm starving, anyone want to head into town and get some grub?" asked Tara.

We all nod. What is it about travelling for just two hours that makes you so hungry?

Hervey Bay is a beautiful little beach town with quaint stores and a lot of seafood restaurants. We stopped at a small, seafood place, slightly out of the main area. It wasn't as glitzy as the bigger restaurants, but it was affordable.

"I'm going to have the lobster," said Danni. "I've never had it before!"

"You know it comes in its shell, don't you?" said Felicity. "You'll have to crack its legs and dig the meat out."

"Shut up! They don't give you an actual lobster! If you think I'm falling for that, you must think I'm really stupid!" said Danni, batting off Felicity's warning.

"I'm being serious!" said Felicity.

"Yeah, yeah, sure you are !" Danni replied.

We had mussels, prawns, sea bass and other fishy loveliness. It was all so beautifully fresh and smelt incredible.

Danni's dish came out last. I had my camera ready.

"You have got to be fecking kidding me! It's an actual lobster! What the hell am I supposed to do with that?" she shouted at the waiter. "I can't eat that, no way!" she said, almost jumping up from her chair.

"Danni, stop," laughed Felicity. "I'm sorry," she apologised to the waiter. "It's lovely, thank you. We'll show her how to do it."

"I thought you were joking," said Danni, close to tears. "I can't eat Sebastian."

"Give it here! I'll cut the meat out for you, just eat that." As I take the dish off her, I pick the lobster up and do a little dance with it, singing 'Under the Sea' in my best Sebastian from the Little Mermaid voice which everyone finds hilarious… bar Danni.

"Louise?" I hear a male voice.

I turn round, still clutching the lobster.

You have got to be kidding me! My ex, in the flesh, is standing there for all the world to see. This must be a bad dream or a parallel universe. Why the hell would he be here of all places? I have not said any of this out loud and am simply staring at him with my mouth open whilst holding a lobster. Use your words, Louise!

"What the hell are you doing here?" Eloquent as always, good job.

"Well, it's great to see you too!" he laughs.

"No, really, why are you here?" The last time I saw this guy he was apologising to me for 'accidentally' sleeping with my best friend. Needless to say, I am not happy to see him.

"We're staying here tonight and heading to Fraser Island tomorrow," he replied, calling a skinny brunette over.

"No, why are you here? As in, you know, Australia?" I'm flailing my arms around. "Of all the places you could have gone to, why here? This is *my* place!" I shout irrationally.

"What can I say, we decided to take a trip and thought Oz would be a great place to start."

"We?" I ask, still trying to fathom how the hell this is possible.

"Yes, my girlfriend Victoria and I," he replies, wrapping his arm around the skinny girl next to him.

And then the penny drops.

"Hang on a minute. Did you say Fraser Island tomorrow?" Please, God, say that I misheard him. I cannot spend one night with that moron on an island; only one of us will come back alive and I'm taking a shovel!

"Yeah," he replies casually, clearly not picking up on my panic.

Felicity clocks my gaze.

"No, no, no, no, no!" I say, chucking the lobster down and pushing my chair back. "No!"

"Louise, no refunds, remember?" Felicity tries to say in a smiley and bright way. "Felicity, by the way!" She extends her hand to the idiot.

"Don't touch him!" I say, slapping her away. "He's a cheating, dirty scumbag! You don't know where he's been… well, I have a good idea and you definitely don't want to touch that!"

"Hey!" said the skinny brunette.

Ignoring her, I carry on.

"You need to change! You need to go to the adventure people and tell them that you need to go at a different time. Yes, that's what you need to do. Go on, do it now," I say, waving him away.

"And why would I do that, Louise? We've had this trip booked for a month, we're not going to change just for you!" he replies.

I need a different angle. I know: the girlfriend.

"Do you really want your man sleeping on a romantic, far away island in close proximity to his ex?" I ask, giving her a crazy, beady eye.

"I, erm…" she replies, clearly battling this out internally, looking from him to me.

"There are lots of dark nooks and crannies, anything could happen." I shrug. "Don't you think it's convenient that, of all the places in the world he could have taken you, he brought you to the exact place where I am? I mean, from choosing, literally, anywhere in the world, he chose where I am!"

"Oh, shut up, Louise!" Turning to her, the idiot says, "Baby, listen to me; I didn't know she was here."

"See, he's already lying to you!" I jump in. "He knew exactly where I was. He came to my Australia leaving party!"

"Is this true?" she sobbed.

I did feel genuinely sorry for dragging her into this, but this guy is a snake and there is no way that I am sharing a country with him, let alone an island.

"Well, yes, I did know she was in Oz," he said in a slimy voice, "but I didn't know she was in this exact spot."

"Cough... social media... cough," I reply.

"How could you!" she said, slapping him across the face.

"I didn't do anything!" he shouted in exasperation. "OK, I knew she was in Oz; I hardly thought we'd bump into her, though, did I? It's a massive country, for God's sake!"

"So why do you still want to go on the same trip as me on the same day?" I interject. I need to nudge this along; my food is getting cold!

"Yeah, why Sam?" she asks.

"Fine! We'll change the date!" he shouts. "Who knows when the next date's available, but we will change it if it makes you happy."

"Very happy!" I say, smugly sitting back at the table. "You can kindly go and stay at least ten thousand kilometres away from me for the rest of your little trip. Oh, and sweetheart," – I direct this at the girl – "I know he's good in bed, but the man is a whore. He's probably already cheated on you; you'd do wisely to cut the cord!" I do a scissor action with my fingers as she runs away crying, with him trailing behind.

"Louise, this is a whole new side of you," said Danni. "I'm impressed!"

"Hell knows no fury like a woman scorned!" I laugh.

"To sisters before misters!" Tara cheered.

"Amen to that!"

Chapter Thirty-One
Better Get the Shovel!

None of us have ever camped before so we are taking a bit of a gamble as to what exactly we should take with us on a desert island. So far, we have:

Entertainment for the evenings (two x bottles of gin and three x bottles of fizz), tinned food (no way we'd survive living off the land!) waterproofs (a bikini), beachwear (also a bikini), hiking shoes (flip-flops), beach shoes (also flip-flops), insect repellent, a shovel (in case the ex turns up), sun cream and five rubber rings (for the lakes).

As we arrive at the adventure HQ, they take one look at us and ask us to go through to the back. Must be the VIP section. We smugly smile at everyone as we strut our way past.

"Ladies, I'm assuming that you don't have camping equipment?" asked the first guy.

"We've actually paid to rent the equipment," Felicity replies.

"OK, we have a large six-man tent or you can have individual tents. What would you prefer?" he asks.

"Definitely the big one," Tara replies, "bet there's loads of perverts out there!"

Rolling his eyes, guys number two ignores that comment and continues: "The issue with the large tent is that it takes some work to erect. You'll need to spend some time studying the instructions,"

"Can't be that hard, we'll figure it out," says Danni. "Stick it in my bag."

Shaking his head, number one says, "It's not going to fit into your handbag, it's a tent!"

"Do you have sleeping bags?" number two asks

"No," we all say, shaking our heads.

"Cooking equipment?" asks number one.

"We've got cans of beans," Danni says. "We'll be grand."

"Have we got a can opener?" I ask.

"Oh, feck, no, we haven't. Can we borrow a can opener?" Danni asks a terrified looking number two.

"Ladies, you are going out onto an island with nothing around for five days. You won't survive on canned food!" he says in an exasperated manner.

"We've got gin as well," said Tara. "We'll be fine."

"Oh God," he said, covering his face with his hands. "How about I pack the van with the things that I think you'll need; how does that sound?"

"Ah, that would be lovely, thanks!" says Danni, oblivious to his horror.

"OK, who's driving?" number two asks.

Felicity and I put our hands up.

"Licenses, please," he asks, holding his hand out. We both pass them over. "Come with me, I'll show you the van. One of you will need to reverse it onto the ferry."

"It took me four times to pass my test because I couldn't go backwards!" I laugh. "Should really be you, Fliss."

"I'd rather you start, Louise; I feel really nervous about it," she replies.

"Me it is then!" I say, much to the dismay of number two. "Don't worry, it'll be fine; I haven't hit anything in ages."

The four by four is pretty old school. There's no power steering and it has the old fashioned sticky outy gear stick and a cassette tape player. I'm starting to wish I'd brought a '90s mix tape for the journey.

"OK, jump into the driver's seat," number one orders. He spends ten minutes taking me through all of the gizmos, and the dos and don'ts for when we're on the island. For example: don't go over twenty miles an hour in the rainforest as it will tip the truck, don't drive across the beach after four p.m. as that's when the tide comes in, and don't leave the lights on or the battery will die.

"It's best if you take your thongs off to drive," he says.

"Excuse me?" I must have misheard him.

"Take your thongs off!" he repeats slowly.

"That's a bit forward! You could at least buy me a drink first!" I say, laughing, nudging Felicity.

"He means flip-flops, Louise!" Felicity whispers. "That's what they call them here."

"Oh! That makes more sense; I was just about to take my pants off! That would have been awkward!" I laugh.

Number one, however, does not find this funny. "Get acquainted with the van. I'll chuck your stuff in, then you're ready to go," he says, slamming my driver door shut.

"He's not very fun, is he?" I say to Felicity. "Do you think we should be worried by the fact that he's so concerned about us?"

"Na, he's just being cautious; we'll be fine!"

Banging on the hood, he tells us that we're ready to go.

Reversing onto the ferry was tricky business, especially with a massive tent blocking the back window. I'm the first to be waved on; I think they have arranged that on purpose as they are worried about me reversing into something.

There is a man in a Hi-Vis jacket waving me into the bay. Yep, got it, got it, nearly there, nearly there. I'm reversing in a straight line heading towards him; I'm nearly in the spot when he suddenly pounds on the back of the truck.

"You nearly ran me over you stupid cow!" he shouts.

"You were telling me to go that way," I retort. "I assumed you'd move!"

"Women drivers!" he mumbles as he skulks off.

After an hour on the ferry, we arrive on the island.

"Ooh, there's a place called Champagne Pools, we have to start there!" said Tara. "It's at the top of the island, if we start there we can work our way back down again."

"Can you believe that we're on an island? Five girls against the elements. It's so exciting!" says Clara. .

"Yeah, five girls, ten other four by fours full of people and, looking through that hedge, around a thousand other people staying in those fancy hotel spas!" laughs Tara.

"There's hotel spas?" asks Danni "Then why the feck are we staying in tents?"

"A hotel would be boring; we're roughing it up in the wild!" says Clara.

"Right, we need to decide which way we are going to go," says Felicity, looking at the map. "We can either go through the rainforest or drive along the beach. We need to take into consideration that we can only drive twenty miles an hour through the rainforest and can't drive along the beach after four p.m. Based on the current tide, I'd say we have two hours, max, of beach time."

"Whatever you think, Crocodile Dundee!" says Danni, laughing.

"OK, let's start on the beach and take it from there," Felicity said, putting her coordinates onto the map.

We're quickly approaching four p.m., so decide to reroute inland to make sure that we don't get caught out by the tide.

Felicity is in full military mode now. "Left, forty-five degrees... Debris up ahead... Hard right..."

An hour of rocky rainforest travel later, we arrive at a campsite for Champagne Pools.

"Hi, ladies," said the guy manning the gate. "Welcome to Champagne Pools. Do you need a hand erecting your tent or are you all good?"

"Nah, we'll be fine," said Danni, before any of us have the chance to say anything.

"No worries, give us a shout if you change your mind," he says, winking at me as he clearly sees the horror on my face.

Dragging the tent out of the boot, we all stand there looking over it with as much disdain as one would look at a dead body.

"Has anyone actually put up a tent before?" I ask, prodding it with my toe.

"Nope," says Danni.

"Me neither," says Felicity.

"I definitely haven't," says Tara.

"We are independent women and we can put up a tent!" says Felicity lifting up the tent cover and dropping it down again. "Where are the instructions he told us about?"

"He gave them to me. I shoved them in my bag," says Danni, rummaging around in her handbag. "Oh crap, I think I left them on the side when I went to the loo!"

"So much for independent women!" Clara mumbles.

"I'll go and get the man," Danni replies, trudging off.

Whilst Danni is looking for help, we take a look at the food supplies the guy at the adventure company has packed for us. I'm pretty sure that we had the basics covered, there can't have been that much more to add. Let's see: water (OK, we totally forgot water), a stove (that will come in handy for the raw cans of food that we packed), air beds, pasta, various meats, juices, fresh fruit, bread, torches and various other camping bits. Hmm, maybe he was right to get involved; next to our gin, flip-flops and rubber rings, this did seem slightly more practical.

The guy put the tent up in approximately thirty seconds. He even set up the stove, made a fire and blew up our air beds for us.

"Wow, thank you!" said Felicity. "That would have taken us hours."

"No worries at all, give us a shout if we can help with anything else. My brother and I will be in the porter cabin across the way. Have a good night!" he says, walking away.

We made some dinner, which mostly comprised of ham sandwiches and gin, and settled into the tent for the night, making shadow animals with our hands against the tent lining.

"What's that supposed to be?" screams Felicity, rolling around laughing.

"It's obviously a duck! Duh!" says Danni, rolling her eyes.

"OK, OK, I got one! What's this?" I say, creating a rabbit shadow on the tent.

"Is it a bird?" says Tara, squinting.

"No, it's a horse!" says Felicity.

"A horse! What are you talking about?" I screech.

"How are you making it so big?" says Tara.

"It's not that big… oh my god, that's not my shadow!" I scream.

There is a massive wolf-like silhouette next to our tent.

"Everybody stay completely still," whispers Felicity, "It will smell our fear; don't move and it should go away."

All you can hear is our breathing as we freeze, clutching onto each other. Nobody makes a sound until Clara shrieks.

"It's on my foot!"

"It's trying to chew her foot through the tent!" Danni screams.

"Pull her back, pull her back!" shouts Felicity.

We all jump behind Clara and start to pull. She lets out an almighty scream.

"It's not letting go, you're going to have to scare it!" Clara is hysterically crying now.

"The shovel!" I shout. "It's in the car!"

I run out to the car, in the opposite direction to the wolf-like thing. Grabbing the shovel out of the boot, I slowly creep around the side of the tent. As I get closer, I realise that it is a dingo. The grumpy guy told us to show them who is in charge and not to act scared if you come across one.

OK, be dominant Louise, you got this! You are the Alpha! Holding the shovel across my body, I charge at the dingo, screaming at the top of my lungs. The bloody thing doesn't move! It's just staring at me whilst continuing to chew on Tara's foot. I'm going to have to hit it. I raise the shovel above my head, close my eyes and bring it down on top of the creature's head. I open my eyes to see it stagger away, whimpering.

"Louise, you did it!" says Felicity, running out.

"I feel horrible, I hit a defenceless animal!" I moan.

"Yeah, that had your mate's foot in its mouth! You saved her!" she says, giving me a big bear hug.

"Clara, are you OK?" I ask, walking into the tent.

"My foot hurts, but yeah, I'm OK," she says, smiling.

The two brothers arrive, running into the tent.

"Thanks for showing up!" Danni says sarcastically.

"We're so sorry, we had to unblock the communal toilet, it was a two-man job!"

"Are you OK?" the younger brother asks Clara.

"I doubt I'll sleep ever again! But yeah, I'm OK. Have you got any ice?" she asks, hobbling on her foot.

"Of course, come this way," the older one says, taking some of her weight on his shoulder.

"I'll come with you," I say.

"It's OK, Louise, I think I'll be fine!" she replies, looking at one of the brothers.

She's looking better already!

After a couple of hours of drinking games, and with the adrenaline subsiding, my eyelids were finally getting the better of me. Drifting off into the land of nod I start to dream that the dingo and his mates have come back looking for revenge, using my body like a giant chew toy. I tighten my grip on the shovel and move all body parts away from the edge of the tent. Not today Mr Dingo, not today!

Chapter Thirty-Two
Famous Last Words

Waking up in a tent in Australia, in the summer, is like waking up in a greenhouse. It was sweaty and clammy with no air. We couldn't stay inside the tent past seven a.m.

"Ugh, thanks humidity, I've always wanted to look like the fricking Lion King!" says Tara, trying to tame the frizz. We were all sporting Dianna Ross style humidity hair. It's the type of weather that makes you sweat even when you're in the shower.

"Just embrace it!" said Danni, shaking her hair "Release your inner wild side! Let's go and find these champagne pools; that should cool us down."

The pools were so relaxing; the waves from the ocean were splashing over into the salt water and filling them with natural sea life.

"Danni, look, it's Sebastian's brother!" I laughed.

"Not funny! I'm so sorry that I ate your family, Mr Crab." She was actually directing this at the crab. "If it makes you feel any better, he was very tasty with the garlic sauce, so he didn't die in vain."

"You're such an idiot!" said Tara, splashing her. "When are we going to get some champagne? That was the only reason I came!"

"There isn't any champagne, you dope!" said Felicity. "They're called the Champagne Pools because of the natural little bubbles. You would have known that if you'd listened to me reading the extract out of the guidebook last night!"

"I was listening; how do you think I fell asleep so quickly?" she laughed.

After a couple of hours of lounging around in the pools, we went back to the site to pack up and move on to our next location. We couldn't find the brothers, so we decided to take the tent down ourselves.

"Just pull that bit, Tara!" Felicity shouts through her legs whilst she's in some form of a twister-style position on the other side of the tent. "Louise, you grab that bit."

"Are you sure we should be taking it down like this? It seems very complicated. He popped the whole thing up in seconds; surely it should go down just as fast?" I say with a mouth full of material, trying to pull the bloody pegs out.

All five of us are in now effing and blinding, trying to get the thing down, when we hear giggling behind us. We turn round to see two kids, who are about six years old.

"Can we have a go?" the little boy asked.

"Oh no, this is grown up work!" said Felicity, jiggling around, trying to pull the rod out.

"You just need to pull that cord," said the little girl.

"Don't you worry, little one," said Felicity, "I know exactly what I'm doing!"

The girl walked over, pulled the cord and the whole thing collapsed in about ten seconds, leaving us red-faced and covered in tent.

"How did you know how to do that?" Felicity asked, completely dumbfounded.

"Because I've got a brain!" the little girl laughed as they ran off.

"Little shits!" said Danni.

Once we'd packed the tent (aka shoved it into the boot), we hopped into the four by four to make our way towards the Maheno ship wreck. It seems so much hotter on the island than it did on the mainland; we all had to wear factor fifty to ensure that we didn't turn lobster red. What was worse was we took the roof down on the car and couldn't figure out how to put it back up again, so we had no shade.

"Can we drive inland a bit, under the trees? I'm dying over here!" said Danni, holding a towel over her head.

"Good idea! Hold on, I'm going to cut in through that bit over there." The girls grab onto the hand rails as I did a handbrake turn, screeching into the forest.

"That was so cool!" shouted Tara from the back.

"Slow down, Louise! You're not supposed to go over twenty miles an hour, remember, or you'll tip the thing!" Felicity nagged.

"I'm not going to tip it; they just say that to scare you! Where's your sense of adventuaaaaaaahhhhh..."

I didn't get to finish my famous last words as I slammed into a branch and sent the jeep somersaulting forward. Suspended in mid-air, I felt like everything had suddenly gone into slow motion. "Noooooooooooo!" I could hear myself shouting, gripping onto the steering wheel. Then I was praying, beseeching with whatever is up there, to "please, please, don't let this thing land on its side!" I was bargaining: "If it doesn't tip over, I promise I'll be a better person – I'll stop swearing, visit my nan more and go to church every day."

It was no good, my prayers were not being heard. God clearly had more important matters to deal with.

We were hurtling towards the ground and the car was tipping over.

I could hear the girls screaming. I glanced across to see Felicity giving me an 'I told you so' stare! Then we hit the ground with an almighty thud.

"Is everybody OK?" I manage to mumble with my right cheek shoved into the dirt.

"They just say that to *scare* you," mimicked Danni. "It won't *really* tip! Nice one, Louise, now I've got whiplash and dirt in my already hideous hair!"

I feel really guilty now. I didn't realise my showing off would literally leave us face down in the dirt. "I'm so sorry, are you all OK?"

"Just perfect," huffed Felicity, climbing out of the side of the car.

We all manage to climb out relatively unscathed. I walk around to each of them, feeling their faces and patting them down to make sure that nothing is broken.

"Get off!" says Clara, pushing me off her face. "I'm fine, I'm fine! We just need to figure out how we're going to get this thing back onto its wheels."

"We need a lever and pulley system," says Felicity. "Grab that big branch over there, Tara; we can put it under the car and lever it up against that rock."

Tara dutifully passed the branch over, we all give it one giant push and, needless to say, it snapped.

"You hear those stories of mums lifting cars to save their babies," said Clara. "It must be adrenaline; maybe if we all get scared and really pumped up we could lift it?"

"OK, how do we do that?" I ask.

"You cannot be serious!" said Felicity, shaking her head.

"We need to try something! Go on, Clara," I say, giving her a nudge to carry on.

"OK, I want you to all visualise someone you love stuck under the car and we have to lift it up or they will die!" she said dramatically. "Louise, you can imagine that it's stuck on HBG's member and that you can never do the dirty again!"

"That would be a tragedy!" I say with wide eyes.

"OK, everyone take a moment and envisage a loved one stuck under the car, they're trapped and fearing for their life." Clara says theatrically. "Close your eyes and really feel it."

Looking at the girls, I could see they were all closing their eyes. I'd better join in; this is my fault, after all. OK, who shall I think of? Zack? Nah, he'd definitely be able to push the car off himself with those ripped abs and big shoulders. Mmmm… Crap, got distracted!

"OK," shouted Clara. "On three; one, two, charge!"

We all charge at the car and push with all of our might; it moves about an inch off the floor and slams back down again.

"Well, there goes my security deposit!" huffed Felicity.

"This is no good, we're not strong enough!" moaned Danni. "We're going to have to find some help."

"We'll have to split up. There are wild animals around; we can't leave all of the food and drink exposed or they might attack the car. I'll get the shovel out and keep watch," said Felicity.

"Why do you get to stay?" whined Danni. "I don't want to go on the hunt!"

"OK," I say, "you two stay. Clara and Tara, you come with me; we'll go and get help."

The girls were less than impressed with their short straw, but they plodded along with me. It took us an hour to walk towards the section of beach where there was life.

"How are we going to choose who to ask?" says Clara.

"We need big guys, not skinny hipsters; they need to be able to lift a truck!" I reply.

"That should be easy enough. I can see how that convo is going to go now: 'Bit hot, isn't it? Fancy getting a bit hotter and lifting a two-tonne truck in forty-five degrees?'" Tara said sarcastically.

"Look, it's my fault, I'll find someone!" I tell the girls as I set my sights on a group of lads and walk towards them.

"Hi, guys!" I shout to the group.

"Hey!" one shouts back. He nudges his mate and they turn to walk towards us.

"We're in a bit of a pickle and could do with some big strapping men to help," I say, flicking my hair at them.

"Ah, a damsel in distress, hey?" one of them asks.

"Exactly!" I reply. "I was fancying myself as a bit of a rally driver and I've flipped our four by four in the forest. Fancy coming to give us a hand to get it back the right way up?"

"Ha, ha, what a bad ass!" one of them says.

"What's in it for us?" the second one asks with a cheeky smile.

"Well," Tara jumps in, "we could make you dinner and drinks. I make a mean ham sandwich with a side order of gin!"

"Sounds good to me, I'm starving!" said the bigger one. "I'm Jay, this is Ro, and we have that bunch of

Neanderthals with us as well," He points to his mates. He does a rally call and all of the guys run over. There are six of them in total. Jay explains the situation; they find it very amusing and agree to help.

Walking back to the car with them was entertaining. They were recounting their travel tales, full of mischief and mayhem. They were definitely a handful, but seemed like a good laugh.

"Hmm, I thought the car was here, we must have gone the wrong way," I say to the group. "Danni, Fliss!"

"There's something over there!" One of the guys points ahead. "I can't make it out."

Looking closer, I can see that it's Danni with the towel over her head.

"This way!" I shout to the group.

As we get closer, Danni looks through the slit in her towel, then throws it on the floor and desperately tries to sort her hair out and pulls her boobs up in her bikini.

"You're welcome!" I say as we walk past her.

"Jesus, you weren't kidding! You really did flip it, didn't you?" said Ro.

"Erm, yeah, not my finest hour!" I reply.

"OK, lads, on three…" said Ro. "One, two, three!"

Wahoo! The wheels were back on the ground!

"Our heroes!" Danni sighs.

"Right, where's this grub we were promised?" asks Jay, rubbing his stomach.

"Let's get the car out of here and have a picnic on the beach, away from the snakes!" Danni says, eying up the sticks on the ground.

"Sounds good; jump in, lads!" says Jay.

The car was packed to the rafters with all of us piled in. Danni was sitting on Ro's knee, Tara was squeezed in between another two in the back, and Fliss and Clara were hair flicking away in the boot.

On the beach, we lay the blankets out and attack the food. One of the guys grabbed his guitar; he has us singing everything from Wonderwall to Aladdin. It was a perfect summer evening; all that was missing was Zack. We couldn't get any signal on the island, so it was five days of no contact. Absence was certainly making the heart stronger for me; I just hoped that it was having the same effect on him. I keep envisaging the 'new arrivals' from Oz, who in my head all look like Pamela Anderson, and for some reason are taking it in turns massaging him. Ugh, I need to stop torturing myself.

"Penny for them?" Ro interrupts my thoughts.

"Oh, it's nothing," I say, wafting my hand, shaking my thoughts away.

"Well it looks like something," he says, smiling.

"It's a guy," I said with a shrug.

"Isn't it always?" he laughs. "Come on, fill me in."

I told him the tale of our long distance love affair. It was actually cheering me up; maybe we could make this work, maybe he really is 'the one'.

"Yeah, that's never going to work!" he said, bringing me back to reality with a thud.

"Excuse me?" I can't believe I'm hearing this; clearly he didn't understand what I was saying. We were meant to be – surely anyone with half a brain could see that?

"Men aren't programmed to be faithful; it's just not in our nature. He'll definitely be banging other girls while you're apart." he said flippantly.

"Just because you haven't found a girl you respect doesn't mean he doesn't respect me!" I say angrily, getting up from the blanket.

"Look, I'm not trying to hurt your feelings, I'm just being honest. It's not about respect, it's about primal instincts. If he's a red-blooded male, he'll need to get his kicks. That's all I'm saying!"

"Well, all I'm saying is that you're wrong!" I say, stropping off into the forest.

Danni comes running after me. "Louise, what happened?"

"That stupid Ro said HBG would be cheating on me because he's 'a red-blooded male'! I mean, what does that even mean? I told him he was wrong and that he doesn't know what he's talking about, but what if he's right?" I ramble, wiping the tears from my eyes.

"The thing is, Louise, we don't know how the story will end with you and HBG. All I know is that you can't give up now, you've come this far! Ro was just saying that to get a reaction and get into your pants. Just ignore him!" Danni says kindly.

"You're right, it was stupid to get upset," I say, trying to shake it off. "It's just so hard not being able to talk to him – anything could be happening."

"Louise, you can't think about that. Just enjoy your time here, don't let it pass you by. Remember, this is your once in a lifetime adventure!"

"You're right. Come on, let's go back; I'll just sit on the other side of the beach to Ro."

"Er, actually, now may not be the best time to move!" said Danni, standing very still.

"What's wrong? Are you OK?"

Whispering, she said, "Look down!"

I look down to see a gigantic snake slithering across her foot. Oh my God, it's massive! It's easily six feet long, if not more. If that bites her, we're miles away from a hospital.

I'm freaking out! What shall I do? OK, stay calm. I resist the urge to scream and calmly take her hands.

"Don't move. Any vibrations will anger it," I whisper. I can feel her hands trembling. "It's going to be OK, just stand really still." There are beads of sweat pouring off her forehead. I need to think of a plan and fast!

"What are you pair of muppets doing?" slurred a very drunk Tara, running through the forest.

Oh no, this isn't good: if she disturbs it, God only knows what it'll do.

"What's this? A fricking séance?" she says, laughing to herself as she stumbles over to us.

I very slowly turn and whisper, "Don't move! There is a snake on Danni's foot! You need to stay still and be very quiet."

"You're joking, aren't ya?" As Tara got closer, she soon realised that we weren't. She throws her drink on the floor, screams an almighty scream and runs for the hills.

This bolted the snake into action and it started to wrap itself around Danni's legs. Shit, shit, shit! I didn't know what to do! Then I hear footsteps running towards us. I turn to see all of the guys coming our way.

"Louise, get out of the way!" shouts Ro.

I jump to the side as the guys run at the snake and pound the floor around it. Unbelievably, the snake unravelled itself and scarpered.

"Oh thank God! Danni, are you OK?" I shout, grabbing her and not letting go. Turning to Ro, thanking him.

"Well, I figured I owed you after making you cry," he said. "Sorry for being an ass, I was just trying my luck!"

"Told you," Danni said through my hair.

Chapter Thirty-Three
I Solemnly Swear

Our amazing five days on Fraser Island have sadly come to an end. It really was an incredible experience, minus the car tipping and wild animal drama. Now that we are back onto the mainland, I must admit I am pretty excited about showering on my own and eating something other than ham sandwiches.

Sitting on the balcony of the hostel, I skyped HBG. I couldn't wait to see his face!

"You're alive!" he answered. "I've missed you so much!" This made me grin like a Cheshire cat. "How was it? Did you have fun?"

"Oh yeah it was great. I hit a dingo on the head with a shovel, tipped the four by four and Danni got herself tangled in a snake, but, other than that, it was a walk in the park!" I laugh.

"Never a dull moment with you girls, hey! Well, I have some pretty amazing news," he says with a mischievous look on his face.

"Really, what?" He's realised that he loves me and wants my babies?

"It's four days until I leave Fiji!" he says with that kilowatt smile. "It was supposed to be two more weeks, but I talked them into letting me leave earlier!"

"Four days? That is the best news ever!" I say, jumping up and down, screaming. "I can't wait to see you! We can go somewhere really romantic and spend some time together."

Danni comes running in from outside. "What's all the commotion?"

"It's Zack; he's leaving Fiji in four days!" I say, shrieking with delight.

"Oh, mega! We'll be at Airlie beach then, are you going to meet us there?" she asked him.

"Yeah, sure! Sounds great!" he replies.

"Great, I'll book you onto the Whitsundays trip with us!" she said, getting caught up in the excitement.

"Awesome! Thanks, Danni!" he says, grinning.

Well, this is awkward! I was really hoping to spend some time alone with HBG, not share him with my friends. How do I bring this up without sounding like a whiny girl?

"Louise? Are you OK?" he asks, full of concern.

"Me? Oh, yeah. I'm, erm, great! Can't wait to see you!" I say, shaking the thoughts away.

"Really? Tell your face!" He laughed. "What's really going on?"

"I guess I was just hoping that, when we met up, it would be just you and me, not you, me and the Brady Bunch." I laughed awkwardly.

"Oh," he said, taking this in. "To be honest, I thought you'd want to hang out with both me and the girls. The best of both worlds scenario! I know you don't have loads of time left with them, so I thought it'd be nice to combine the two. If I've read that completely wrong, then I'm more than happy to have you to myself."

There he is, being the sweetest guy ever, and I'm acting like an over clingy moron. Get your shit together, Louise!

"Now I feel bad. I never should have said anything!" I say, inwardly cringing.

"Look, how about I meet you at Airlie Beach, we get our own room, go on the Whitsunday's trip with the girls and then take it from there?"

"That sounds perfect," I say, beaming.

"OK, babe, see you in three sleeps!"

I allow myself another ten minutes to daydream about HBG, before I pack up and leave the hostel.

Lugging our bags onto the bus, we get comfy for our next journey towards Agnes Waters. We only have four more stops together before we all fly back home; I wasn't sure I was ready to leave this beautiful country or these amazing girls. We'd become so close; we were past friendship now, we were sisters. I knew more about these five girls than I did about myself, and I'd certainly seen way too much of them after sharing bathrooms for the last five months. Then there was the thought of leaving Zack. Ugh, that fills me with dread. Realistically, my brain understands that we have only spent two weeks together in total, but my heart is overruling it by saying, "This is it!" I've played the scenario out in my head a hundred times and it goes like this:

He comes to Airlie Beach, realises that I am the love of his life, asks me to marry him, I say yes, and we set up in Australia and have four gorgeous little children that all have his looks. He is a professional surfing instructor that wins loads of medals and I am the trophy wife!

My daydreaming is interrupted when we pull into a gorgeous little town called 1770 in Agnes Waters. I've got no idea why it's called that (although I can't admit that as Felicity has already told us, in great detail, from the guidebook that she read out loud from front to back.)

The hostel is a cluster of small huts that are named after countries from around the world. It has a really cool rustic vibe to it. We are allocated the British hut (obviously) and invited to join the United Nations Drinking Games this evening. For the first time in a long time, they'd actually managed to fill the huts with the correct nationalities and wanted to celebrate in the time honoured tradition of beer pong.

"Right, girls, we need to get it together and bring our A-Game tonight!" Danni says, standing in the middle of the room like a drill sergeant. "If you need a nap, do it now. If you haven't eaten, feed up. Keep the water intake high; we've got to be on point!"

"I don't think I've ever seen her so passionate!" Tara whispered.

"That's because this is serious! We are representing a nation, our great nation, so we have to put our all into this!" she replied, pacing up and down the room.

"Jesus, she's going to have us singing the national anthem in a minute!" laughed Clara.

"Brilliant idea, Clara. Right you lot, on your feet," she ordered.

"For God's sake!" said Felicity, resisting Danni pulling her up off the bed.

"OK, you don't have to sing the national anthem, but you do need to take an oath! Everybody stand and repeat after me."

Begrudgingly, we all stand and raise our left hand, with our right hand on our hearts.

"I solemnly swear… come on, repeat it," she jibed.

"I solemnly swear," we all repeat, rolling our eyes.

"That I will bring all that I have…"

"All that I am…"

"To this game..."

"I swear to ruin the other contestants..."

"In the name of the United Kingdom!" Danni said, pounding her fist into the air. "I'm pumped! How about you guys?"

"Sure, sure," we all mumble.

"Come on, let's line our stomachs."

We have been advised that the best way to get into the town from the hostel is to ride a bike; apparently, the local bus service is inconsistent at best. The driver is regularly spotted taking a nap by the side of the road or pulling over to eat his sarnies.

We find a lovely little café that does homemade food, where we fill up on quiche and cake, the lunch of champions according to Danni, who wouldn't allow us to look around the town as we had to go back and 'prepare'. I'm not sure what preparation goes into beer pong, but she was so insistent it was hard to say no.

Back at the hostel, we had to 'scout out the competition'.

"There are a lot of guys. That's going to put us at a disadvantage," says Danni with her hands on her head.

"Depends which way you look at it!" laughed Felicity.

"There'll be no time for any of those shenanigans!" Danni chastised. "We've got a game to win!"

"Think about it," said Felicity. "The best way to disarm a bunch of guys is to flirt with them! We could actually win if we do that!" She winked at us.

"You're right! Solid plan, Fliss! Louise, you need to brush up on your flirting skills, your game is terrible," Danni said.

"Hey! I resent that! I got HBG, didn't I?" Cheeky cow.

"OK, fair cop," she said putting her hands in the air. "Let's go and get ready so we can arrive early." With that, she marches off.

"Organised fun, my favourite!" Tara says sulkily.

The tension was palpable at the United Nations game; each country was scoping each other out, circling, picking out the weak links. Everyone was talking to each other in hushed tones, sussing out their game plan. Anyone would think this was the Olympics!

"Ladies aaaaand Gentlemen," said the compère in the style of a Master of Ceremonies at a boxing match. "Here, tonight, you are representing your nation! It is your time to put your country on the map!"

"Told you it's a big deal!" whispered Danni, getting more and more excited by the second.

"If you look to your left, the first round has been mapped out. Please see which country you are playing and head to the allocated table," he says, pointing to a large chart.

Our first match is against Germany. We are met at our table by six sullen looking faces.

"They look like a barrel of laughs, don't they?" laughed Clara.

"All the beer they'll have to drink will cheer them up!" shouts Danni. "It's psychology!" She tapped her temple with wild eyes. "I'm psyching them out!"

"On your marks..." shouts the compère.

"Right, girls, head in the game! Take no prisoners!" Danni shouts giving each one of us the eye.

"Get set... go!"

Danni goes first. The ball goes straight into one of their cups.

"Yeeesss! In your face, losers!" she gracefully shouts, doing the loser sign on her forehead.

"Danni, chill," Felicity says pulling her back. "You're going to burst a blood vessel at this rate!"

On their turn, the ball went straight in. Tara took our second shot, I was up next; God, this is nerve-racking!

OK, here we go... Come on, Louise, you got this...

"Yes! Hole in one!" I shout.

"It's not golf, Louise, but good shot," Danni says, patting my arm.

"They haven't got any cups left, what does that mean?" asked Clara.

"It means we've fudging won!" Danni screams "Wahoo!"

We absolutely blitzed it through our first five games, knocking people out left, right and centre. Danni was right, it really was a buzz. I needed a time out, though; I'd drank way too much beer in a really short space of time. We hit the snack table with drunken abandon.

"If I'm going to survive this, I need carbs and I need them fast," slurred Tara.

"Me too," hiccupped Clara.

We shoved as much food and water down us as we could and shuffled over to start the next round.

We made it down to the remaining eight (out of sixteen) countries. I was really starting to feel it now, but Danni was right, we needed to keep our head in the game. The first team that we had to face was France.

"Oh bollocks, the French can outdrink anyone," says Tara, swaying around.

"None of that negativity, Tara!" slurred Danni. "We've got this. Your baguettes don't scare me!"

We somehow beat twelve other countries and were now in the heats with just three countries left to beat: USA (of course), Australia (it's their homeland, so I'm OK with that) and Russia (who were mildly terrifying).

Our team was starting to look a bit limp. Tara has thrown up all down herself; she says it's tactical as now she feels fine. Felicity has hooked up with some Danish guy, we had to extract her from his face to get her to throw the ball. Danni was verging on full hysteria. I've never seen anything like it. She is pacing up and down and giving herself little slaps across the face 'to keep herself fresh'. As for Clara, she is slumped on a chair in a drunken haze; we had to pretty much resuscitate her to get her to take her shot. In short, I didn't like our chances.

First up was the USA. They look nimble and fresh, like they've been sipping lemonade all night and not chugging beer.

"They must be cheating," I said to Danni.

"I've been watching them. I couldn't pick up how they are doing it, but they must be, there's no way they can stay that sober," said Danni.

"Well, they won't be able to get away with it in front of all of these people," hiccupped Tara. "Let's take them down!"

We were killing it, absolutely going for gold, when suddenly it was like they had a second wind. They woke up and started to kick our asses. We were literally handed to them on a plate, annihilated. Danni was distraught; she dropped to her knees, raised her arms to the sky and screamed "Nooooooooooooo!" We were out, the dream was over.

As we were licking our wounds, the tables were moved, and an epic party kicked off.

"Don't know about you guys, but I'm excited to drink something that's not beer!" I slurred to the girls.

"Amen to that! Ah, come on, Danni, cheer up," Tara said to a beaten Danni, who is slumped on the floor.

"Leave me be, I just want to lie here," she said dramatically.

"No chance!" said Clara. "Come on, girls! Lift!"

We picked Danni up and dragged her to the bar.

When the party died down, we invited a bunch of people to come back to our hut for our own United Nations shindig. I learned how to say 'piss off' in seven different languages.

Felicity was still sucking the face off the Danish guy. When she came up for air, she turned to me and whispered, "I'm going back to his, OK?"

"OK, be safe!" I replied, blowing her a kiss.

She dragged him down the stairs from the hut, and they both took a massive tumble and hit the floor with a thud.

"Are you guys OK?" I shouted from the porch.

"We're fine, we're fine!" Felicity waved me off.

I could hear the Danish guy shouting that his foot hurt. Fliss was clearly in no mood to hear this and told him to man up and dragged him back, caveman style, to his hut!

I eventually went to bed at around four a.m. There were various bodies scattered around our room and on the porch. I kicked them all out and clambered into bed. My head was going to hurt tomorrow.

Chapter Thirty-Four
The Backpackers Are Here!

At eight a.m. the following morning, I woke to Felicity's boozy breath in my face.

"Louise, wake up! It's an emergency!" she said, shaking me.

"Is someone dead?" I mumbled into my pillow.

"No," she replied.

"Then come back in four to six hours!" I sighed.

"I'm serious, it's the Danish dude. I think his foot is broken, we need to get him to the hospital!" she said, rolling me over to face her.

"Are you serious? How did that happen?" I said, attempting to sit up.

"I think it was when I dragged him down the steps last night. I told him to man up, but it's now four times its usual size and he's in agony!"

"Oh, Fliss!" I said, rubbing my eyes. "How are we going to get him there? We haven't got a car."

"He has, we just need to drive him. I asked the manager and he said the hospital is only fifteen minutes away. Please, Louise, I'm begging you!" she said with her big blue eyes pleading.

"Ugh, OK. I need a cold shower, toast and lots of coffee!" I replied, dragging myself over to the bathroom.

"Thank you, thank you. I'll get your toast and coffee, you shower and we'll meet you at the front in fifteen!" she said, running out of the door.

I chucked myself into a freezing cold shower; it was so cold it made me do an involuntarily yelp.

Danni came staggering in with crazy hair. "What's up? What's going on?" she asked, rubbing her eyes.

"Fliss broke the Danish dude's foot when she dragged him down the stairs last night! I need to drive them to the hospital."

"You are kidding?" she laughed "In that case, budge up, I'll come with you."

She jumped into the freezing cold shower with me.

"Shit the bed! This is some way to sober up!" she shouted.

"What's going on?" asked Tara as she staggered in. "Are we having a shower party?"

"Fliss broke a dude's foot; we're sobering up so we can take him to the hospital," said Danni, shivering in the shower.

"Seriously? Hilarious! Room for a little'un?" she said, squeezing in.

Fifteen minutes later, we met Felicity and the Danish dude (no one actually knew his real name, including Felicity!) at the front of the hostel. His foot was massive; it definitely was broken. We demolished about three cups of coffee each and six rounds of toast, attempting to soak up the gallons of beer that were consumed last night.

It took us longer than fifteen minutes to get there as I drove the whole way at thirty miles an hour. I was terrified of being pulled over.

When we finally made it to the world's smallest hospital there was a man sitting outside on the step. As we pulled in, we heard him say, "I'll have to call you back, a bunch of backpackers have just turned up!"

"How did he know we are backpackers?" asked Tara.

"Beats me!" I replied, looking around at us all in our PJs.

Danni somehow managed to squash Danish Dude's foot as we pulled him out of the car, so he was screaming by the time the doctor ran over to us.

"What happened?" the doctor demanded.

"He's broken his foot," I replied.

"How did that happen?" he asked with a big, booming voice.

We looked at one another. I finally answered, "He fell down the stairs."

"Hmm, I'm assuming alcohol was involved?" he asked with a look of disdain on his face.

"Well, you can't have a United Nations drinking game without it!" Danni scoffed.

We all rolled our eyes at her.

"Bring him inside," he demanded, looking unimpressed.

His foot was X-rayed, which showed that it was broken in three places. He was going to have to stay overnight and have a cast put on. We promised that we'd be back tomorrow morning to drive him back to the hostel.

"I feel awful!" said Felicity. "He kept moaning about it last night and I told him to stop being such a pansy!"

"You were not going to be deterred, that was for sure," laughed Danni. "You were a woman on a mission!"

"How embarrassing," she moaned. "I'm going to be remembered as the horny girl that broke a poor guy's foot!"

"If we've got anything to do with it, yes, you will!" laughed Clara.

"Come on, there's nothing we can do here, let's go back and we'll come and get him tomorrow," I said, wrapping my arm around Felicity and heading back to the car.

Back at the hostel, everyone was asking after Danish Dude. It turns out his real name is Frederik. We filled them in on the cast and that he needed picking up tomorrow.

"We'll get him tomorrow; you've done enough!" huffed one of his friends in Felicity's direction.

"I didn't see any of you leaping out of bed to take him to the hospital this morning!" Danni accused. They all shuffled around, looking at their feet. "Yeah, as I thought! Come on, girls, let's get out of here. You're welcome, by the way!" She shouted in their direction.

We were all in the mood to do something seriously relaxing after the hectic start to the day. Agnes Waters is known for its beautiful beaches and national parks, so we grabbed our bikes and went on a mini adventure.

Agnes Waters truly is a hidden gem, there are hardly any tourists around and the natural elements have remained unspoiled. We saw so many beautiful waterfalls and natural surroundings, it was just the peace and serenity that we needed for the day. We spent most of the day splashing around in waterfalls and napping. By the time that we arrived back at the hostel, we were feeling much more chilled out.

"I'm going to catch up with Frederik's mates and check that he is OK" said Felicity when we got back.

"OK, need some back up?" I asked.

"Nah, I'll be fine, thanks," she said, smiling.

We'd bought some local delicacies for dinner, so the rest of us headed over to a garden just outside the hostel with a picnic blanket.

"Well, they can kiss my ass!" said Felicity ten minutes later, marching over in a huff.

"What happened?" asked Clara.

"Danish Dude has told his mates that he doesn't want to see me again! I said fine, pick him up yourself!" she said, pacing around. "I just feel like such an idiot; I mean; I literally broke a guy's foot and dragged him back to a hut because I wanted sex!"

"He just needs to learn to stand on his own two feet, if you ask me!" Danni scoffed, making us all roll around with laughter.

"Let's just hope he can foot the bill!" screamed Clara joining in.

"Don't listen to them, Felicity," I said, putting my arm around her. "You're never going to see him again, you just need to move on and put your best foot forward ha ha."

Chapter Thirty-Five
A Little Pampering Never Hurt Anyone

My nerves are really starting to kick in now. I can't wait to see Zack, but I can't deny that there is a tonne of pressure. We've been amazing on the phone, but what if that's all this is? Just amazing pen pals. What if our chemistry totally sucks when we're together? What if he remembers me to be ten times hotter than I actually am and he's seriously disappointed? This is too much; I need to sit down!

"Louise, you're hyperventilating! Come on, I know you're going insane with the internal monologue!" said Felicity with her hands on her hips.

"I'm fine," I manage.

"Uh huh!" said Danni in the background. "Come on, Louise, we all know you're freaking out. You're seeing HBG tomorrow, it's a big deal, we get it! Come on, what will make you feel better?"

"Lipo?" I say, pinching my stomach.

"Not enough recovery time," said Danni seriously.

Felicity stared at her. "You don't need lipo! You look gorgeous as you are!"

"I need to primp and prime, but I don't know anywhere and I'm scared of something going wrong the day before he gets here!" I say, biting my nails.

"We'll all get on our phones on the coach and find you a beautician with a good recommendation, it'll be fine! You'll feel all glowy and lovely by the time he lands," she said.

"Ah, thanks, girls," I say, giving Danni and Fliss a hug.

"And you've forgotten another major event happening tomorrow," said Fliss.

"What?" I ask.

"Hannah is back!" she screamed

"Oh my gosh, I'm so excited to see her! I hope she had the best time with James; I can't wait to hear all about it. Where is she meeting us?" I asked.

"At the bus station, she gets in at the same time as us," Fliss replied.

"The gang is back together again!" shouted Danni.

On the coach, the girls are reading through the local directories of beauticians.

"You should get a vajazzle, Louise!" laughed Tara.

"What's a vajazzle when it's at home?" asked Felicity.

"You know, it's where you stick little gems on your foof to make it look all sparkly? Look, here's a pic!" Tara showed Fliss an image on her phone.

"Now I have officially seen everything!" Fliss laughed.

"That's a firm no on the vajazzle!" I laugh. "Anyone found any good ones? This one has four stars from reviews, I'm thinking of going there."

"Let's see," said Danni, leaning over. "Yeah, that looks good. We should get there in a few hours, book yourself in!"

I did just that. I was going to get my nails done, my foof, legs and armpits waxed. I might even get them to do a strip over my lip. I haven't got a full tash, but just to be sure; I want him to be the only one with facial hair!

Four hours later, we arrive at Airlie Beach.

"Look, there's Han!" shouts Danni. That got us all jumping up and down screaming on the coach. I couldn't wait to get off and give her a big hug.

Shoving everyone one out of the way, we all jump onto Hannah.

"Look at you, you're glowing!" said Felicity. "Did you have the best time?"

"Oh, girls, it was the greatest! I've fallen so madly in love, it's ridiculous!" she laughed. "I can't wait for our last few girlie weeks together, but I must admit, I'm excited about going home to James!"

"I'm so happy for you!" I said, giving her a big squeeze. "You look like you could walk on water!"

"I feel like it!" she replied, laughing. "It's an incredible feeling."

"Well, HBG is coming tomorrow, so I hope I feel the same," I say, clinging onto her. Just saying that he is coming tomorrow makes me unsteady on my feet.

"Ahh, how exciting, Louise! Bet you can't wait," she said, beaming.

"I'm mildly terrified, but yes, mostly excited," I said. "Let's go and find the hostel, I've got some vajazzling to do!"

I was having one last night in the dorm with the girls, then tomorrow night HBG and I are getting our own room for a night before we take off for the Whitsundays. The hostel was actually really nice. There was a section that was in a hotel style with loads of rooms; and there was another section that had little cabins dotted around in a forest. It was very enchanting! We paid a little extra to stay in that part.

"Right, girls, I'm going to go for my appointment. Be back in an hour for dinner, OK? Can't wait to hear everything, Han, make sure you don't spill all the details before I'm back!"

The salon looks nice enough; it is clean and fresh.

"Good afternoon, madam," the lady greeted me from behind the counter. "Do you have an appointment?"

"Yes, I do, Louise Johnson at four p.m.," I reply.

"Perfect, let's do your nails first then, waxing last, OK?" she asked.

I picked the colour for my nails. I was going with a lovely bright yellow as it would look really nice with my tan. It was such a treat to have my feet soaked and have someone fuss over me. I haven't had a wax in ages; I always find them really painful and that half of my skin disappears with the hair.

"OK, let's start with your legs. Just lie back and relax," she says.

Yeah, like that's going to happen!

She puts the hot wax on my legs and it actually feels quite nice. She places the strips on, then rips.

"Jesus fricking Christ!" I shout.

"The first one is always the worst," she says. "Just lie back, it'll be over before you know it!"

Ten minutes of torture later, my aluminous red legs were looking pretty sorry for themselves.

"OK, open your legs please, I will now do the bikini area," she says.

"Yeah, after the legs, I'm having second thoughts!' I say, pulling my top down, trying to cover my foof.

"It's OK it's much quicker in this area. It'll be over in a jiff!" she says, pinning me down.

She was right; for some reason, the foof was far less painful. She finished off by quickly doing under my arms and upper lip. I was red raw everywhere, but apparently this was normal and it would calm overnight. She gave me some cream to take away and advised me to lather myself in it regularly for the next few hours.

I got back to the hostel and Danni jumped as she saw me.

"Jesus! What happened to you?" she said, staring at me.

"It's just a bit of redness!" I waved away her concern. "It'll go down in a few hours, apparently."

"I've never seen a wax look that sore before, Louise. Are you sure about the place you went to?" she asked.

"There were loads of people in there and they seemed to know what they were doing," I replied.

Glancing in the mirror, I saw that she was right: I was very red. I lathered on more lotion and hoped that it would go down as the night wore on. I wore some nice baggy trousers to cover my legs and popped some foundation on my tash area. There we go, good as new!

We found a gorgeous little restaurant for dinner; it was very quaint with nice low lighting. I should definitely come here with HBG, it had a really romantic feel to it. Hannah was telling us in detail about her trip with James; it was lovely to see her so happy.

I'm not sure what is going on in my nether regions, but my foof is on fire and really itchy. It must be the wax.

I need to have a look at what's going on. I excused myself and aimed for the ladies.

The ladies loo has a really brash strip lighting that's a real shock on your senses after the nice dim lighting of the restaurant. I went into a cubicle and pulled my pants down. Oh my God! My foof is bright red and has got lumps all over it; it looks like I've got herpes! It looks beyond sore; it looks angry, like 'someone stole your last chocolate style' angry. I had to get one of the girls. As I run out of the cubicle, I glance into the mirror and catch sight of my reflection. The whole bottom half of my face has swollen; my lips are about four times their original size. Oh my God! This is a disaster!!

I run out of the bathroom, close to hysterics.

"Girls, bathroom, NOW!" I scream, then run back in again.

All five of them come racing in.

"Louise, what's the... aaaaah, your face!" Danni shouta. "What the hell happened?"

"I don't know," I manage to say with tears pouring down my face. "Look at this!"

I pull my pants down just in time for a little old lady to walk in and then run out just as quickly.

"Well, she's never going to sleep again!" said Tara.

"What am I going to do?" I was close to hysteria. "Zack is arriving tomorrow morning and I look like a leper!"

"OK, calm down, it's just a reaction," said Felicity. "It's not, erm, that noticeable!"

The girls nod dutifully.

"Oh shut up! Of course it's fricking noticeable! Fliss, help!" I scream, shaking her.

"We need to go to a chemist. Come on, let's go," said Felicity, dragging me out. "You guys stay here; there's no need for us all to go."

"I'm not missing this!" said Danni.

"None of us are," said Han; "Come on."

Tara lent me her scarf and I tied it around my face as we scarpered out of the restaurant.

We got to the chemist just as it was closing. They weren't going to let me in, but one flash of my face under the scarf made them reconsider.

"What happened? Is it herpes?" the pharmacist asked.

"No, it's not fricking herpes!" I spat at him. "I went for a wax a few hours ago and I must have had a reaction."

I showed him my legs and the surrounding areas of my foof. He actually took a step back and said, "Jesus!" Thanks for the professional reaction!

"OK, we need to give you an antihistamine, aspirin and cream to stop the itching. It would also be a good idea to ice the affected areas," he advised.

"So my whole body then!" I sob.

Danni put her arm round me. "Will this stop her looking like a plague victim Doc?"

"Danni!" Felicity and Tara shouted.

I took as many tablets as I was allowed and we went back to hostel.

I lay myself down on the bed in the hostel, covered head to toe in cream and about seven bags of ice. It was blisteringly cold, but this was preferable to the alternative.

"Girls, what am I going to do about tomorrow? I can't let HBG see me like this!" I said, sobbing.

"If you still look like this, then we'll come up with a plan," said Danni. "I'll distract him and take him on a massive detour or something. But don't worry, it'll be fine, it'll have gone down by then."

The tablets are starting to kick in and I start to think back to when my fat rolls were my only problem. I hope that things look brighter in the morning. As I am dozing off, I can hear the girls talking in muffled voices in the background.

"You know that's not going down," I hear Danni say. "We need to come up with a plan."

"Maybe we should text HBG and tell him to postpone a day?" Felicity replied.

"I think he's already on the plane," said Tara.

"I'll wake up early and take a look at her," said Danni. "If she still looks like Quasimodo, we'll come up with a backup plan."

Chapter Thirty-Six
Is the 'Leper Look' in Fashion Yet?

I can feel the light on my skin; oh God, it must be morning. Please say that last night was a bad dream and everything is as it should be! I gently raise my hand and touch my face. Hmm, doesn't actually feel so bad. Ripping the covers back, I take a look at my legs. OK, just looks like a mild sunburn, I can get away with that. Now it's time to check out the foof…

"Louise, don't," Danni said, grabbing my hand.

"Danni, what are you doing?" I ask, fighting her grip on my arm.

"I woke up early to assess you," she said. "The good news is that your face has pretty much gone down, it's just your lips. With a bit of lippy you'll look like you've had your lips done, and what man doesn't love a fuller pout?"

"OK, that's not so bad," I said, gently touching my lips.

"Exactly. Then, if you plaster your legs in fake tan, you shouldn't be able to see any difference there. They just look like you've stood too close to a kilowatt lamp."

"Ok… Where's the 'but'?" I ask carefully.

"Well, your foof is another issue entirely. I'm sorry to say that it's still a horror show down there!" she says matter-of-factly.

"What were you doing looking at my foof?" I say snappily, pulling the duvet off myself to inspect the damage.

"Damage control!" she replies, holding my hand down over the duvet. "Louise, when you look, you are going to freak out. I tried to force feed you antihistamines but you kept gagging."

"Who left you in charge?" I say, shaking my head. By this point, all of the girls are awake and are giving me the sympathetic look. Ugh, this is bad. "I need to look in private!" I say, pulling the duvet back over me.

I slowly lift up my pyjama bottoms, take a deep breath and look down.

"Holy mother of Christ! It looks like herpes on steroids! Look!" I say to the girls, about to get out of bed.

"We've already seen," Felicity replies sombrely.

"What? You all woke up early to check out my bits? That's weird, even for you lot!" I say, swinging my legs out of bed.

"We just wanted to see before you did, so that we could help you to manage it," Hannah said kindly.

I shakily make my way to the mirror to look at my face. Well, it's not ideal, but Danni is right, it has enhanced my pout. At least the rest of the swelling has gone down. In the natural light, my legs don't look that bad. Not ideal, but not horrendous either. My foof, on the other hand…

"What am I going to do?" I moan to the girls. "This is the first night in five months that I'm seeing HBG and I look like a plague victim! He can't see me naked like this!"

"We've come up with a solution to that!" said Tara.

"What? A foof-ectomy?" I ask, sobbing.

"Well, we were thinking we could tell him that there aren't any private rooms available, so he'll have to stay in the dorm with us! He won't want to bump nasties with a room full of people!" Tara says proudly.

"Then, we go out on the catamaran for two days on the Whitsundays," said Danni, joining in. "You have to sleep in a room full of people then, as well. So, by the time we come back, your foof will have had three days to calm down and look like a normal vag again!"

"That's actually not a terrible plan," I say, wiping my eyes. "What if he asks at the reception, though, about the double rooms?"

"We'll go and fill the guy in!" said Han.

"Don't tell him about my plague ridden foof!" I shout.

"No, no, don't worry, we'll think of something else!" says Hannah reassuringly.

"Well, I guess that's as good a plan as any. I'd better go and get some tan for my legs," I say, giving them a closer look.

"Already done!" says Han. "I popped out for you as soon as the shop opened this morning."

"You girls really are the best," I say, pulling them in for a group hug. "Lord knows what I'd do without you!"

"Come on, chuck yourself into the shower. HBG will be here in two hours, we need to make you look semi-normal. There is work to be done!" said Danni.

After two hours of tanning, YouTubing how to minimise lips and seventeen outfit selections, I was finally ready and looking semi-normal.

"You look amazing!" said Felicity. "Honestly, he'll never be able to tell."

Chapter Thirty-Seven
A Lumpy Secret

Sitting at the train station waiting for HBG, I've bitten nearly all of my freshly painted nail varnish off. I'm so nervous, I feel like I'm going to throw up. I need to calm down and think non-foof-scratching rational thoughts.

Rational thought number one: if this does in fact turn out to be a holiday romance, then I had an amazing time and I will always look back at it fondly. Yes, very mature, good thought.

Rational thought number two: if we don't gel, then it is a pretty big country. The chances are that I will never see him again - also a very good point!

Rational thought number three: I have already named our children, chosen the wedding venue and written the guest list, so the big decisions are already taken care of… I think I am venturing into the irrational side.

Rational thought number four: I actually saw a wedding dress in a store window by the beauticians the other day. I could casually ask his opinion as we walk past, just to get an idea of his sense of style… OK, lost it, I'll just go back to sitting quietly.

The train is pulling in… The train is pulling in! Ferociously wiping my sweaty palms on my trousers, I'm standing on my tip toes, looking through the crowd, trying to pick him out. Is that him? No, that's a lady with big hair. Ooh, ooh, over there? No, that's another lady…why do I keep picking out women!

As the crowd clears, I see him. We lock eyes and I'm pretty sure my heart has just skipped a beat. He gives me that lazy smile; I beam like a Cheshire Cat in response. I'm pushing people out of the way, running towards him; I feel like time has stood still, all I can see is him.

He drops his bags and holds his arms out to me. I run and jump into him; he pulls me towards him and gives me a knee-buckling kiss. We take a step back and look at each other.

"Hi," he says with a smile.

"Hi," I reply.

I have no idea how long we are standing there, staring at each other. We are interrupted from our bubble by a sweeper budging us out of the way to clean around us. The spell is broken and we both snap back into reality.

"You look incredible!" he says, sizing me up. "Different, though, I can't put my finger on it."

Sucking my lips in, I reply. "Hmm, not sure, it has been a while!"

"Too long!" he says, gently kissing me. "So, where to?"

"Let's go back to the hostel and drop your stuff off, then I can show you around. The girls are dying to see you!" I say, holding his hand.

"Perfect! Although I'm not too bothered about the scenery, I'd much rather see the inside of our room, if you know what I mean!" he says, nibbling my ear.

Must remain strong and not let him see manky foof!

"Yeah, about that… erm, all of the single rooms were sold out, so we'll have to stay in the dorm with the girls tonight," I say, looking at my nails.

"Oh, well, maybe if we ask at reception they may have a cancellation? Or we could go somewhere else?" he asks, gazing into my eyes.

"I already checked with reception, they definitely don't" I say, shrugging and ignoring the question about somewhere else.

"OK, cool, no worries," he replies. I can see him in the corner of my eye, weighing me up. This was going to be harder than figuring out the square root of pi.

Back at the hostel, the girls run out to greet him.

"HBG!" Danni was first. "Sorry about the whole mix up with your boss, hope she was OK!"

"Water under the bridge." He laughs.

"I feel like we've never been apart after my daily updates from Louise!" said Felicity, giving him a hug.

One by one he made his way round the girls.

"We'll show you to your bed," said Danni. "Sorry about you having to share with us, bummer about the single rooms!"

"Yeah, I think I'll double check with the manager, just in case" he says, kissing me on the cheek.

"I'll come with you!" I shout in a panic.

"Me too!" says Tara. Zack looks at us both strangely. "Safety in numbers and all that!" She laughs nervously.

Zack confidently strides up to the guy behind the desk and asks if there are any single rooms available.

"Yeah, should be, mate,'" he replies. "Let me check."

Tara coughed in the background. The manager looks up, spots Tara and surreptitiously replies, "Ah, just checked the old system and there's nothing, mate. Sorry about that!"

Zack turned to look at Tara. She shrugged nonchalantly and said, "Oh no… that's… erm… terrible!"

"Hmm, indeed." he replied, looking from Tara to me.

Zack was starving so I took him to the quaint little restaurant that we went to the evening before. I'm hoping that the mood lighting would distract him from looking too closely at my lips.

"Hello, welcome back!" said the server.

Crap, he recognises me!

"Your food was so good I had to bring Zack!" I replied, laughing. OK, now shut up, no need to say anything more! Grabbing Zack's arm, I steer him towards a table.

"Great! How is your face?" he asked. Shit. I saw Zack look bemusedly from the waiter to me.

"Great! How's yours?" I laugh. Walking away, I whisper to Zack, "What a weirdo!"

As we take our seat at the table, I see the little old lady walking towards us who saw my manky foof last night. Oh no, she must work here! I snatch the menu from Zack's hands and hold it up in front of my face.

"Good afternoon," she says. "Can I get you any drinks?"

"I'm not sure, I haven't looked at the menu!" says Zack, clearly confused as to why I rudely snatched it from his hands.

"It's all the usual stuff," I shout from behind the menu. "Just pick whatever you usually have."

"Okay," he says warily. "How about a bottle of wine? We're celebrating getting back together after four months apart!" he says to the waitress.

"Oh, how wonderful! Here, let me point out a nice bottle for you," she replies, trying to pull the menu away from me. I've got such a grip on it, it's turning into a really awkward tug of war. Oh God, just let go, I'm screaming in my head.

"That's OK. I'm pretty fussy, I'll pick one." I say, still hiding.

"Are you OK behind there, Louise?" Zack laughs awkwardly.

"Yep, I'm great!" I reply. "How about the Sauvignon Blanc?"

"Great, I'll get you a bottle," she replies.

I accidentally loosen my grip, just enough for her to whip the menu away from me. I try to snatch it back, but it's too late; I'm exposed! She stares at me and slowly makes the connection. I see the look on her face change. She steps back and physically gasps, throwing her hand to her mouth. Thanks for the theatrics, Grandma!

"Do you two know each other?" Zack asks.

"No!" We shout in unison as she scarpers off.

"Louise, what's going on?" Zack asks. "I feel like you're behaving really strangely."

"Really? I feel totally fine," I say, in a much more high pitch than I was aiming for!

He looks at me with wide eyes. Oh God, he thinks I'm a total crackpot! Why did I bring him here? Of course they would recognise me; stupid, stupid, stupid!

"Louise?" He asks, looking concerned.

"Hmm?" I say, trying to snap out of it.

"Never mind. So, fill me in on everything, where you've been and what you've been up to. Tell me all!"

And I did just that. We sat in the same spot, talking for four hours straight and filling each other in on our travels, the highs, the lows and the in-betweens. He moved to sit next to me and held my hand, telling me how much he's missed me, how he couldn't believe the connection that we have.

At six p.m., we finally left. As soon as the fresh air hit, I realised how much wine we'd had.

"Whoa, easy there!" he said, pulling me back up to a vertical position.

"We drank a lot of wine!" I hiccupped.

"You can really put it away!' He laughed. "Come on, let's take a walk on the beach and sober you up a bit."

We splashed around in the sea and sat talking on the beach until the sun went down.

"I've got to tell you, Louise, I've never felt this way about anyone before," he said, pushing my hair behind my ear, "and I've been with a lot of women!"

"OK, it was cute until the last part!" I laughed.

"Sorry, no idea why I said that!" he says covering his face laughing. "My point is that you are special."

"OK, that's better. Lead with that next time!" I laughed.

"Shall we go back?" he asked, stretching his hand out to me.

I held his hand as he pulled me up towards him and led us back to the hostel.

As were walking we bumped into the girls leaving for a night out.

"Here are the love birds!" shouted Danni. "We're going clubbing, want to come?"

We looked at each other and, still fuzzy from the wine, we giggled. "No, I think we'll stay here!"

"Are you sure?" said Felicity, giving me the beady eye.

"Of course!" Why wouldn't I be sure? "Have fun," I say.

Back in the room, we lock the door and start to tear each other's clothes off. This is amazing! I've missed him so much. I'm down to my undies when I suddenly remember the horror show in my pants.

"Stop, stop, stop!" I say, pushing him away and pulling my dress in front of me.

"Why, what's wrong? Are you OK?" he asks, his face full of concern.

"I'm fine, it's just… I can't do this right now," I mumble.

"What? Louise, what is going on? You're acting like a schizophrenic tonight! I don't know where I am with you one minute to the next!" he says, pushing his hair back off his head. "You were weird in the restaurant and now you're being weird again. Just tell me, what is it?"

"Oh God, it's really embarrassing," I say, flopping onto the bed and covering my face with my hands.

"It can't be that bad. Come on, tell me!" he says, kneeling on the floor in front of me and cupping my face in his hands.

"OK, OK," I say, pushing him off, and pacing up and down.

He sits on the bed, giving me his full attention.

"OK, well, before you arrived, I wanted to make sure that I was perfectly preened for you!"

"OK…" he says, looking confused.

"I found a salon online and went for a wax."

He is looking at me intently; God, this is awkward. Just say it!

"Well, it turns out that I had an allergic reaction, my whole face swelled up last night, and my legs got horrible bumps on them. That's why you thought I looked different, my lips have puffed up!"

He stood up and walked over to me. "Seriously, this is what's bothering you? I think you look beautiful!" He kissed my neck.

"I haven't finished!" I say, stepping back.

"Carry on," he says, looking frustrated now.

"Well, my legs and my upper lip weren't the only thing I had waxed," I say, biting my lip.

"Ooh, I like where this is going!" he says cheekily, walking over to me.

"Trust me, you won't!" I say. "My foof is like a car crash! It's all lumpy and vile!" I moan.

Laughing, he says, "Oh, it can't be that bad! Come on, show me! Bet I don't even notice!"

"Really?" I'm not sure that this is a good idea. Mind you, guys are weird. It might not be a big deal to him.

"Really! I know; how about, on three, we both drop our pants?" he says.

Giggling, I reply, "OK, but you have to prepare yourself. It's really terrible, like chickenpox-style awful!"

"Louise, nothing can turn me off you," he says sincerely.

"OK, here goes nothing. One, two, three..." I drop my pants.

"Good God!" he shouts.

"I knew this was a bad idea!" Close to tears, I'm scrabbling around, pulling my dress back on over my manky foof. What was I thinking? Of course I shouldn't have shown him that, what man would ever think that was attractive? Oh God, this is beyond embarrassing. Ground, please swallow me up!

I'm now covering my face with a pillow, sobbing on the bed.

"Shit, Louise, I'm so sorry. I never should have reacted like that, that was horrible of me," he says putting his hand on my shoulder. "I was just not expecting… well, that."

"I told you it was bad." I sobbed through the pillow. "I look like a leper!"

"You don't look like a leper," he says, laughing. "Come here, look at me," he says cuddling me.

I look up at him with my panda eyes and a heavy heart.

"It is bad; I'm not going to lie to you," he says seriously.

"I thought you were trying to make me feel better!" I moan.

"But," he continues, "you are still the most beautiful girl that I have ever met and you have the best foof in the room!"

"I have the only foof in the room!" I sob.

"Exactly!" he says, laughing.

We spend the rest of the night cuddling and chatting. By the time the girls get home, we are fast asleep.

Chapter Thirty-Eight
A Little Chop

The following morning, Zack was the perfect gentleman. He took himself off to breakfast whilst the girls and I got ready in the room.

"So how was it?" Tara asked, as soon as he walked out of the door.

"It was so amazing!" I sigh.

"Did you bang?" Danni asked incredulously.

"With this in my pants? Erm, nope!" I reply, laughing.

"How did you get away with it?" asked Felicity. "We were convinced you'd forgotten when we saw you!"

"Oh, I did!" I say. "I suddenly remembered just before my pants came off!"

"No! What did you do?" asked Clara.

"I ended up showing him and telling him everything!"

"Showing him?" shouts Hannah. "And how did that go down?"

"Not well, at first! But he saw the funny side and was fine; we just cuddled and talked all night. He was great!" I say.

"You've got yourself a good one there," says Danni. "Most men would run a mile with a vag looking like that!"

At eleven a.m., we boarded the catamaran for our adventure out to the Whitsundays. My experiences with water so far in Oz have not been the most tranquil, so I was a little nervous. I know that Zack is a complete water baby, so I'm putting on my big girl pants and attempting to act cool and collected.

"I'm so excited to see the Great Barrier Reef!" he says, visibly pumped. "You're going to have a go at diving with me aren't you?"

"Absolutely! Wouldn't miss it!" I say over cheerily.

As he walks off, I turn to the girls. "I've never dived before. How the hell am I going to get out of this?"

"Fake the shits?" said Tara.

"I think I've had enough real ailments to last me a lifetime without throwing fake ones into the mix! I'm already doing a weird shimmy with the towel to make sure no one sees the manky foof!" I replied, doing a little jiggle.

"We'll have to cause a distraction," said Danni. "Ooh, I know, tell him you're not going when standing in front of something shiny, he'll get distracted looking at his abs and won't listen to you!"

"It's us that gets distracted by his abs, not him!" I retorted.

"Oh yeah!" Danni said, staring off into the distance.

"Ah, seeing you with HBG is really making me miss James!" said Hannah.

"We've only got a month to go; you'll be home soon enough!" I say, putting my arm around her.

"Have you and HBG discussed what you're going to do in a month?" she asked. "You have flights booked home, don't you?"

"To be honest, this was something that I was putting off. Now that he's actually here, I don't even want to think about what comes next, especially if it involves me on a flight back to the UK and him staying here."

"Sorry, Louise, I didn't mean to upset you," said a forlorn looking Hannah.

"Don't be silly, you didn't," I reply, attempting to brush it off.

"Here you go, babe, I got you some snorkelling equipment," Zack said, handing me a pair of flippers and a mask.

I don't want to admit that I have never worn flippers before, so I subtly watch everyone else and then give it a go. OK, it seems simple enough; hold them down at the back and slide your foot in. Bingo, easy. One thing I didn't notice, however, is that everyone else is sitting on the edge of the boat; I put mine on in the centre so I have to Charlie Chaplin my way over to the side.

"Ready?" Zack asks, turning to face me.

"Sure am!" I say in my new overly chipper manner. Reel it in, Louise!

"The best thing to do is to spit in your goggles and smear it around the plastic" he says, proceeding to do a massive grot in his. "It'll stop them from steaming up."

"OK, got it!" Gross! Definitely not doing that!

We all jump in whilst holding our noses, much to Zack's amusement.

"You know, before I came away, I had a checklist of what I was looking for in a girl. May as well burn that list now that I've met you!" he said, laughing.

"Why, what was on it?" I asked, doing a doggy paddle.

"Water baby was one!"

"Check. What else?" I say, desperately trying to do a more sensible stroke than doggy!

"Loves the gym," he said, holding up two fingers.

"Gym or gin?" laughed Felicity. "Because she has the latter nailed."

"They both work your arm muscles if you think about it!" I laughed. "What else?"

"Natural, Ozzie and a beach babe," he said as the final three.

"Well, I'm natural sometimes!" I protest.

"Yeah, when you get out of the shower! My point is, babe, that the list is irrelevant. I've found the girl of my dreams," he says, winking at me.

It's a good job that I'm in water so that he couldn't see my legs going weak.

"God, I'm knackered!" said Danni. "How much longer do you reckon we have to splash around for?"

"You can go back onto the boat at any time, it's not going anywhere!"

"Well, if I'd known that I wouldn't have bothered getting in! You coming?" she asked, swimming back.

"Nah, I've got to pretend I like this; remember 'the list'!" I say mockingly.

After an hour of splashing around in the ocean, we all clamber back onto the catamaran to continue on our tour of the Whitsundays. The evening is drawing in and the colours in the sky are incredible.

"Penny for them?" Zack interrupts my thoughts.

"I'm just enjoying being in this bubble, away from real life, with you!" I reply, cuddling into him.

"It's pretty incredible here, isn't it?" he says, pulling me into him.

This moment couldn't be more perfect. I'm snuggled into the man of my dreams, my girls are here and we're in these beautiful surroundings. What more could a girl want?

"Guys, we're just about to go through a bit of chop. Can you all come inside, please? You can go back out once we have passed, but, for your own safety, please head inside now," the deck hand announced.

Oh no, this isn't good. I literally get seasick on a pedalo.

Ten minutes later, we find ourselves slap bang in the middle of a terrifying storm. The boat is doing some massive dips as it navigates its way over the humongous waves. Everyone is clinging onto whatever they can for dear life, but the current is too strong and we are being flung from one end of the boat to the other. I feel like I'm going to throw up. I need to look at the horizon; a steady line in all of this chaos should help. Clutching onto a table, I look out of one of the little round windows. I can see the horizon roughly every ten seconds; the boat is going so high, then so low over the waves, ugh it isn't helping at all. The toilets are crammed with people chucking up, so I can't seek refuge in there. I really need some fresh air!

"Are you OK, Louise? You've gone an off shade of green," said Felicity, clutching onto the column in the centre of the boat.

"I'm going to throw up. I need to go outside," I reply, feeling the bile rising.

Against the Captain's orders, I stagger out onto the deck, sliding around and attempting to clutch onto the railings. I feel like I'm on a merry-go-round and I want to get off! The dips were getting worse; my stomach was doing somersaults. I started to wretch and, just as I was about to throw up, I hear Zack behind me.

"Louise! What the hell are you doing? Get inside, it's not safe!" he shouts, staggering out towards me. I tried to talk but it was too late, the vomit needed to be free. As I'm barfing over the side, I realise with absolute horror that I am facing the wind. My puke is not only splattering back all over myself, it is also covering Zack. Batches of sick are literally splashing all over us from head to toe.

I can hear Zack shouting, "Louise, turn around, for Christ's sake! Face the other way!"

I was too far gone, I couldn't. I was gripping onto the railings like a lifeline. I couldn't let go.

"What the hell is going on here?" I hear the deckhand shout.

"She's projectile vomiting everywhere! She can't stop!" Zack said, sounding majorly distressed.

"You need to come inside, now!" he shouted, over the crashing of the waves.

The puke was relentless; it was literally pouring out of me.

The deckhand staggered over and shoved a bag under my chin. "Throw up into that, we need to get you inside."

Both guys, one on either side of me, steered me inside whilst my vomiting persisted at a ferocious rate.

"We're approximately five minutes away from steady waters. You just need to hang in there until then, OK?" the deckhand says, holding my shoulders and staring at me square in the eyes.

I try to answer, but I can't stop throwing up.

Five minutes later, the sea has calmed. I look around and see a plethora of dishevelled faces. The inside of the boat is completely trashed; there are chairs and tables everywhere. My stomach has finally settled but I still have sea legs.

I am absolutely covered in sick. Much to his dismay, so is HBG.

"Are you OK?" I reach out to him.

"Just give me a minute!" he says, pulling away from me. "I just need a minute."

I look to the girls, who are all giving me the 'yikes' face.

The deckhand came over. "Are you OK?"

"I've felt better," I reply. I still feel like I'm on a seesaw.

"The best thing you can do is chuck yourself into the ocean; it'll lower your body temperature and make you feel better. If I were you, I'd jump in with your clothes on, because, well, you stink," he said, walking away. "You too, buddy," he said, tapping Zack on the shoulder.

I turn to Zack. "Do you want me to take your clothes in with me?" I ask in a little voice.

"I'll go in a minute, Louise; you go ahead," he says with his back to me.

"Come on, I'll jump in with you, stinky!" says Tara.

"I feel so crappy; I really don't feel like going in at all, I just want to go to bed."

"Come on, Louise, just jump! You'll feel loads better!" shouts Tara from the water.

OK, here goes nothing. I hang my legs off the side of the boat and, on three, jump. Hurtling through the water instantly snaps me out of sickness. It is so refreshing, who knew that would work?

"Better?" Tara asks.

"Loads," I reply. "I just need to get this vom out of my dress now."

I give it a good rub in the water and the sick'll come out in no time.

"I know I hurled some pretty serious chunks, but I didn't think it would make Zack so mad," I say to Tara.

"He was covered in it, Louise, even in his hair!" she laughed. "I'd be pretty pissed too. Speak of the devil, here he comes."

I turn to see Zack fluidly dive in. How can someone so big be so elegant?

"Are you OK?" I softly ask. Even in the water, I could feel my face burning.

"I'm OK. Not going to lie, though, that was pretty gross. I'd say even it was even worse than your foof horror show!"

"I'm so sorry, I'm so embarrassed!" I say. "Once my puke had its exit strategy planned, there was no stopping it."

"Don't worry about it, it's OK," he said, leaning over to kiss me. "On second thoughts, you can brush your teeth first."

I instantly close my mouth. God, I get more attractive by the second!

Chapter Thirty-Nine
So, This Is Rock Bottom?

The next morning was clear, beautiful and, thankfully, storm free. Today we had an opportunity to dive around some of the Great Barrier Reef's coral. Zack was so excited, and I didn't want to burst his bubble, but I really feel like Mother Nature is telling me that the ocean is just not for me.

"Listen up!" shouts the instructor. "If you want to dive, please move to the right hand side of the boat. If you want to snorkel, please move to the left. Again, that is diving right, snorkelling left."

I surreptitiously started to shuffle to the left.

"Louise!" shouted Zack. "You're going the wrong way, it's this side for diving."

"Silly me!" I reply, desperately trying to think of an exit strategy.

"Here's your equipment," he said, dumping a wet suit, tank, snorkel, mask and flippers onto me. "Pop it all on and I'll show you what to do next, OK?"

"Great!" I replied through a false smile.

Fully kitted up, the instructor gave us a play by play of what to expect when we're under water. I start to slowly manoeuvre myself backwards to fade into the crowd with the hope that Zack will jump in and be so enamoured with the beautiful ocean bed, he won't even notice that I'm not there. The instructor tells everyone to put on their eye mask and insert their oxygen tube as a test to go through the various stages of pressure as you go further down towards the ocean floor. As I stepped slightly behind Zack, he reached out and held the hand of the girl next to him. I was just about to storm over there and tell her to get her grubby little hands off my man, when it dawned on me that he thought she was me. With all of the equipment on, he couldn't tell. This was my ticket out!

The instructor tells everyone to remove their mask and oxygen to go through the next steps. I quickly shimmy back into position next to Zack and bump the confused looking girl next to him away.

The time has come for everyone to get ready to jump in for the first dive. While Zack is preoccupied, I grab the girl in question and drag her around the corner.

"Hi, we haven't met yet, I don't think. What's your name?" I ask, gently manoeuvring her to a position where Zack couldn't see.

"Chloe," she replies, looking very suspicious of me. "You were the girl that just shoved me out of the way, weren't you?"

"Er, yes, that was me. Look, I'm sorry about that, but that's what I wanted to talk to you about," I say looking over my shoulder.

"I get it, he's your guy," she said, holding her hands in the air. "I was surprised when he held my hand, I was just about to pull away when you jumped in. I think it must have been the gear, he thought I was you! Hope there's no harm done? It's a small ship, I don't want any trouble."

"No, no, no harm at all. So, are you any good at diving?" I ask, trying to gauge exactly what I was dealing with here. I couldn't have her flailing around; I could do that myself.

"I'm pretty good, yeah," she replied. "I've been diving for about five years." Perfect! "Do you need a hand learning?"

"Not exactly…" I replied. "See, the thing is that Zack and I are in a new relationship, you know the stage where you say you can do things that you actually can't to impress, hoping that it'll never actually come up? Well, that's kind of where I am with diving…"

"Okay," she replied, looking dubious. "So what's that got to do with me?"

"Well, when he grabbed your hand with all of the equipment on, it made me realise that he couldn't tell who was who! From the side and the back, we look quite similar. Which brings me nicely to my point… will you pretend to be me?"

"What? Are you crazy?" she asks, taking a step back.

"Look, I'm not asking you to shag him! Just, when you're underwater, give him a little wave, do some occasional hand holding, make him think I'm there with him!" I finish.

"You're serious?" she asked incredulously.

"Deadly," I reply.

She stood staring at me for a moment, weighing me up.

"OK, on one condition," she replies.

"Name it!" I say.

"I really fancy the captain! Whilst I'm down there, I need you to big me up to him and get me a date," she says.

"Done!" I say, taking a picture of her on my phone.

We shake hands and the deal is done.

The instructor lines us up on the side of the boat, ready to fall in backwards. One at a time he goes along the line, telling people to jump. Chloe is positioned next to me; when my turn comes, she will fall instead.

"See you down there!" Zack says as he falls back.

The instructor gets to me and tells me to fall in. I kindly decline and point at Chloe for her turn.

"Good luck," I whisper.

I step back from the side and watch as Zack is giving her the thumbs up underwater. This is a perfect plan! I peel my kit off and make my way back to the girls.

'What are you doing?" said Danni. "I thought you were going in?"

"I have the perfect cover," I say, tapping my nose. "Be back in a jiff, I need to speak to the captain."

It took me a good twenty minutes to convince the captain that he should go on a date with Chloe. Lord knows why, she was a stunner... well, I thought so anyway, but that's probably because she looked like me! As I made my way back to the deck, I could hear the people on board cheering. Oh crap, they are coming back! I quickly threw my oxygen tank on my back, put my mask and flippers on and waddled over to the side.

I could see Chloe in the distance popping her head up and signalling for me to go to the right. I jumped in and hovered around there until she tagged past me. We managed to switch just in time for Zack to pop his head up.

"Wow! That was awesome!" he shouted. "What a buzz!"

"Oh yeah, it was top notch! So glad I was there," I reply.

"You, my lady, have being lying to me!" he said wagging his finger. Oh balls, we are busted. I knew the plan was too good to be true.

"I can explain…" I started.

"You don't need to be ashamed!" he said, stroking my face. "I'm actually flattered."

"You are?" Wow, men really are from Mars.

"Yes! I can't believe you took lessons!" he said, laughing.

"Lessons?" I ask bemusedly.

"Don't you try and tell me that was beginners luck! There is no way. You don't have to be shy about it. Honestly, I'm really proud of you. I know water isn't your thing and the fact that you would take lessons so you could do this with me is incredible. Thank you, Louise!" He kissed me.

So, this is rock bottom.

I have to tell him. I can't have him believing that it was me the whole time. But look at his face. He's so happy, so proud to have shared this moment with me; I can't take that away from him. I'm going straight to hell, that's for sure!

Back on the boat, Zack told everyone that would listen how proud he was of me. He couldn't believe that I'd gone to so much trouble to learn something that he loved; he was blown away by me and wanted everyone to know.

"Feel like shit yet?" asked Tara.

"Definitely getting there!" I replied. "I didn't think it would be such a big deal, I thought it would be a little switcheroo, we'd all move on and that would be the end of it. But no, he has to be *proud*! Ugh, it's humiliating – even bloody Chloe is giving me pitying looks."

"It's OK, you just have to never go anywhere near water ever again, for as long as you are together, and he'll never ask you to dive again!"

"Helpful," I replied sarcastically.

I spent the rest of the evening feeling like a piece of dirt. The more Zack told people how proud he was of me, the more I recoiled in shame. What was worse, there was an underwater camera! He will actually treasure photos of him and the 'non-me' forever. I would have to take this secret to the grave; there is no way he would forgive me for letting it get this far.

Chapter Forty
Karma's a Bitch!

The following morning, we left the boat and piled onto the coach to Mission Beach.

"So, how's the foof looking? Are we disaster free yet?" Zack laughed.

"You will be very pleased to know that I am healed and back to normal, no more tickets to the horror show required!"

"Great! That means I'll have an amazing birthday present then," he said nonchalantly.

"Birthday? When? Today?" I ask, aware that I am screeching.

"Shush, it's not a big deal, I'm not big on birthdays." He spots the expression on my face. "Louise, please don't make a fuss! Promise me?"

With my fingers crossed behind my back, I reply, "Promise. We can't do nothing, though. Is there anything at all you'd like to do to celebrate?"

"I have a few ideas" he says, nibbling my ear.

"OK, apart from that?" I giggle.

"Dinner, just the two of us, would be perfect!" he says, playing with my hand. "Don't tell the girls, OK? I really don't want a fuss."

"Brownie's honour," I reply. I didn't happen to mention the part where I got kicked out of Brownies, so technically it didn't count.

We have three hours until we get there and that doesn't leave me much time. I need to coordinate the girls to arrange a surprise party without him knowing. I know he says he doesn't want a fuss, but no one actually means that! I tell HBG that I need the loo and subtly nudge Fliss as I walk past.

"What?" she whispers.

I nod my head towards the toilet. She squeezes into the horribly cramped and stinky loo with me.

"What's wrong?" she asks. "Have you come on?"

"No, this is a non-toilet related matter," I say, holding my nose.

"Then why are we squidged into this disgusting little room?" she says, also holding her nose.

"I'm hiding from HBG; this is a covert operation," I reply.

"Not another one! Who are you bribing to be you this time?" she chastises.

"Ha ha, very funny!" I mock. "It has just been brought to my attention that it is Zack's birthday today."

"Today?" she shouted back.

"Shush! Covert, remember? He says he doesn't want a fuss, but I think that's rubbish. Who doesn't want to be the centre of attention on their birthday?"

"Erm, lots of people!" she replies.

"Pish posh," I say, wafting my hand. "This is my opportunity, Fliss! If I can pull an epic party out of the bag, with literally no warning, he will see how important he is to me!"

"If you're sure," she says. "If he distinctly said he doesn't want a fuss, shouldn't you honour that?"

"Na," I reply, refusing to be deterred. "We need to think of a theme!"

"A theme? Where on earth are we going to get fancy dress costumes from this late in the day?" she says exasperatedly.

"Haven't you ever seen Blue Peter? We'll have to whip them up," I say, full of enthusiasm.

"I don't know, Louise. This is a lot. Why don't we aim for tomorrow, give ourselves twenty-four hours to do it right?"

"Because his birthday is today, not tomorrow," I whisper. "We need a brainstorm; can you subtly tell the girls to think of a theme? I'll walk back to the loo in a couple of hours and we can decide!"

As we both leave the loo, a guy clocks us and gives us a knowing wink.

"You wish," I whisper as I walk past.

"Are you OK?" asked HBG. "You were gone for ages."

"I'm all good. I was, erm, just checking the foof was in full working order."

"What?" he asks, with wide eyes.

"Oh, not like that! Never mind," I say, trying to hide my rosy red cheeks. Let's hope my surprise parties are better than my cover ups.

Ten minutes outside of Mission Beach, I tell HBG that I'm popping to the loo again. As I walk by the girls, I duck down and squeeze onto the seat with Danni and Tara.

"Ouch! What are you doing?" Danni hisses at me.

"Operation Brainstorm!" I said. "What have we got?"

Fliss turns round from the seat in front. "OK, we have a few ideas. Water theme?"

"Pass," I reply.

"You didn't even hear me out!" she whines.

"I'm not giving him any more chances to tell everyone how proud he is of 'me' diving! The deceit is killing me!" I reply.

"OK. Wrestlers theme?" Fliss says, shrugging her shoulders.

"Wrestlers? Why wrestlers?" Zack has nothing to do with wrestling!

"Because he looks like a wrestler... with the hair," Danni adds.

"Pass."

"He likes dressing up in dresses; what about a cross dressing party?" adds Tara.

"What? No! He did that once for ladies night! Come on, girls, we need to think outside of the box." Drumming my fingers on the seat in front, I suddenly have an idea. "I know, what about a breakfast party? He finds it hilarious that we call him Hot Breakfast Guy. Everyone could come dressed as their favourite breakfast food."

"It's so ridiculous, it might just work!" said Clara.

"Breakfast party it is!" said Fliss.

"OK, we will reconvene at the hostel and see where we can hold the party. Yey, excited!" I say as I scurry back off to Zack.

We arrive at two p.m. The hostel's like an American motel. It has a pool in the centre with two-storey rooms circling it all the way around. The reception is managed by a bunch of party boys wearing oversized sun glasses, bright bowler hats and tiny shorts. They instantly got along with HBG, doing the 'bro' greeting. You know; fist pumping, chest bumping, muscle flexing.

This was the first time that Zack and I were able to share a room, now that the foof had officially healed. I was more than a little bit excited.

"What side of the bed do you want?" I asked.

"I don't really care," he shrugged.

"You have to care! This is our first couple decision! The side of the bed that you choose will be yours for as long as we are together, it's not something that should be taken lightly!" I say seriously.

"My apologies, I underestimated the importance!" he said, grabbing me and pulling me onto the bed, making me screech with delight. "Which side have I landed on? The left! This is officially my side of the bed!"

"I'm going to go and see where we can go for dinner around here. Be right back!" I say, blowing him a kiss.

At the reception, I filled the guys in on my plan.

"This idea is epic! It's going to be so cool!" said dude number one.

"You have to use the club here!" said number two. "The music is pumping and you can pretty much do what you want to it!"

"We have loads of blow-up bananas and flamingos. Want us to bring them?" asked an excitable number one.

"Yes, that's perfect! Do you think breakfast food is going to be too tricky last minute?" I asked.

"Maybe it should just be any food, as that's easier at this late stage?" said dude number two.

Danni popped up behind me. "Yeah, that's way easier, let's do that."

"OK, done! So, how do we get everyone else involved?" I asked the guys.

"Well, girls, you will be pleased to know that this is a party hostel! You get your man out of the way for a few hours and leave the rest to us! There is a fancy dress store down the road, we can show the girls where to pick up outfits," number one replied.

"I'll go!" shouted Danni, acting a little too keen.

"OK, I'll leave it in your hands. Try and get me something semi-sexy, OK?" I said.

As I didn't have time to buy a birthday present, I had to give HBG something that money couldn't buy… well, you can buy it, but you know what I mean! After a few hours in bed, we finally surfaced to go to dinner. There was a lovely little place just down the road from where we were staying, so we got dressed up and headed out.

"I'll just give the girls a quick knock to let them know we're going out," I told HBG.

I knocked on the door. Danni opened it just a fraction.

"Hey, girls, just letting you know that we're going out. We'll be back by eight p.m. sharp," I shouted loudly through the door.

"Yeah, yeah, no bother. See you at eight p.m." Danni winked through the door crack.

"Text when you leave," shouted Fliss from the back of the room.

"Will do!" I replied, swinging round to HBG and leading the way out.

"That was a bit weird," Zack said, pointing back towards the door. "Are you and the girls OK? I'm not getting in the way, am I?"

"Of course not! Can't believe you would say that, they love having you here!" I reply, brushing him off.

"It's just Danni didn't even open the door properly?"

"Ah, that's Danni, she's a weirdo! You'll get used to it."

We found a gorgeous restaurant right on the ocean. We ordered lobster and drank copious amounts of wine; it was indulgent to the point that I'm hoping the old bank balance could handle it!

At quarter to eight, I asked for the bill and suggested that we should head back.

"What's the rush?" Zack asked. "Don't you fancy a nice stroll along the beach?"

"I'm just eager to get you back!" I say, pulling him closer to me.

"Roger that!" he said, giving me a kiss.

I surreptitiously sneak my phone from my bag and text Felicity to say that we are on our way back. She replied to say that both of our costumes were waiting at the bar and to head straight there.

"I'm so glad we did something just the two of us," Zack said. "I was really worried that you would plan some big stupid surprise and I'd have to pretend to like it, but secretly hate it! How awkward would that be?" He laughed.

"Ha, ha! So awkward!" I fake laugh back. Oh God, maybe this was a mistake. I must probe further. "Wouldn't you think it was sweet, though, if I went to all of that effort?"

"Yeah, of course I would. But it's really not me, you know, and I'm glad you can see that."

Shit.

As we get closer to the bar, I'm racking my brain, trying to decide what to do. We are approaching around the corner and I see massive inflatable bananas, hot dogs and burgers hanging from the roof. Oh crap, I'm going to have to tell him; I can't keep any more secrets.

"Zack, wait," I say, putting my hands on his chest. "I screwed up."

"What are you talking about? Tonight has been perfect!" he says.

"Well, it has been so far…" I mumble.

"I don't understand," he says, shaking his head.

"When you said you didn't want a fuss for your birthday, I just thought you were being modest! I thought, who doesn't want a fuss on their birthday? That's ridiculous!" He's looking at me intently. "So I arranged a surprise party," I say, cringing. "The girls and I arranged it all in secret and put loads of effort in for it to be something special for you. I'm so sorry, I feel stupid now, I never should have done it!"

He doesn't say anything for a minute.

"Ah, Louise! Really?" he asks.

"Really," I reply.

"Well, I suppose it is pretty sweet, the effort you put in. I just really don't like surprises," he says, looking genuinely upset.

"Well, now it's not, because I told you!" OK, this is good; I can work this angle. "Now, you are part of the surprise, so it's not a surprise anymore, it's just a party! And you love parties, don't you?"

"I can see the angle you're working here." He laughed. "I am actually really glad that you told me. Who is going? We don't know anyone here!"

"Just a few of your closest strangers! We can't back out now, everyone has made such an effort. What will make you feel more at ease?"

"Shots," he says seriously, "and lots of them."

Back at the room, I blast some music to get him in the mood and we take it in turns doing shots. On the third shot, I build up the courage to tell him the full surprise.

"How many shots have you had?" I ask.

"Four," he says.

"Are you feeling it yet?" I ask meekly.

"Starting to… Why?" he asks suspiciously.

"Because I maybe haven't told you the full surprise," I say, hiding behind a pillow.

"Oh God, Louise, what is it? It's not fancy dress, is it?"

There's no way to sugar coat this, I just need to go in. "Yes, it is," I reply. "It's a breakfast food party because you're Hot Breakfast Guy…"

"Everyone is dressing up like breakfast food? You have to be joking!" He laughs.

"Nope! Us included."

That stopped him in his tracks.

"Oh God, what do we have to wear?" By this point, he has picked up the bottle and is just downing it.

"That's the fun part. I don't actually know, the girls arranged it," I say, laughing.

"Bloody hell, Louise! You owe me!" he says with a cheeky look in his eye.

"Come on, down the rest of that, and let's go. Remember, look surprised!"

Round the corner from the bar, we are propping ourselves up, giggling like a pair of school kids.

"Ready?" I ask.

"Let's do this!" he says, laughing.

Booze, the answer to most first world problems.

We burst through the door to everyone yelling, 'Surprise!' Zack does an amazing job of faking his surprise. The bar is covered in inflatables and the DJ is playing The Breakfast Club track. I have to hand it to the guys, they really packed the place out. Everyone had made such an effort!

Danni is dressed as 'beans on toast'. She has actually poured beans over a massive piece of cardboard and glued it on. She's even painted her face orange and is wearing an aluminous orange wig!

Fliss is a bowl of cereal. She has hired what looks like the bottom half of an Oompa Loompa outfit, complete with braces, and accessorised with a bowel of cornflakes.

Tara and Clara have bacon and egg costumes with frying pans in each of their hands.

Hannah is a giant bottle of tomato ketchup.

They all look amazing.

"OK, enough of the suspense! Where are our costumes?" I ask.

"Come with us," Danni says. The girls lead me into the ladies and the guys take Zack into the gents.

"Sorry!" I shout over to him, laughing.

"You owe me, big time!" he shouts back.

In the cubicle is a giant hot dog costume.

"So when I said 'sexy', you lot heard 'hot dog'," I say, looking at them incredulously.

"It's the best we could do on short notice! The only size left was a small, so it might be a bit of a squeeze with your baps," laughs Tara.

Good job I had some Dutch courage. "Come on, let's stick it on." I manage to wiggle myself in; they were right, it is tight. I try to straighten up a bit, but, as I push my shoulders back, I hear this almighty rip. Covering my eyes, I say to the girls, "What was that?"

"It's ripped!" says Clara.

"Oh no, it looks like..." starts Hannah.

"Like what?" I ask in a panic.

"Let's just say that your foof woes may not be over..." says Tara.

I push them out of the way to look in the mirror. Not only had I managed to split the centre of the hot dog, the layers of fabric made it resemble a giant fricking vagina.

"It's karma!" I say to the girls, throwing my arms in the air. "He told me he didn't want a fuss, but would I listen? Nope! And now my penance is to spend the entire night looking like a giant walking vagina!"

"Hang on, I've got an idea," says Felicity, running out of the loo.

She comes back in with three pink balloons. "We can cover the hole with balloons!"

"It's worth a try," Danni says.

As they are strategically placing the balloons, one of them pops and I now have what looks like a flaccid condom hanging out of my oversized vagina. This has quickly escalated from bad to worse.

"On the plus side, I don't know many guys that would turn down a giant vagina on their birthday!" says Danni. This makes us all cry with laughter. I now had make -up running down my face and looked like a giant walking vag; Zack is not going to be able to keep his hands off me!

I peer around the door to see Zack with his top half bare and a large triangular piece of cheese covering his nether regions.

"Let me guess, you chose the costume," I said to Danni.

"I don't know what you're talking about!" She laughed.

"So, just to get this straight… Zack looks like a fricking Greek god and I look like a walking vag?" I ask the girls.

"Yup! That about sums it up," says Felicity, doubled over laughing.

"Here goes nothing," I say, wiping the laughter tears from my cheeks.

As I walk across the dance floor, Zack glances at me, then looks away. Clearly his mind is telling him that this couldn't possibly be the girl that he has travelled thousands of miles for. He glances again and realises, oh no, it really is!

"Here I am, the VAG of your dreams!" I shout across to him.

Zack bends over double, doing massive belly laughs, slapping his thigh, tears rolling down his face. He's really going to town on the old point and laugh action. When he finally manages to pull himself together (approximately fifty years later in hot dog years), he struts over to me and plants the biggest kiss on my lips.

"Louise, you are officially the coolest chick ever!" he screams, laughing. "You did all of this to take the attention away from me, after I said I hated it! You really are the best" He wipes the tears from his eyes.

Sure, let's go with that!

All in all, it was an amazing evening. It turns out that Zack actually doesn't mind surprise parties as long as they're not technically a surprise. The 80's tunes were pumping and we danced until we couldn't feel our feet.

Chapter Forty-One
You Have to Kiss a Few Frogs to Find Your Prince!

We were local legends in the hostel. Everyone had had such a banging night, they couldn't stop talking about it. Zack got up early and went to the shops to buy ingredients for pancakes and made them for everyone who wanted them, just to make him even more charming, if that is even possible.

Felicity had booked a sky dive, but was seriously regretting it, based on the enormous hangover that she was tackling.

"Come on, you have to do it!" Zack pushed. "A bit of wind in your hair will sort you right out."

"I woke up with a man dressed like an oversized frying pan this morning, I am hardly in a position to be making life decisions!" she moans, "He kept asking if I wanted my cereal fried or poached! He picked me up with a pick-up line that didn't even make sense!"

"Come on, Fliss, you've been talking about this skydive for ages. You have to do it! Get some pancakes down you, and we'll come and cheer you on, OK?" I say, pushing a plate over to her.

"Ugh," she replied.

"I'll take your place if you don't want to go," Zack says, chomping on his mega stack.

"Really? You'd do that?" she asks with a glimmer of hope.

"Of course I would! It would be epic! What time is the jump?" he asks.

"Twelve o'clock," she grunts.

"Done! Louise, will you come and cheer me on?" he asks, whipping me with the towel.

"Ouch! Yes, I will, I'm going to jump in the shower first," I say, clearing my plate.

"Mmm, fancy some company?" he asks cheekily.

"Don't be late, you two," Felicity shouts after us, "or I'll lose my deposit."

Felicity managed to make it to the beach with us. She was clutching onto me as I dragged her along. The instructor pulled Zack to one side to go through the safety procedures and what he should expect on the plane.

"Do you think I'm an idiot, missing out on this?" Fliss asked me.

"It's not too late if you still want to go," I say. "Zack would understand."

She sat for a good few minutes, contemplating, and then said, "Screw it! This trip is all about experiences, I'm going!"

"Good girl!" I shouted after her.

I saw Zack's face; he looked so disappointed when she told him. I can't let him miss out.

I ran over to the booking hut. "Is there any chance you could fit another person on the plane for this dive?" I asked the girl behind the counter.

"Actually, we've just had someone pull out." She pointed over to one of the guys from the party last night, who was throwing up in a bush.

"Amazing! Can I please book that slot for my boy… erm… Zack? He's the guy over there with the instructor." I pointed Zack out.

"Yes, sure, I'll just take his details," she says, clicking away on the keyboard.

"How much will it cost?" I'm going to be rivalling the national debt after this trip!

"Well, this guy has paid in full and it's non-refundable, so Zack's good to go."

"Really? That's amazing! Thanks, mate!" I shouted to the guy throwing up in the corner.

He replied with a thumbs up.

Zack trudged over to me looking forlorn; I could tell that he was really disappointed.

"Happy birthday," I said, handing him the ticket.

"What's this?" he replied grumpily. It took him a second, but, when he realised what it was, his whole face lit up. "Are you serious?" he asked.

"Deadly!" I replied. "Go, go! You need to go to the briefing!"

"Louise, I lo..." Oh my God, was he just about to say he loved me? "This is erm, amazing, thank you. I'll wave from the plane." He kissed my cheek and ran off.

My face is burning; was he really just going to say that he loved me?

I ran over to the pad in time to get some great shots of Zack landing.

"Did you get it?" he shouted.

"Yes! Where's Fliss?" I shouted back.

"She was looking a little green up there." He laughed. "I'm not sure if she'll jump."

I stepped back and looked up. "Here she comes."

Camera ready, I was in position. Near enough at the ground, I'm clicking, clicking, clicking.

"Wahoo, you did it, Fliss!" I shouted from the other side of the pad.

From a distance, I could see that she was covered in strange, coloured splats. The instructor, whom she was strapped to, unhooked himself from her and practically shoved her off before storming away. As he stomped in my direction, I could see that he had the same splats all over his face and matted into his hair. When he got closer, I got a very pungent whiff and realised, with horror, that he was covered in puke.

"Are you OK, Fliss?" I ask, running over.

"I'm so embarrassed! He was literally swearing at me to stop chucking up the whole way down!" she says, wiping the sick from her cheeks. "I couldn't stop. As soon as we jumped, my stomach flipped and that was it! It was awful, Louise, I could feel it coming out, but it was kind of flying past me. I think he got the brunt of it!"

I was trying so hard not to laugh; she looked like a scarecrow!

"How are you feeling now?" I ask, biting my lip so my laugh doesn't escape.

"I actually feel much better," she says, the colour slowly coming back into her cheeks. "Have you got any tissues?"

"You're going to need more than tissues, love! Come on, let's get you back and chuck you into the shower."

Once Fliss came back from her shower, she looked much more human.

"Soz about the vom, Fliss; are you OK?" Danni asked thoughtfully.

Laughing, she replied, "Yeah, I'm OK, just feeling a bit delicate. I need to lie still for a while!"

"Soak up the sun and enjoy the view," Danni said, peering over her sunglasses at the guys in the pool.

As Felicity lay down on the sun lounger, Clara whispered, "Girls, look!" She pointed next to Felicity's head.

"What are we looking at?" Tara whispered.

"The frog!"

There was a florescent green frog with bright red eyes and red feet. I'd never seen anything like it before; it looked like some kind of scientific experiment gone wrong. It was perched on the plant pot right next to Felicity's sunbed.

"Fliss slowly try and take a pic, don't scare it!" Danni whispered.

Felicity slowly rolled onto her side, carefully picked up her camera and... snap! The flash from the camera must have startled the frog, because it leapt from the plant pot towards the light and splatted right onto Felicity's cheek!

"It's on my face, it's on my face!" Felicity screamed.

She was shaking her head vigorously from side to side, desperately trying to get it off. The frog, however, would not be deterred; it was clinging on for dear life.

"Do something!" Felicity shouted.

So we did what any good friends would do: we rushed to our cameras and took as many pictures as we physically could whilst creasing up with laughter.

"What's going on?" Zack asked as he ran over. "I can hear you lot from over there."

"Look at Felicity's face!" Tara screamed.

"What the hell? Is that real?" he asked, clearly thinking this was some kind of elaborate joke.

"Of course it's bloody real!" Felicity screamed. "Get it off."

Zack gently pulled it off her face. "There you go, he's nothing to worry about, he's only a little frog." He laughed.

"Little bastard!" Felicity spat at the frog.

"You never know; you might find your prince now," said Hannah.

"What?" said Felicity, frantically wiping her cheek.

"You know, the old fairy tale; the princess had to kiss a frog to find her prince," Hannah explained.

"OK, well, I'll let you know if that happens!" Felicity replied huffily. "I've only just cleaned puke off my face, now I've got frog juice! Today is not my day. I'm going to go back to the room and take a nap, where hopefully nothing else will go wrong."

"Make sure you say goodbye to your prince!" Zack laughed, holding the frog up to her face.

"Goodbye, you horrible little thing, I hope to never see you again!" she said, sticking her fingers up at it.

"Let's take a pic of you and the frog as a keepsake!" Danni laughed.

"No!" Felicity sighed. "I've had enough of today."

Zack quickly held the frog up next to Felicity's face.

"Say cheese!" Danni shouted.

As the camera flashed, it happened again! We couldn't believe it; the frog jumped straight back onto Felicity's face.

This time she didn't scream, she just stood there. "You have got to be shitting me," she said in disbelief.

My stomach was hurting from laughing so hard.

"Maybe he really is your prince!" Zack spluttered, holding onto his sides, laughing.

Felicity gently pulled the frog off her face, looked at it intently and said, "Maybe he is!"

Chapter Forty-Two
The Last Hurrah

The mood on the coach is sombre. This was our last stop together. What we've been through together these last six months has been life-changing and I'm just not ready for it to end. The thought of going back to the drizzly UK, to the old nine to 5, is filling me with dread. I want to stay here, carefree, with my best friends and Zack. I haven't actually broached the subject with him yet that I have a flight booked back to London in a few days. I know that the clock is ticking on that bombshell. I guess the reason that I haven't told him yet is that I'm more terrified that he will encourage me to take the flight rather than stay, and confirm my deepest fears that this really is a holiday romance and nothing more.

Zack is resting his head on my shoulder, gently snoring. Looking into his face, I know that I have to tell him today, I can't put this off any longer.

I look across the aisle to Felicity and Danni and get a lump in my throat. Felicity, clearly feeling the same, reaches over and takes my hand. I can feel tears trickling down my cheeks.

Zack is stirring and slowly starting to wake up.

"How long have I been out?" he asks, stretching.

"An hour or so, not too long," I reply, kissing his head.

He turns to look at me. "Hey, are you OK? You look like you've been crying."

"Ah, it's just stupid hay fever," I reply wiping my eyes. I can tell that he doesn't believe me, but thankfully he lets it go.

We arrive in Port Douglas, north Cairns, at twelve thirty p.m. It is beautiful. What a place to end our trip. I ask the girls if they would mind Zack and I popping off on our own.

Sitting on the balcony of the restaurant there was a gentle breeze and the sun was beating down, it was perfect.

"OK, let's do this!" Zack says.

"Do what?" I ask, cutting up my kangaroo sausages.

"I know you're freaking out about the girls leaving, and you and we haven't discussed what comes next for us yet, so… let's discuss!" he says, with his arms open.

"OK" I say, building up the courage.

"Ladies first," he says, kindly putting all of the pressure on to me.

"Well, there's no easy way to say this; I just need to get it out of the way," I start.

"OK," he says, looking scared.

"I have my flight booked back to London in three days' time," I tell him, looking down at my hands.

"Three days? Louise, are you kidding me? When exactly were you going to tell me about this?"

"I don't know, now!" I fumble. "There wasn't really ever a right time. I didn't want to *assume* that you'd want me to stay, just like I didn't want to *assume* that you'd expect me to go! Help me out here, which way am I leaning?"

"Three days! Shit!" Do you want to go home?"

I don't say anything. I can't. I'm afraid of what will come out of my mouth.

"So you want to go!" He sulks, pushing his seat back from the table.

"Zack!" I say, grabbing his wrist. "Please, stay."

"You need to tell me what you want, Louise. Now is the time for you to be really clear!" I could see the hurt in his eyes and it was killing me.

"I want... you. I want to be wherever you are!" I blurt out.

He stares deeply into my eyes. "Do you mean that?"

"More than anything!" I reply earnestly. "Where do you want to be?" My knuckles are going white from squeezing the chair so hard waiting on his answer.

"I want to be with you too," he replies.

We jump up and hold each other, I can't believe how lucky I am to have found this guy "OK, that's the easy part," I say, breaking the spell and sitting back down. "Now we need to decide which continent."

"I don't know about you, but I'm not ready for the UK yet," he says.

"I agree. So do we stay here or move on to somewhere else?"

"Hmm, I hadn't really considered somewhere else," he says, looking intrigued. "I always assumed I'd end up back in Melbourne, but you're right, we're free to go wherever."

"So the question is: do we want to start living or do we want to stay in the bubble and keep travelling?"

We both look at each other and say "travelling" at the same time.

"Good job we're having the same thoughts on that one." He laughs. "So where do you fancy? More of Oz? Or we could go to New Zealand or Asia?"

"Ooh, Asia! That would be so magical. I probably have enough in the bank to do flights and travelling around for one more month. How about you?" I ask.

"I'd love to go to Asia with you!" he says, with a big grin on his face.

I run to the other side of the table and jump on him. "We'll be a real couple!"

"How the hell did I get myself into this mess?" He laughs.

"Hey!" I say, hitting him playfully. "I'm a catch and you know it!"

Zack took himself off surfing for a few hours. I can't wait to tell the girls! I burst into their room, about to explode with excitement, when I catch their faces. It looks as though they have all been crying.

"What's wrong?" I ask in a panic. "What's happened?"

"Nothing," Clara says, sniffing "We're all just going to miss each other so much!"

"Oh, girls!" I pull them all together for a group hug.

"Where's Zack?" Danni asked. "You didn't split up, did you?"

"The opposite, actually! We're going to travel around Asia together for a month and see how we work as a proper couple!"

"Louise, that is amazing!" Hannah jumps off the bed to cuddle me. "I'm so happy for you!"

"Don't forget our invite to the wedding when you become Mrs Hot Breakfast Guy!" says Fliss, giving me a big hug.

"Oh, you'll all be there, front row, there's no doubt about that!" I laugh.

"Come on, girls, we need to go out in style!" says Tara. "Let's sort our faces out, get dolled up and go and get some champers."

Zack bro'd up with the guys who ran the hostel for a lad's night out, leaving us ladies to have our last hurrah together.

"A toast!" says Felicity, raising her glass. "To the weirdest and most wonderful bunch of girls I have ever had the pleasure to meet."

"Let's go around the group and do the peaks and troughs of our trip. Anyone who starts to cry has to take a sip!" says Danni.

"OK, I'll start," says Hannah. "my peak was my time away from you girls with James."

"Ah, that's rubbish!" Tara shouts at her.

"We're not even included in your peak? That hurts!" jokes Fliss.

"Let me finish!" says Hannah. "It was a peak because I was missing James so badly, but when I was with him he made me see that he will always be there. He pointed out that this is my time to embrace new people and create memories for life, and thanks to you girls I can hold my head high and say that I did that."

"Ah, Han, you made me cry! Now I have to take a sip," I say, hugging her.

"And your trough?" asked Clara.

"Hmm, that has to be when that stupid boy pretended to be a ghost pirate in mine and Louise's room. He scared the crap out of me!"

"OK, I'll go next," says Danni. "The peak of my trip was meeting you girls!"

"Aww!" we all mock.

"Only kidding, it was shagging that Spanish guy on my second week in. Think his name was Pedro, which was mind-blowing!"

"That sounds more like it!" I laugh. "And your trough?"

"Honestly, it's flying home the day after tomorrow; I don't know how I'm going to cope without you girls. I can't even go to the bloody loo on my own now!"

"OK, now me!" said Fliss. "My peak was that week at Auntie Cassandra's."

"Good shout!" says Tara.

"When Louise attacked that poor guy on the yacht, that was beyond hilarious! Also the prison tour, I really thought we were locked in there with a nut job!" Felicity laughed.

"Oh my God, I was terrified!" I say. "I remember me and Danni trying to kick the door in!"

"And your trough?" Tara asks.

"That definitely has to be throwing up all over the really hot skydiving instructor," she says, shaking her head. "That was a new low!"

"Now that was hilarious!" I say, bent over laughing.

"Tara, your turn" says Fliss.

"OK, my peak was stealing pizza from that place in Surfers! And Felicity throwing her shoes at the poor guys chasing us!"

"Yeah, I can't remember much of that night, to be fair," laughs Danni.

"You were the reason we stole the pizza!" screams Tara. "After you got us kicked out for shouting 'Gay FL' in the players' faces!"

"And your trough?" asks Fliss.

"That has to be getting punched in the face outside of Stevie's house in Brisbane!"

"Oh my God, I totally forgot about that!" says Danni.

"OK, Clara, you're up!" Danni orders.

"My peak was camping on Fraser Island."

"Yes!" says Tara.

"I'd never even walked through woods before, let alone erected a tent, so that was a massive first for me. And the fact that Louise knocked out a dingo, who was using my foot as a chew toy, made it extra special!"

"I did, didn't I?" I said. "I'd forgotten about that. Poor dingo!"

"Poor dingo, my ass! You saved my foot!"

"True!" I replied. "And your trough?"

"That definitely has to be when we got stranded on top of the Blue Mountains and that stupid chirpy group leader man forgot about us, and Louise told us we couldn't run in Sydney, so we missed the bus."

"That was so funny!" laughed Hannah.

"OK, Louise, last one, make it good!" says Tara.

"This is so tough, there are so many! OK, peak has to be meeting the most incredible bunch of girls ever… and my future husband." We all screech, laughing.

"Don't tell him that! You'll terrify him!" laughs Felicity.

"And for my trough… jeez, where to begin? It has to include being hunted by Australia's two biggest killers: a shark *and* a spider!"

"You do seem to attract the wild!" says Danni.

"Also firmly up there in the trough department is my horror show of a foof and the fact that I showed it to HBG!" The girls are now rolling around laughing. "AND the fact that I ripped the stupid hot dog costume to remind HBG of that fact by looking like a giant walking vagina! It's been pretty disastrous in the foof department!"

We laughed and drank all night, swapping memories, cutting shapes and filling every room we went into with nothing but drunken love! It was the best send-off that we could have asked for. At around midnight, I had a text come through from HBG.

Hey baby, just checking in on you. I know tonight will hard; stay strong and remember that you will all meet up in the UK. I'm drunk, hope you are too. See you later… my girlfriend! ☺HBG x

"Ah, girls! He called me his girlfriend!" I gush.

"You two are the cutest!" says Hannah.

"Makes me want to vom," hiccupped Danni.

Chapter Forty-Three
The Cake Will Have to Keep!

Now that I have decided to continue travelling for another month, I need to tell my parents.

"Hello?" Mum answered.

"Hi, Mum, it's me,"

"Who is it?" she shouted down the phone.

"Your only child!" "Have you got your hearing aid in?" *This could take a while!*

"Hang on a minute, whoever you are; I haven't got my hearing aid in." she bellowed to my Dad; "Frank, someone's on the phone. I haven't got my hearing aid in, so I don't know who it is."

"I think Birmingham knows we've had a bloody phone call! Want to shout a bit louder, love?"

Here we go!

"Hello?" Dad came on the phone.

"Hi, Dad," I answer.

"It's Louise. Hurry up and put your hearing aid in; I don't want massive call charges," he shouts to Mum.

"Dad, I'm paying for the call. I'm in Australia, not prison!" I laugh.

"Why the hell are you in prison, Louise Shirley Johnson? How much is bail over there? We'll have to get the bank to convert our cash into funny money!" shouted Dad.

"It was a joke, Dad..."

"A joke! Don't make bloody jokes about prison! You know that's how Australia started, don't you? Whole bloody place is full of convicts; don't want them leading you astray."

Oh God.

"I'm here now" Mum jumps in. "Louise, why are you in prison? What did you do? Australia is full of convicts, you know, that's how the country started!"

"That's what I just said!" shouted Dad.

"Well, I didn't know you said it, did I? I wasn't here!" Mum screeched back.

"Mum, Dad, calm down! I am not in prison; I just need to talk to you both for a minute," I say, trying to calm them down.

"*I* will. It's her that's the problem," Dad huffed.

"Me?" Mum shouted. "Why don't you tell Louise what you did this morning if you're so clever? Go on!"

"That's not important, Shirley, just leave it."

"OK, I'll tell you," Mum replied primly.

This was going to be a long call.

"Your father has built a beautiful shed in the back garden," she began in a voice that one would use for a Shakespearean play. "I went outside to examine the finished product and do you know what the dozy sod has done? He has built the bloody thing without a door! So now, we have a wooden box at the bottom of the garden that you can't get into!"

Mum is now crying with laughter and Dad is shouting at her to shut up; we're fifteen minutes into the conversation and I still haven't managed to say anything.

"Mum, Dad, I've got something to tell you. Can you please just listen to me for a few minutes? Then you can tell me all of your stories."

"Jesus, she's pregnant!" Dad whispered.

I heard a thud.

"Dad! Are you OK?" I ask.

"I just need to sit down, love. We knew this would happen." He sighed. "When you sent us pictures of that 'hot dog guy', I knew you wouldn't be safe!"

"I'm too young to be a grandma, Louise!" Mum joined in. "What will the neighbours say?"

"Jesus, I'm not pregnant! And, for the last time, it's Hot Breakfast Guy!" I moaned.

"Oh thank God for that!" Mum rejoiced. "We were going to cancel the surprise party if you came back with a baby bump!"

"Surprise party?" I asked.

"Oh, well now you know about it. Just act surprised, OK? Your nan's been baking cakes for three weeks solid."

Pants, a surprise party? They're going to be really annoyed now.

"Well, this is why I am calling you…" I say gently.

"What? You don't eat cake now?" Dad asks incredulously.

"No! Just listen!" I shout.

"This had better be good! You've eaten cake all your life and now you stop," says Dad. "You're not going anorexic, are you?."

"For the love of God, I can eat bloody cake!" I shout down the phone. "I'm calling to tell you that I'm not coming home yet!"

OK, probably could have handled that a bit more tactfully, but they'd pushed me too far.

"What?" Mum asked in a little voice. "But what about the party?"

"I'm sorry, Mum, I really am. Can't you push the party back by a month?"

"What about the cake your nan made?" she asked, genuinely more upset about the cake than the fact that I am not coming home.

"It'll keep! Listen, the girls are flying home tomorrow so I'm going to continue travelling with Zack. We're going to travel around South East Asia for a month, I'm so excited!"

Big silence.

"*Zack?*" Dad said incredulously. "We don't know anything about *Zack*."

"Well, I do, and he's great, Dad, you'll really like him!"

"What if he's an axe murderer?" Mum asks.

"Hang on, I'll ask him... Zack, are you an axe murderer? He says he's not, we're good!"

"That's not funny, Louise; an *axe* murderer is unlikely to admit to being an *axe* murderer!" Mum whispers conspiringly down the phone, clearly now envisaging Zack as some sort of international spy.

"Well, what are the signs of an axe murderer? Tell me and I'll do a double-check!"

Zack is sitting in the background, packing his surf bag and laughing.

"Stop being a smart arse!" Mum chastised. "You don't know anything about him. How do we know you'll be safe?"

Zack walks over and motions for me to hand over the phone.

"It's your funeral!" I mumble.

"Hello, Mr and Mrs Johnson, this is Zack, Louise's non-axe-murdering boyfriend."

"Hmm, we've seen your pictures. What's your interest in our Louise?" Dad asked.

"Hey!" I shout from the background, "low blow!"

Zack replied, "Well, Mr Johnson, you clearly did an excellent job raising her as she's an incredible young woman, and, frankly, she's swept me off my feet."

"Smooth!" I mouth.

"Ah, well, thank you for saying so," says Dad. The buttering up is clearly working.

"I'll ensure that I am with her at all times in Asia, Mr Johnson," he continues. "I'll keep her safe."

"Well, thank you, young man, that would mean a lot," Dad replies.

"So you're definitely not an axe murderer?" Mum asks.

"Definitely not!" Zack laughs.

"And Louise is your only girlfriend?" she asked.

"Mum!" Jesus!

"Yes, she is my only girlfriend; I can assure you, Mrs Johnson. And I really am sorry about the surprise party," he finishes.

"Don't worry, love, it's not *your* fault…" Mum is leaving the guilt hanging in the air for me.

I take the phone back from Zack.

"Are you both OK now?" I ask.

"When will you be home?" Mum asks.

That's a question that we haven't really figured out ourselves yet. I have no idea if I'll be going back to

Manchester and Zack back to London, or if he'll stay in Oz. We look at each other, knowing that's another subject that we need to tackle at a later date.

"I'm not sure yet, Mum. I'll let you know, OK?"

"Well I suppose we'll have to accept that," says Dad sadly. "Can you give us a couple of weeks' notice so we can plan the surprise party again?"

"Of course! Speak to you both soon, love you." I walk across the room to sit on Zack's knee and ask him, "How does it feel to have your first dose of crazy?"

"You haven't spoken to my parents yet!"

Chapter Forty-Four
A New Chapter

The girls had managed to book onto the same return flight to London. Our flight to Phuket was four hours later, so we were leaving separately. We all hugged for one last time and they had to peel me off them as they piled into the minivan.

"Be safe, Louise," says Felicity, pushing my hair off my face. "Stay with Zack at all times in Asia, don't leave his side, even to pee! I mean it!" She forced a laugh.

"Have the best time! Soak it all up, OK?" Han says, balling her eyes out.

"I got you a leaving gift!" said Danni, chucking a box of condoms at me. "Won't need them in the UK, all the fitties are over here!"

"Take photos of everything!" said Tara. "We want daily updates!"

"I'm going to miss you so much!" said Clara, hugging me tightly.

Zack popped up behind me and slowly pulled me back for the van to take off.

"I love you!" I shouted after the van.

"We love you!" they all shout from the windows.

I turn to Zack and ball my eyes out.

I was still sobbing when our airport transport arrived.

"Are you sure you want to do this, Louise?" Zack asks taking hold of my hands standing in front of me.

"Yes, I'm one hundred percent sure!" I said, shaking it off. "I'm sorry if I made you doubt that. These girls have been my life for six months. I'm so excited to start this chapter with you, beyond excited! It's just an adjustment."

"It is for me, too, you know, we're in this together." he said, cupping my face and giving me a soft kiss. "Now, stop crying because we're going on an adventure!"

As soon as we took our seats on the plane, Zack passed out. I couldn't believe it. People were still finding their seats and putting their bags into the overhead compartment and he already has a patch of drool on his shoulder. This is going to be a long flight!

Left to my own devices, I was given way too much time to think. My mind is racing. I mean, when all is said and done, what do I really know about this guy? He's hot, yes, great in bed (two ticks for that one), but substance wise, what do I really know? Oh God, was this a mistake? I was flying to a country where I know absolutely no one with a guy that I know little or nothing about. What if Mum was right? What if he is an axe murderer? I'm starting to hyperventilate, I need to calm down.

I squeeze past Zack to go for a walk around the plane. At the back of the plane, I'm taking deep breaths, trying to relax and channel rational thoughts.

"Are you OK?" a concerned looking flight attendant asks.

"Oh, yes, I'm fine, thank you," I said, still consciously taking large deep breaths in and out.

"Why don't you have a little sit down here," she says kindly, pulling me behind the staff curtain. I've always wondered what went on behind here. Sadly it's not as exciting as you would think, just rows of metal boxes filled with dodgy plane food.

"Are you flying with anyone today? Would you like me to get them for you?"

"No, I'm fine, honestly, no need to panic anyone!" I said hastily.

"Is this your first time on a plane?" she asked.

"Oh no, I've flown lots of times." I replied. "I'm just evaluating some of my life choices!" as I get these words out, I start to hyperventilate again.

"Why would you want to do that?" She laughs. "Here, breathe into this." She says handing me a paper bag.

I've seen people in movies do the old breathe into a bag thing; I didn't think that it actually worked. I managed to calm my breathing down back to a normal rate and rested my head on the metal drawers behind me.

"Maybe this would be more helpful for a life crisis?" she says, handing me a glass of wine.

"My hero!" I laugh, taking a sip.

"Who are you travelling with today?" she asked.

"My boyfriend… well, very new boyfriend, hence the freak-out!" I take another sip, well, if I'm honest it's more of a large gulp.

"I see. How long have you been together?" she asks, sitting next to me.

"Officially? A couple of days!"

She raises her eyebrows in a 'tell me more' way.

"We actually met six months ago when I chucked a bowl of cereal over him! It's a long story." I shake my head.

"I've got time! 10 hours, actually. Go on," she encouraged.

"Well, we had a couple of incredible weeks together and then went our separate ways to pursue our own adventures. I have to give him credit though; he called me every day during the six months we were apart."

"This is so romantic!" she gushed. "What happened next?"

"He flew from Fiji, where he was for the time that we were apart, to meet me in Australia. We travelled with my friends for a couple of weeks and now we're off on our own adventure around Asia." I could feel myself relaxing.

"This all sounds wonderful! So, why the freak out? It sounds to me as though he proved himself by flying to you in Australia and travelling with your friends. I'm assuming that they were all female friends? That has to be tough for a guy to come into, especially after you've formed a bond with these girls for six months. He must have been very anxious."

"I'd never really thought of it from his perspective." She was right, that must have been really intimidating. Am I so self-absorbed that I haven't even taken a second to contemplate how he must be handling this?

"Was it his plan to travel around Asia?" she asked.

"Actually, he was going to stay in Australia and work," I reply, slowly letting this thought sink in.

"So, he left a country that he wanted to stay in for you?" she asks with a knowing look.

She was right. What more did I want him to do? Walk on fire? I have a wonderful man who has changed all of his plans for me. I have basically turned his world on its head, and I hadn't even given that a second of consideration.

"In my experience, dear, this kind of love is as rare as rocking horse poop! Grasp it with both hands and enjoy the ride!"

"Thank you," I said, turning to hug her.

As I squeeze back into the seat next to Zack, he is starting to wake.

"Everything OK?" he asks sleepily, squeezing my hand.

"It's perfect, go back to sleep," I reply , kissing the top of his head.

She was right, this is rare. What I feel for this guy, I can't put into words. It's a deep unexplainable feeling that I can't let go of, the type of feeling that I'd move mountains for. I need to get out of my own head and enjoy the ride. Here I am, sitting next to Hot Breakfast Guy and freaking out. My teenage self would be ashamed!

Chapter Forty-Five
Dirty Balls!

Bangkok is a far cry from Australia. The hustle and bustle of the place, coupled with the humidity, gives it an overwhelming congested feel. There are constant horns honking, people touting, selling food or knock-off clothing. I'd had a gentle warm up in Oz and I was now thrust into the chaotic world of real world travel. It's down and dirty, but, most of all, full of adventure. I can't wait to sink my teeth in!

I've never even eaten Thai food before. I let Zack lead the way and hoped that I liked what ended up on my plate. We people-watched from a local restaurant at the side of the main street, waiting for our food and letting it all sink in.

"Ping pong show for you, lady?" a man asked, approaching our table.

"Ping pong? No thanks!" I laughed.

"You don't fancy it?" Zack asked. "It could be a giggle. These things are famous all over the world!"

"Ping pong shows are famous? I couldn't think of anything duller!"

Laughing, Zack said to the guy, "We'll take two tickets, thank you."

"Why did you do that? I've got no interest in going to a ping pong show!" I said in disbelief.

"Trust me, you will love it!"

The food arrives, and I have to say that it was delicious. The flavours are incredible; I've never tasted anything like this before!

"Louise, quick, turn round!" Zack shouts. "There's an elephant behind you!"

"Do I look like I've just fallen off the top of a Christmas tree? I know the second I turn around, you're going to nick my food! I wasn't born yesterday!"

"I'm serious! Turn around!" he shouts, getting way more animated. .

"Ten out of ten for effort, but no chance."

As I continue eating, he walks around to my side of the table, picks me up on my chair and turns me to face the road.

"Oh my God, it's a real elephant! Why didn't you say?" I jump off my seat to run over and stroke it.

The guy riding it laughed at my enthusiasm. "Every day!" he says.

I turn to Zack as I didn't understand what he meant.

"He means that elephants walk down the street every day," he explained. "He's laughing because it's not a big deal to him."

I tried to explain that this is brand new to me as we don't have elephants in Manchester. He found my explanation hilarious - it must be the language barrier!

"So, are you ready for the boring ping pong show?" Zack asks with a cheeky grin.

"Do we really have to go?" I sulk.

"I promise; it'll be better than you think!" he replied, grabbing my hand.

The venue was some seedy back door boozer; it didn't look like the kind of place you would have a ping pong show. I imagined people in headbands with pristine white shorts and socks pulled up to their knees.

"Am I missing something?" I ask.

"Just wait!" Zack says, holding a velvet curtain back for me to walk under.

"Ladies and gentlemen, please take your seats, the show is due to commence," The compère in a top hat and tails announces.

"This is a bit fancy for a ping pong show, isn't it?" I turn to Zack and ask.

He winks at me with a little smirk. OK, my spidey senses are tingling now; There is definitely something strange going on.

The compère introduces a Thai lady who walks over to her ping pong table (so far so good), climbs onto it (bit strange, but I'll go with it), pulls down her pants... (erm), and opens her legs!

"What is this?" I whisper to Zack. "Is this a sex show?"

I can't believe he's brought me to this! My cheeks are burning with embarrassment.

"It's not a sex show! I promise you'll think it's hilarious!" he said, pulling me back down onto my seat.

A second lady walks onto the stage in a Moulin Rouge-style getup with a tray of what looks like darts. Lady number one, with her legs akimbo, takes five darts and inserts them... into her vagina! The Moulin Rouge lady then walks to the other end of the stage and holds up five balloons. Lady number one then fires the darts from her foof like a fricking tommy gun!

"What the hell is this?" I say.

Zack isn't even watching the stage at this point, he's just crying with laughter as he watches my reaction.

"I think you are the only person in the world who doesn't know what a Thai ping pong show is!" he howls. "Your face is a picture!"

"I don't understand!" I say, still trying to figure this out in my head. "How the hell do they do that? As someone with a vag I can tell you, that's not a talent that you are born with!"

"I have no idea! But it's really famous in Thailand, like the Lady Boys."

"Lady Boys? What's that?" I ask, downing a glass of wine as I try to remove the sights that I have just witnessed.

"Oh, Louise, I have so much to show you!"

On the second act of the show, they scan the audience for volunteers, and of course, land on Zack! They pull him onto the stage and hand him a bucket. They manoeuvre him to the side and tell him that he has to catch the balls…that come firing out of a random ladies vagina…perfect! Zack of course, is loving it; he's goofing around on the stage, playing up to the audience.

The lady starts to fire the balls out of her vag at a rapid rate. Five men on the stage are running from one end to the other, desperately trying to catch them. It's like a warped Benny Hill sketch. Zack is laughing so hard that he is bent double, with tears rolling down his face.

As Zack is laughing, she fires a ping pong out of her vagina. It flies across the room, hurtling towards the bucket that one of the guys was holding. The guy somehow trips and falls in front of Zack. The ball, however, keeps on hurling through the air.

As if in slow motion, it all plays out before me and I can see what is going to happen. I stand and shout "Noooooooo!"

It's too late; the ball has landed…in Zack's mouth!

The whole audience freezes.

Oh my God, oh my God, oh my God! I jump onto the stage and drag him straight to the bar, order four large vodkas and immediately make him swirl them around in his mouth and spit.

"What am I going to do? She could have all sorts!" he says with wide-eyed terror.

"Just keep slushing the vodka! We're going to have to take you to a hospital!" I reply, frantically looking around the room for an exit.

A guy approaches us mid-slush and spit.

"I'm a local doctor at the hospital, do you need some help?" he asks.

"Oh thank God!" I say, holding onto him. "This is a nightmare! What do we need to do? Wait, what is a doctor doing here? You know what, never mind! Just help Zack!"

"So you're the fella that caught the ball in your mouth? That was a one in a million shot, you have to give her that!" he laughs.

We both just stare at him.

"Too soon?" he asks. "Look, we always keep an ambulance service on the main strip as tourists tend to get a wee bit out of hand over here. Let me take you and we'll give you a quick check over, OK?"

"Yes, yes, absolutely. Let's go!" I say, pushing them both out of the door.

My mind is spinning out of control. What if she has herpes or chlamydia? Or worse, AIDS? I can't even think about it.

At the ambulance station, the doctors are finding the story quite hilarious.

"Let's take a quick look at you," says a nice lady doctor. "I'm assuming you had all relevant injections before you came here? Typhoid, hepatitis, tetanus?"

"Yes, I did." Zack answers.

"OK, that's good, and I understand that your girlfriend had the sense to get you swilling a spirit around your mouth before you left, is that correct?"

"Yes, doctor," Zack replied.

"OK, as you've had all of your injections and you immediately cleaned the impacted area, you should be fine. To be sure, I'm going to suggest a quick booster injection to make sure that all of your cells are protected. Have you had much to drink tonight?"

"I only had two drinks. I just did the old slush and spit with the vodka, Louise even made me gargle it!" he says.

"Very good, that should have killed most local bugs. Where did you get that idea from?" she asked me.

"Movication! I watch loads of gangster movies," I reply. "They're always cleaning wounds and their knives with alcohol!"

"I see," she says, raising her eyebrows. "Well, it's a good job that you do. OK, Zack, can you please sign these forms to say that you agree for me to give you this booster?" She says handing him a form and a pen. "Now, this will make you a little woozy. How far away are you staying from here?"

"Not far, about a fifteen-minute walk," I tell her.

"OK, you should be fine, although he's a big lad, isn't he? You may need to get a cab."

Outside of the van there are hordes of people; there's no way a cab was getting through there. We'll just have to manage.

After sitting for ten minutes the doctor told us that we were good to go.

"Thank you so much, doctor," Zack says, shaking her hand.

"No worries, keep your mouth shut from now on, OK?" She laughs.

"Excellent advice!" I agree.

Walking through the crowd, I have a firm grip on Zack's hand.

"How are you feeling? Woozy yet?" I ask.

"I feel fine, don't worry!"

We are only about ten minutes away from the hostel; I need him to continue feeling fine until we get there. As we're walking up the hill, I can feel his hand slackening slightly.

"Zack, are you OK? We're almost there, just hang on."

"You're the best!" he slurs.

"Just hold on, baby, we're not far now. I just need you to focus on what you're doing, OK?" I say, pulling his arm around my shoulders.

"Louby-lou, I never thought I'd end up with a girl called Louby-lou!" he slurs. "Have you ever thought about calling yourself Madonna?"

"Not recently," I reply. He's really leaning on me, god this guy is heavy! "I need you to stand as straight as you can, OK?"

He attempts to straighten himself up, which in turn causes him to lose his balance and fall straight onto his face on the dirt track.

"Oh Zack, I'm sorry! Are you OK?" I ask, trying to pull him up.

Giggling like a school boy, he pulls me on top of him, right in the middle of the street.

"Let's just sleep here!" he says, snuggling into me.

I can see the hostel in the distance; I just need to get him there. He's started snoring now. Crap! I need to get him up. Oh, I know: I have a bottle of water in my bag. I unscrew the lid and chuck it over his face.

Spluttering, he comes to. "What the hell are you doing?" he says, wiping the water from his face.

"I need you to get up and keep walking, OK? We're nearly there."

"OK." He replies, sulking like a child.

The hostel doesn't have any lifts, and of course we are on the top floor. It takes me ages to get him up the stairs whilst he's singing Spice Girls at the top of his lungs. I finally manage to wrestle him into bed, where his parting words of wisdom are:

"Do you know that God spelled backwards is dog?"

Chapter Forty-Six
One Very Bad Decision!

Zack wakes the following morning with no recollection of anything after the injection, which is probably for the best. I miss out the part about the one-man Spice Girl concert and tell him that he handled the whole situation like a pro. Today we are moving on from Bangkok across the border into Cambodia.

The coaches in Asia are nothing like the coaches in Australia. There is no air con or loos. We're shoved into a minivan with ten other travellers in the 40°C heat, with the occasional stop at local 'restrooms', aka holes in floors behind brick walls. You just had to pray that you didn't need a number two until you got to the hostel! The trip was supposed to take six hours. However, they stopped at pretty much every relative's house en route to entice you into buying some sort of crap that you didn't want. It was like a jumble sale road show.

We eventually stopped for food two hours outside of the border. We all piled out of the van into a wooden shack on the side of the road that had plastic tables and chairs outside. I wasn't convinced about the hygiene, so I had some sticky rice wrapped in a bamboo leaf with vegetables. Zack went to town on the undisclosed meat dish. I hope he's been doing his squats to prepare him for the poop in a hole scenario.

"Mmm, this is actually really nice, want to try some?" he asks, shoving the unidentified meat in my direction.

"I'm good!" I reply, dodging it like the proverbial bullet.

Back on the van, Zack starts to complain about his stomach.

"I told you not to eat it," I said shaking my head.

"I know, I was just so hungry!" he whined, clutching his stomach.

"We'll be at the border soon, just hold on."

"Hello, team!" The guide was now addressing the group. "Can you all ensure that you have your visas ready for inspection, please. Border patrol is very strict. You need to have your Cambodian visa, Thai visa and passport for clearance before they let you through."

Hmm, this might be a problem.

"Excuse me!" I shout over the group. "We haven't actually got Cambodian visas yet; we were advised that we could pick them up at the border. Is that not accurate?"

"You will have to ask border patrol; they may not let you through," he replied.

"What happens if they don't let us through?" Zack asks, "Is there anywhere to stay round there?"

The guide laughed and turned around. Not a good sign.

"Don't worry, we'll figure it out," Zack assures me. "These lot are always up for taking cash; we may have to pay a little extra, but it'll be OK."

Oh, how I hope that's true!

Off the van, we were separated from the group into the naughty line.

"Visas here," the man behind the desk yelled.

"We actually need to purchase two Cambodian visas, please," Zack says with as much authority as he could muster.

"You no have visa?" he replied.

"Ah, no, we don't, we'd like to pay for two now," Zack says, holding old a bunch of notes.

"Wait here," he replied walking off.

As I turn around, I see our van driving off back to Thailand as the rest of our group pass through the border.

We've been abandoned, at the Cambodian border.

"Come with me, please." A man taps us on the shoulder.

"Where do we need to go?" Zack asks.

"Government building. Get in van," he says, pointing at a pickup truck.

Glancing at each other, we bend down to pick up our bags.

"Your bags stay here with security." He points towards a group of children with headscarves and machine guns.

I look at Zack, terrified.

"It's OK, just leave them," he said, smiling kindly at me. I could see in his eyes that he was as scared as I was, but he was putting a brave face on. "We have our backpacks with all the important stuff in, the rest is replaceable."

Shakily, we climb into the pickup truck that bombs through the jungle at a ferocious speed. Neither of us speak. I'm too busy trying to hold onto my pee that was desperately trying to escape; I couldn't bring myself to breathe, let alone speak! What felt like hours later, we arrive at the 'government building', aka a shack in the middle of nowhere.

Zack jumps down off the back of the van and turns to help me out of the truck.

We're greeted by a Cambodian guy wearing an army beret and smoking a cigar. "So, you need visa?"

"Yes, we do. Two, please," Zack says, much more calmly than I know he was feeling.

"Two hundred dollars," he replies.

"We know that the visas are sixty dollars each, that's all we have on us."

Zack's voice was starting to tremble a little now and I was clutching onto his hand for dear life.

"You go to bank, get more money." He waved his hand dismissively. "Then you come back."

"OK, where is the nearest bank?" I ask.

"Ten minutes on moped, one stay, one go," he replied.

"I think it's safer if you stay here," Zack says. "There's only one guy. I'd feel better you doing that than jumping onto a moped and going into the middle of God knows where."

I could feel myself physically shaking.

"It's OK, Louise, just go and sit over there on that chair. I'll be twenty minutes, tops." Zack says giving me a massive cuddle and then turns to leave.

I walk over to the chair that Zack pointed at and hold onto it for dear life. As Zack drives off into the jungle and disappears, I smile meekly at the cigar smoking man. As I turn to my right I see about eight guys walk out from behind the hut.

Oh my God. I am going to be on the news!

I've seen enough spy films to know that the art of survival is to keep moving; I need to channel my inner Jason Bourne. I get up from my chair and slowly move around looking like I'm taking in the nuance décor of the inside of the shed, then leisurely navigate my way outside. Breathe in, breathe out, breathe in, breathe out. I glance over my shoulder to see that they have followed me. Oh God, I need to do something, I need to distract them.

"Beautiful day, we don't get weather like this in the UK. Do you wear sun cream or are you used to the heat? I burn like crazy, factor thirty all day long for me!" I've somehow channelled Hugh Grant rather than Jason Bourne!

They don't look deterred at all. In fact, they are practically salivating over me like a piece of meat. I need to turn it up a notch, I need to scare them; "Do any of you know karate? I happen to be a black belt. Oh yeah, karate and judo, I'm actually *pretty* deadly!" I say, showing them some of my fly swatting moves.

As I'm flapping my arms and legs around, I bump into one of them behind me and I quickly realised that I am being circled.

Another touches my face, saying, "Pretty girl."

I am close to tears, terrified. It's that kind of fear that clutches you from the inside, clamping down on your chest so you can't breathe.

I can feel tears spilling out of my eyes. Come on Louise, shake it off, don't give into your fear; this is about survival. I continue to move in zigzagging lines. There is a little opening; I manage to squeeze through, outside of the circle. I just need to keep moving whilst I figure out my plan. Do I run into the jungle? No, Zack will never find me, I just need to keep moving. I turn my steps into some sort of weird barn dance, constantly shifting direction.

My prayers were finally answered; I can hear the moped in the distance screeching back. A guy with black teeth winks at me and nods his head for the rest to follow. I let out a breath for the first time in what felt like an eternity. Zack pretty much leaps off the moped whilst it is still moving and runs towards me.

"Louise, are you OK?" he asks, gripping my arms and looking intently into my eyes. He looked like he is going to cry. "Where the hell did they come from?"

"Behind the wall after you left." My words came out shakily and quietly, I wasn't sure that I even managed to say it out loud.

"Did they hurt you?" he asks with a fire in his eyes that made me glad that they didn't.

"No, just give him the money; we need to get out of here!"

Zack threw the money at the cigar smoking man, much to his amusement. He hands us the visas and gives the nod to the driver to take us back to the border. I still can't breathe. Zack is holding onto me so tightly I feel like I'm going to pop, but I didn't ask him to let go; I needed him to hold on.

The kids bring our bags back to us, looking filthy and battered. They'd obviously tried to get in and failed. Thank God I put about a hundred padlocks on each case.

"How do we travel into Cambodia?" Zack asks one of the guys.

"Where you want to go?" he replied, chewing a piece of grass.

"Siem Reap."

"Come," he replied.

At this point, we literally have no choice. It's getting dark and we are in the middle of nowhere. Frankly, I'd like to get as far away from those men as possible.

He directs us to a black car and bends over to tell the driver where we wanted to go.

"How much?" Zack asks.

Looking us up and down "Thirty dollars." He replied.

"Done," said Zack.

We throw our bags into the boot and climb in.

It's pitch black. There's literally not a light in sight. I can't tell if we're travelling through desert or fields, or along a dirt track; all I can feel is rough terrain underneath the tyres.

After an hour in darkness, there is light in the distance.

"Where are we?" Zack asked.

"Change money!" he replied.

"We don't need to change money; we have US dollars," Zack said.

"No work in Cambodia," he replied.

We knew for a fact that they did. I took the money from Zack; he had drawn out five hundred dollars. I passed him fifty dollars back and hid the rest in my bra.

"Just tell them that's all we have," I whisper.

We pull up into a little shanty town and a guy with gold teeth opens my side of the door. "Friends, friends, welcome to Cambodia. I hear you need to change money?"

"I think there has been a misunderstanding, we have already changed our money into US dollars. Sorry to have wasted your time." I smile.

"Ah, you are misinformed!" he replied theatrically. "US dollar no longer work in Cambodia, you need Cambodian riel. How much money you have?"

"We only have fifty dollars," Zack replied.

"You only travel with fifty dollars?" he asked suspiciously.

"Buying visas at the border cost us more than we were expecting, so that's all we have left," I reply, squeezing Zack's hand.

This makes him roar with laughter. "You buy visa at border? You crazy!" He slaps his thigh. "Come, come!" He pulls Zack and I out of the car. "I do special deal just for you!"

He gave us fifty Cambodian Riel for fifty US Dollars, he'd just made himself a five-hundred percent mark-up. But I didn't care, I was happy to do it to get back in the car. He waved us off and we continue driving. I close my eyes to try and settle my breathing. There is nothing we can do now; we are where we are.

"Louise, wake up!" Zack pokes me.

I must have nodded off. "What, what's happening?" I say, clutching onto him.

"It's OK, we're not in danger. Look out of the window!"

I look out to see what can only be described as the Vegas of Cambodia. There are rows of ridiculously extravagant hotels with water fountains and Bentleys parked outside. It's unreal, a far cry from the mayhem that we had just been through. The further we drove the more down-market the hotels became. Our cab stopped outside of a lovely mid-range hotel.

"Ah, sorry, this can't be ours, we're staying in a hostel." Zack repeated the name.

"Yes," he says, pointing to the sign.

Wow, six dollars a night gets you pretty far in Cambodia!

We enter the hostel/hotel to an ornate marble sweeping staircase sitting proudly in the centre of the room with beautiful large golden Buddhas and flowers everywhere. It was so elegant and relaxing. I finally felt so safe that I burst into tears.

"Hey, hey; shush, shush," said Zack, nursing me like a baby. "It's OK, we're safe now. Louise, I promise I will never put you in that situation again, I'm so sorry," he hugged me tightly.

As I was crying, a lovely Thai lady ran over with a 'special' tea. I have no idea what was in it, but after a few sips I was finally able to breathe again. I don't think I'm cut out for Cambodia!

Chapter Forty-Seven
Life's a Beach

Flying with Zack's kite surfing equipment is interesting, to say the least, especially when you're flying from Cambodia to Thailand. Lord only knows where the bag will turn up! As soon as we arrived in the Phi Phi islands, Zack ran to the baggage claim and asked where the oversized luggage collection was. It took us two hours and six people to locate it. By the time we found the bag, it looked as though it had been through hell and back. I feel like attaching a camera to track its journey; I wouldn't be surprised if we found out that it had done a stint on the front line.

I have to say, I was really excited to be back on the beach. Travelling around inland Asia in this heat is an absolute killer; I was massively looking forward to a dunk in the ocean. It looked as though Zack was on the same wave length: within ten minutes of being in the hostel, he had unpacked his kite surf equipment and was standing in his boardies, grinning like a child.

"Time to go to the beach yet?" he asked with his megawatt smile.

"Definitely! Come on, let's go!" I said, running out of the door.

The local kids were pretty excited about Zack's kite; I don't think they'd ever seen anything like that before. He was like the Pied Piper: wherever he led, they followed. As he was zipping along in the water, they were having a whale of a time chasing after him and splashing around.

Whilst Zack was keeping himself occupied, I went for a little wander around the beach shops and tour venues to see what there was to do around here.

"You want tour, lady?" a man shouted from across the beach.

I took a leaflet from him. "Where can we go?"

"We take you on tour of Phi Phi islands, see where The Beach was filmed, have lunch, go diving, many fun to be had!" he replied.

"Sounds great. Have you got any slots tomorrow?" I ask.

"Yes, we leave ten a.m. How many peoples?" he asked, taking my details.

I told him two.

"OK, you booked for tomorrow, ten a.m. sharp. You no arrive by ten a.m., you no go. No refund!"

I could see Zack making his way back onto the beach. I stopped at the bar to pick us up some nice cold cocktails and met him at the sun loungers.

"You are a mind reader!" he said, gratefully taking the cocktail from me.

"It's one of my many skills!" I replied, giving him a big kiss. "Are you going to introduce me to your friends?"

Zack turned to see about ten of the local kids all patiently waiting for him to go back out again. He bent down to speak to them. "Hey, guys, I'll shout to you when I go back in, OK?"

"OK, mister," the ring leader replied, pulling them away.

"Ah, they are so cute!" I laughed.

"That's one word for it."

"I've booked us on a tour of the islands tomorrow; we can see where The Beach was filmed!" I told him, handing over the leaflet. "If I'm lucky, Leonardo Di Caprio may stop by!"

"Oh really? You're already trading me in for a movie star, are you?" he said, tickling me.

"Well, my dad did always tell me to go for money first, then love the second time round!" I said, wriggling around and giggling.

"Love, hey?" he asked with a cheeky grin.

Dig up, Louise, dig up! "Well, I'm still on plan A, going for the cash. You don't have a secret stash I don't know about, do you?" Good save!

"Sadly not, no. You may have to skip plan A and go straight to plan B," he said, looking into my eyes.

Neither of us said anything, we just let that hang in the air between us.

"I'd better shout the kids to go back out again," he said, with that cheeky smile and sparkly eyes.

"Yep, you better had!" As he turned around, I knocked back both of our cocktails in one go.

Chapter Forty-Eight
A Case of Mistaken Identity

After a serious amount of cocktails, we woke up a little groggy.

"What time is it?" I asked Zack. My mouth is so dry and my head is killing me.

"Nine thirty," he replied.

"Crap! We've got the boat trip in half an hour. Come on, get up; we need to go!" I said, throwing a pillow at him in an effort to get him to move.

"Are you wearing that?" Zack asked as we were leaving the hostel.

I looked down and realised that I had thrown on a gold going out dress. With my hair up on top of my head and large black sunglasses, I looked as though I was going to St Tropez rather than a boat tour in Asia.

"We only have ten minutes, there's no time to change. I've got my bikini in my bag, it'll be fine."

We arrived at the beach to a plethora of yachts and boats with locals touting their trips. I had no idea which one we were supposed to get on and I couldn't remember what the tour guide that had booked the trip looked like. As I was rummaging around in my bag for the leaflet, a man came running over to us.

"This way, lady, please," he said, bowing in front of me. He must have recognised me from yesterday.

We were ushered along a red carpet onto this incredible yacht. I felt like a star. As we entered the yacht, a lady greeted us with a tray of mimosas and invited us to sit at the front. Not bad for a fifty dollar trip!

The Phi Phi islands were just incredible; the scenery is filled with naturally vibrant, bold colours. With all of the hype that surrounds these islands, I wasn't sure that they would deliver, but they had exceeded my expectations.

Zack has passed out next to me, gently snoring. Lightweight! I squeezed past him to go to the loo. As I was washing my hands, I heard a commotion outside the toilets. I opened the door to a lady who launched her baby at me, screaming, "Photo, photo!" As I was trying to grasp what the hell was going on, I was blinded by flashing lights from several cameras. I'm not ashamed to say that I used that baby as a human shield! As I held him up in front of my face, they stopped snapping for a second, long enough for me to ask what was going on.

"You take photo now!" one man shouted. "With baby!"

"A photo?" I asked, dazed and confused.

"Yes, smile!" they shouted.

Maybe they are not used to seeing many blonde Western women. Whatever the reason, there are now several photos of a crying baby with a terrified looking English woman making their way around South East Asia. One for the family album.

I woke Zack to tell him what had happened.

"Maybe it's because you look like you're about to have breakfast at Tiffany's!" he said, poking fun at my dress.

They invited us to leave the boat first, rolling out the red carpet. I could get used to this! First stop was a beautiful quaint little restaurant for lunch; the food was divine. When we finished, three little girls came up to me and handed me pictures that they had drawn.

"For me?" I asked.

They all nodded and curtsied. The Thai people are so polite!

"Thank you," I replied. "I will stick them on my fridge!"

We were told that it was time to get back onto the boat for our next island.

Zack asked for the bill. "No, no! No charge, our honour," the man in the restaurant replied, bowing.

"It must be included in the trip cost," said Zack.

As we walked back to the yacht along the red carpet, rows of people on either side are handing me gifts: I am given hand carved Buddhas, fans, scarves, you name it. They must be so busy to do this for their guests every day. I love that they go to this much effort; it makes the trip so memorable.

We spend the afternoon island hopping, visiting where The Beach was filmed, popping in and out of the ocean, and stopping at various shops and restaurants, all of which gave me a parting memento.

"How are we going to travel with all of this stuff?" I say to Zack, with a bulging bag.

"I didn't get anything, some severe favouritism going on here!" He grinned.

"It must be a female thing." I turned to a lady next to me and asked her what gifts she had received.

"Oh no, madam, all for you!" she said, curtsying.

"All for me? I don't understand. Why is that?" I asked.

"Because you are queen!" she said, again curtseying.

Queen? Slowly but surely, the realisation sank in. The photographers, the gifts, the curtseying...

"Zack, I don't think that is a turn of phrase, I think they think I am an actual queen!" I whispered to him.

"You wish! I know in your head you are lady of the manor, but I really don't think they think you are a Queen," he scoffed.

"Then tell me, why do they keep referring to you as my security?" I said.

"Clearly, they are joking!" he said, shaking his head.

"Really? Then why did they ask if I was OK with you sitting with me at lunch? Think about it, their behaviour has been really weird!"

Zack took a step back and looked around. I could see the reality of the situation starting to sink in. "Hmm…" he said.

"Hmm, indeed," I replied. "We have literally hijacked a Queen's yacht, eaten her food and taken her gifts!"

"Well, it's too late to say anything now! We're near enough back to where we started," he said, looking slightly harassed. "When we get off the yacht, thank them for a wonderful day and then we need to get the hell out of dodge!"

Literally everyone on the yacht was smiling and bowing at me every time I looked at them. This is bad! They have probably been preparing for this for months. I wonder where the Queen is from? She'd better not be ugly!

As we left the yacht, I did as Zack said and thanked them all for a lovely day. I had one last group photo and scurried back to the hostel.

As soon as we walked into our room I jumped onto the Wi-Fi to see who I had been impersonating today.

"Oh my gosh, Zack, look!" I said, pointing at the news page.

"No way!"

The Queen of the Netherlands was due to arrive today. However, she had some urgent family business to attend to, so didn't make it. Word mustn't have gotten through to the Thai people quickly enough.

"Oh God, she's having a family emergency and I took all of her gifts!" I said. "This is definitely not helping with my karma points!"

"Well, you know what they say; you go to heaven for the weather and hell for the company!" He laughed. "Don't worry, I'll see you there!"

Well, that's comforting!

Chapter Forty-Nine
It's 'All Go'!

The following day we had planned to take a boat to Surat Thani to visit the party islands Ko Samui and Ko Pha Ngan. However, I was paranoid about leaving the hostel in case we got arrested for impersonating the Queen. I didn't fancy spending the next twenty years in a Thai prison!

"Just stick a big hat and sunglasses on, I promise they won't recognise you!" said Zack, laughing.

"Stop laughing, this is serious!" I said, throwing my hairbrush at him. "What we did was unethical and I'm pretty sure illegal."

"Louise, we got on the wrong boat! There is nothing illegal about that," he said, kissing my cheek.

"What about all the gifts I took?" I whined.

"Again, not illegal. Immoral, maybe, but not illegal! Come on, we have a boat booked, we need to get going," he said, walking me over to my case.

"OK, but if we get caught..."

"We won't! Just relax," he said, rubbing my shoulders.

I threw on a pair of denim shorts, vest top, cap and sunglasses. My hair and face was covered and my outfit was a far cry from the gold dress of yesterday. I am praying that they don't pick me out in a crowd! Slumped behind Zack, I dragged my case onto the beach.

"Tickets, please," a man asked at the boat.

"Here you go," said Zack.

The man peered around Zack to look at me hiding behind him.

"OK, on you go," he said, ushering us on.

Phase one complete, although I couldn't fully relax until we were on our way. We were on a small fishing boat; apparently we had to wait for another couple who were late, so we remained sat on the beach with all the other boat owners running around us. I was sweating more than usual; it felt as though someone had cranked up the heat a notch. I faced out to sea and kept my head down, praying that we could depart any second. After twenty minutes, the other couple didn't arrive, so we were free to leave, thank God!

Being on a little fishing boat in the middle of the ocean is hot! Like, 'stuck in a greenhouse with someone directing a magnifying glass at you' hot. We were grabbing clothes out of our bags to cover our shoulders, trying to find a small amount of shelter from the sun.

Once we made it to Surat Thani, it took us an hour to find the hostel. Zack was doing the usual man thing of not asking for directions, so we wandered around in circles for what felt like eternity in the blistering heat. When we arrived, we were burnt, hungry and cranky.

"I'm starving, want to come and get some food?" Zack asked.

"Actually, I'm gagging for air con, would you mind picking me something up and I'll stay in the room?" I feel a little space would be a good idea right now!

"Sure," he said, visibly relieved. "Be back soon."

Whilst he was away, I jumped online to check on any emails from home. There was one from Mum.

Hi Louise, it's your mum.

I hope you are having a good time.

It's 'all go' here, as they say. I had my hair done yesterday whilst Dad was at the match; they came second (I made sure I was out when he got home! Hashtag LAUGH OUT LOUD).

Anyway, I have some 'scandal' to inform you of. When the hairdresser arrived she couldn't turn her car around at the top of the cul-de-sac, because there was a car parked there. She had to park facing up the street instead of facing down. When she told me, I asked if anyone was in the car. "A woman," she says. "What did she look like?" I said. "Dark hair with sunglasses," she says. "Well, that could be anyone," I said, so we looked through the net curtain to 'scope her out'.

I couldn't get a 'confirmed visual' from our window so decided to investigate further. I went 'incognito' with a headscarf and sunglasses (so she couldn't identify me in a line up) and casually walked across the street to Mrs Winkle's house (not really going to Mrs Winkle's house you see; it was a cover). I lowered my sunglasses to take a good look at her face (like they do in the spy films), but I think I rattled her as she quickly started her engine and shot off down the street like a 'bat out of hell'! I threw my headscarf off and ran inside. "Did you see that?" I said to the hairdresser. "Yes," she said. "Very suspicious," I said. "Yes," she said.

That's as far as we got for now; stay tuned for my next findings!

Anyway, your dad was rambling on about something to do with pirates when I said you were in the Kung Samurai place. It's on the news; they are lopping tourists' heads off on boats to the party islands. So be safe and hold onto your heads! LAUGH OUT LOUD!

Hope you are having fun with Hot Bounty Man, but not too much fun. Remember the deal: bun in the oven, no surprise party.

Love, Mum
PS – The cake didn't keep for your party so we ate it.
PPS – Nan will make you a new cake when you come home.

She really needs to stop watching so much Sherlock! What she said about pirates concerned me, though; surely they wouldn't use boats across to the party islands if it was unsafe?

Chapter Fifty
Pirates

I still had my lumo outfit from the party that I went to in Sydney and Zack had covered himself in florescent green and pink body paint, so we were Full Moon Party ready! I was really excited for tonight; this was our first proper party together with just the two of us and no back up.

As we were staying on Surat Thani, we had to get a boat to and from Ko Phangan where the Full Moon Party was being held. Pulling onto the beach, I could see thousands of people covered in body paint, five DJs spread along the full width of the beach playing different styles of music, and bars on every corner. This was going to be some party!

"Drink?" Zack asked.

"Hell yeah!" I shouted.

I was listening to the different DJs to see where I wanted to start. Ooh, disco! That could be fun!

Zack pushed his way over to me through the crowd and handed me a bucket.

"What's this?" I shouted over the music.

"Vodka and coke! It's how it's served here, apparently."

The boat trip home is going to be interesting!

Zack nudged me and pointed to a really gorgeous girl dancing on the table next to us. "She's hot, isn't she?" he said.

Is he serious? We're in a brand new relationship and he's pointing out good-looking girls. This was clearly some sort of test; must play it cool.

"Erm, yeah, she's pretty," I replied, taking a big glug from my bucket.

"I mean, she's *really* hot! Look at her!" he said with a twinkle in his eye. I hope he's not implying what I think he is implying; three's a crowd and all that.

"Yes. Like I said, she is pretty," I said with warning in my voice and a glare that could wipe out a small village.

Laughing, he turned me to face her. "Notice anything unusual?"

"Unusual? Like what?" I have no idea where this conversation is going. Does he have a Thai sister that I don't know about?

"Look at her shorts!" He pointed.

She was wearing a bikini top and tiny shorts. Nothing unusual about that, we were on a beach. But wait, what's that? There's some sort of bulge in her pants, it looks like…

Wait a minute. "Is that a ding dong?" I whisper.

"Bingo!" He laughs. "She's what they call a 'ladyboy' over here… as in, she started off as a dude!"

"No!" I said with genuine shock.

"Lots of people come to Thailand to get sex change operations. They're called 'ladyboys' because they look like a woman on the outside, but have male plumbing, if you know what I mean!"

"Wow! I've got to say, she looks amazing! Maybe I should ask her for her surgeon's details?" I said, laughing.

"There are some really famous shows in Phuket; maybe we could go to one when we're there?" Zack asked.

"Oh God, it's not like the ping pong show, is it?" I said, shaking my head.

Laughing, he said, "No, they're like a West End show, all big feathers and diamantes!"

"You had me at feathers! But seriously, she is amazing," I said, turning back to the girl dancing on the podium.

We started in the disco section; it was so much fun. Everyone was going wild, cutting some serious shapes to 70s grooves and knocking back copious amounts of alcohol.

We worked our way along the beach, stopping to dance and sing our hearts out at every DJ. We came up with a game: every time one of us didn't recognise the song, we had to take a swig from our bucket. Needless to say, we got pretty hammered!

"I need to pee," I slurred at Zack.

"OK, I'll lead the way, let's do a conga!"

I grabbed his waist and we conga'd to the loo… well, at least we tried to. Within a few minutes of starting to conga, a girl latched onto me, five girls latched onto her, and a massive group latched onto them. We had accidentally started one of the biggest conga lines in Full Moon Party history! The whole beach was involved; there were literally thousands of people doing the conga. Cameras were flashing and all of the DJs had changed their music to 'Let's all do the conga!'

"Zack, look!" I tapped him on the shoulder. He was so drunk he hadn't even noticed.

"Yeah, conga, woo hoo!" he was shouting.

Someone had stuck a massive pink hat on his head and thrown a giant candy cane at him.

"I'm the conga master!" he screamed, followed by thousands of cheers.

The conga went on for much longer that I would have liked as I was gagging for the loo. As soon as it died down, I grabbed Zack's hand and made a bolt for the ladies. One of the tribulations of being hammered as a girl in Asia is that the toilets are holes in the floor. Trying to stand up without swaying around was hard enough, let alone trying to squat without falling over. I handed my bucket of vodka to Zack so at least I couldn't knock that over, but I now needed to navigate the hole. OK, steady, steady. Ugh, my stupid Bambi legs were failing me.

I was flailing around from one side of the cubicle to the other, trying to drunkenly pull my pants down.

"Louise, are you OK in there?" Zack shouted concerned by all the banging and groaning.

"I can't stoop without falling over!" I hiccupped.

"Open the door, I'm coming in!" he slurred.

"No! You can't see me like this! Wait out there!" I said in a panic.

"Open the door!" he said, banging on it. "I can help!"

Well, there goes the mystery in the relationship!

"OK, babe, I got you!" he said, putting the buckets down and staggering over to me. "Take your pants off so you don't pee on them."

"I don't want you to see me do this!" I whined.

"We are a TEAM!" he shouted dramatically. "I got your back. Now take your pants off!"

I swayed around, trying to pull my pants off; I didn't want to put them on the dirty floor so I stuck them on my head and bent down in the squat position with Zack holding my hands for balance. He was even helpfully making splashing sounds to make me go. As he was swaying around singing to me, he slackened his grip and I went flying into the hole on top of my pee.

"Eww, it's on my bum!" I whined.

"Oh no! Babe, I'm so sorry I let you down!" Zack said with drunken sincerity.

"It's OK," I slurred. "I'll just go into the sea and clean up."

We staggered out of the cubicle, me with my pants still on my head.

"You need clean up?" a Thai lady shouted, holding up a hose.

"Ooh, a hose!" said Zack excitedly.

"I have pee on my legs!" I hiccupped.

She really went for it and completely drenched my bottom half, but I no longer smelled of pee so it was a win. Zack helped me to put my pants back on and pulled me outside.

By five a.m., we were propping each other up and slumped on the beach.

"I think we should go home now," I said.

Zack couldn't even speak; he just slowly got up and pulled me with him. We arrived back at the speed boat with six other English couples, who were all equally hammered. Some were throwing up over the side, others were asleep, and one guy was really wired and annoying.

"This was the best night ever!" he kept shouting; "Woo hoo, I'm pumped!"

The boat let rip and we zoomed across the ocean. It was pitch black, so I couldn't see anything other than the lights on our small boat. I was taking deep breaths, trying my hardest not to throw up, when the boat came to an abrupt standstill. We all looked around at each other. I squinted towards the guy who was driving the boat, trying to focus on him. He had a bandana and one gold hoop earring. Oh my God, he's a pirate! This was exactly what my mum warned me about!

All of a sudden, the lights shut off and we heard a giant splash. We all scrabbled around for our phones, trying to get some light.

"Where did he go?" one woman shouted.

"He's jumped into the sea!" a guy responded.

What? Oh my God, we were abandoned, in the middle of the ocean, in the pitch black!

"Pirates!" I whispered to Zack, with wide eyes.

"What did you just say?" A guy shouted to me.

"My mum sent me an email saying that pirates are targeting tourists on the ocean between the party islands."

Mass hysteria broke out.

"We're going to die!" one woman screamed.

Zack instantly sobered up. "Everyone stay calm." He stood up and shouted, "Does anyone know how to drive a boat?"

We all shook our heads.

He clambered over everyone to get to the driver's seat. "The keys are gone," he quietly said.

Everyone started to panic.

"We're going to have to swim!" I said to the group.

"Which way?" a man shouted back to me.

"We were travelling that way; we'll just have to keep going in that direction," I replied, close to tears.

"We can't even see any land, Louise," Zack said, now completely sober. "I have no idea how long that will take."

"Well, the options are we stay and face the risk of getting our heads chopped off by pirates, or we jump!" Everyone is now crying. "Whatever we do, we need to stick together. Let's take a vote."

It was six to two to swim.

"There's a boat coming!" a woman shouted. "Let's flag them down!"

We were all jumping up and down waving. When the boat got closer, we realised that there were about ten guys, all with bandanas and hoop earrings.

"Oh my God, they're pirates!" a woman screamed.

"JUMP!" Zack shouted. He grabbed onto my hand, dragged me to the opposite end of the boat and we jumped. The coldness of the water took my breath away; it completely snapped me out of my vodka slump.

"OK?" he asked.

"Yes, just go!" I shouted.

I was terrified, but the fear pushed me to swim as fast as I could.

I turned to see that the boat was following us. "Oh my God, Zack!"

"We need to split up!" Zack shouted. "There's more chance of survival. Everyone break into pairs."

We followed his orders and started to swim in opposite directions. I was sobbing and struggling to catch my breath.

"Keep pushing, baby, it's going to be OK," Zack shouted reassuringly.

A man was shouting from the pirate ship, but I couldn't hear what he was saying.

"What is he shouting?" I said to Zack.

"Doesn't matter, just keep swimming!" he said.

They were gaining on us; of course they followed us rather than anyone else, just our luck!

"What you doing?" I heard a man shout. "Get back in boat, is dangerous!"

"Ignore them, Louise, they are trying to lure us in," Zack said.

We stayed steadfast in our quest.

"Lady, we have petrol!" he shouted.

"Petrol?" I looked at Zack.

"Boat have no petrol; we get petrol!" he shouted, holding up a can.

"What?" I shouted.

"Your boat have no petrol, driver swim to shore to get help, we help!" he replied.

Zack and I looked at each other for a good ten seconds, back to the boat, and back to each other. Treading water, we both howled with laughter.

"What are you doing?" the man asked us. "You crazy!"

"We thought you were pirates!" I mumbled as he pulled me onto the boat.

"Pirates? Why would you think that?" he asked looking genuinely confused.

"Because of the bandanas and the earrings," I whispered, feeling really stupid now.

"Is fashion!" he replied.

"Why didn't the guy who was driving our boat tell us what he was doing? He just jumped in and swam off!" Zack said, clambering on board.

"He no speak English," he replied.

"So, to get this straight," I said to Zack, "we jumped into the ocean to escape from pirates, when in fact the poor guy had swum all the way back to shore to get help and petrol? I feel terrible!"

"I have a feeling that the rest of the group is not going to see the funny side!" Zack said, pointing at them climbing aboard.

They all individually glared at me in complete disdain.

"So, maybe my pirate intel wasn't totally accurate!" I tried to joke.

They did not find this funny.

The ride back to Surat Thani was made in silence. Judging from their faces, I think I preferred that!

Chapter Fifty-One
The Songkran

We were both completely wiped out by the time that we got back to the hostel at seven a.m. When we finally woke up that afternoon, we decided to catch the coach to Phuket. We agreed that it would be better to get a day of hangover and travelling hell done in one fell swoop. First on my to-do list for Phuket was an elephant ride. As soon as we decided that we were coming to Asia, it was all I could talk about. We asked at the hostel reception and they pointed us in the direction of the booking centre five minutes down the road.

"Hello! How may I help you?" said a smiley Thai lady at the booking centre, aka a wooden shack.

I told her that we'd like to book an elephant ride for today.

"OK, you get pick up in thirty minutes from here. Lovely restaurant across the street if you want food while you wait," she advised. "Anything else I can help you with today?"

"No, that's it!" I said, smiling.

"OK," she replied, bending down behind the desk.

I turned back to smile at her, before she picked up a large bucket of water, stood on a chair next to me and chucked it over my head!

"What the hell?" I spluttered.

"What did you do that for?" Zack shouted.

"Because is funny!" she replied, laughing.

Zack and I stared at each other in disbelief. Why would she do that? I don't understand! I could tell that Zack was just about to lose it, just as a pick-up truck full of men drove past us and completely soaked us with water guns! We were literally soaked through to our pants. Zack was jumping around, shouting. I was just standing there with my mouth open. It was like we had woken up in some sort of parallel universe. I looked along the street and saw restaurants and hotels dragging massive vats of water outside their properties with piles of small buckets stacked next to them.

I turned to the lady. "Is this because it is so hot?"

"Because of Songkran!" She smiled.

"I'm sorry, I have no idea what that means."

"Songkran is Thai New Year," she explained.

"But it's April?" I asked confused.

"Yes, our new year is April 13th," she explained. "The water is for purification, a cleansing of your sins and bad luck. Festival lasts for three days."

"So the water throwing will last for three days?" Zack asked.

"Yes," she replied.

"We need to arm up!" Zack said. "Where can we buy water pistols?"

"All shops this time of year. Elephant transport arrive twenty minute. Must hurry!"

Zack was in full Liam Neeson mode: he had 2 pistols tucked into the back of his shorts and a machine gun style pistol strapped across his chest.

"Wow, you're really going to town for this, aren't you?" I laughed.

"Oh, it's game time, Louise! The next punk that wets me is going to get a soaking! Are you going to get a pistol?" he asked.

"I'm too much of a klutz, I'll hurt someone!" I laughed. "I'll just stick to the buckets and throw water at people."

"Louise, get ready!" Zack shouted, getting into position. "There's a load of mopeds coming."

"Ready!" I shouted from the opposite side of the street.

I had filled my bucket and was ready for action.

"Now! Throw it!' Zack shouted.

As they whizzed past, I swung the bucket, but somehow let the whole thing go. My bucket, filled with water, hurtled through the air towards some poor unsuspecting man on a moped. Time seemed to stand still. I ran across the road, desperately trying to intersect it, but it was too late. It smacked him round the head with such force that he went flying off the scooter.

"I'm so sorry! Are you OK? How many fingers am I holding up?" I asked, holding four fingers.

"Dozy bitch! Why would you let go of the bloody bucket? Smacked me right across the chops!" he said, wiggling his jaw around.

Zack came running over; I could see in his face that he was desperately trying not to laugh.

"Are you ok?" Zack shouted.

"Is she with you?" he asked. All twenty stone of bald headed, tattooed man stood up and faced Zack.

"Yeah, she is. Look I'm sorry about that, it was her first attempt. I'm sure she'll get better with practice!" he said, with a twinkle in his eye.

"Practice?" he scoffed. "If I were you, I'd sit this one out, sweetheart!"

He jumped back onto the moped, rubbing his face, and screeched away, the poor bike struggling with the sheer volume of the man.

"Maybe you should just accept that you're going to get wet for three days and there's nothing you can do about it." Zack laughed.

The tuk tuk arrived to take us to the elephant sanctuary shortly after the chaos. We were whizzing through tight spots, dodging trucks with animals on one side and massive vats of water on the other. I was pretty relieved when we got stuck in traffic; my knuckles were white from holding on so tightly. I was giving my hands a rest, taking a breather, when Zack shouted:

"Look out!"

I turned to see about ten young Thai boys racing towards us with water guns.

"Drive, drive, drive!" we were shouting to the driver.

But there was nowhere to go, we were stuck. They jumped into the back and absolutely soaked us. I nearly drowned, I was laughing so hard. Zack was giving it his best shot with retaliation fire, but it was no good, we were outnumbered.

We arrived at the elephant sanctuary dripping wet.

"Happy Songkran!" The guide laughed as he walked over.

"Yeah, you too!" We laughed back, wringing our tops out.

We followed him to a reservoir filled with elephants, all cleaning themselves with their trunks.

"Wow." I sighed.

"They are beautiful, aren't they?" he said proudly.

"They sure are!" Zack replied. "I've never seen anything like this."

"Our sanctuary is pretty special. Come, I introduce you to your elephant."

I was blown away by how peaceful the elephants were; even though they were ginormous, they were so gentle in their approach. Our elephant was called Boon-Mee, which meant 'Lucky' in Thai. We were helped up onto Boon-Mee and he gently walked us around the forest.

After an hour, we were invited to jump off and watch an elephant show. I was a bit worried about this, as I'd heard stories of animals being mistreated in these kinds of environments. However, none of the elephants had any kind of chains or ropes around them and they genuinely seemed to love their carers.

The first part of the show, they asked for volunteers to receive an elephant massage. There was no way that I was going to miss this, so I jumped up and shoved the kids out of the way to go first. I was instructed to lie on the ground, face down. They covered me with a rug and told the elephant to 'massage me.' The elephant lifted his leg and gently patted my back with his foot. It was amazing. When it finished, I asked if they could do Zack.

"End of the show! Special!" He winked at Zack.

The elephants were soaking the audience with their trunks, headbutting balls and even singing… well, ish. When they finished, the ring leader signalled Zack to join them for the grand finale.

They asked him to lie on the floor; he got down and lay on his front like we had done for our massage.

The instructor said, "No, no, other side!"

Zack slowly rolled over onto his back, looking mildly terrified. The instructor quickly threw bananas inside of Zack's board shorts and signalled the elephants. The elephants quickly sniffed out the food and went straight up inside of Zack's shorts, sucking to retrieve the bananas. All I could hear Zack shout was, "I'm not wearing any pants!"

I did what any dutiful girlfriend would have done, and live streamed the whole thing.

The elephant sanctuary was incredible. We spent the day washing the elephants, learning about their habitats and riding them. If it was up to me, we would have never left.

We had to rush back because we had decided to go and see a Ladyboy show. The decadence is something else, they could put shows on the West End to shame!

"So, what do you think?" Zack asked me at half time.

"I think I seriously need to get their plastic surgeon's number! They look unbelievable!" I said with my mouth still gaping open.

"They really do!" Zack said, shovelling his popcorn.

"So, if one of them approached you on a night out, would you?" I asked with a cheeky smile.

"Depends. Are we talking pre or post ding-dong op?" he asked.

"Post," I replied.

"And do I know or not?" he asked, still shovelling.

"Hmm... not!" I reply after consideration.

"That's a tough one," he said seriously. "Well, if a girl approached you in a bar looking like that and you had no clue, you'd be mad not to pursue that!"

I nod.

"However, they are so overly effeminate that I think you'd be able to suss out that they are a ladyboy. In that instance, I'd say no."

"Fair enough!" I said, sipping more of my wine.

"Anyway, I don't need to worry about meeting girls in bars any more as I have my lady," he said, with a gentle kiss.

My legs have gone again.

Chapter Fifty-Two
An Uninvited House Guest!

The coach ride to Kuala Besut took twelve hours, and of course, the air con on the coach was broken. The heat had pretty much reduced us to pools of water by the time that we arrived. Who needs Bikram yoga when you can sweat out a stone by sitting still on a bus?

Besut is a quick pit stop for our transfer over to the Perhentian islands. The islands aren't even on the map, so we have no idea how we are actually going to get there or how long it will take. We find someone at the bus station, who kindly draws us a map on the back of a napkin, showing us how to get to the port where we need to catch a boat to the island. Napkin in hand, we set off on foot, dragging our bags along the forty-minute walk in what feels like a million degrees' heat.

"I think I'm starting to see a mirage!" Zack moaned. "I honestly don't think there's any more fluid left in my body to sweat out."

"According to the napkin map, we should be there in about ten minutes," I reply, dragging myself and my case along. "Just keep pushing."

At the port, we ask several old men with no teeth how we can get to the islands. They all kept pointing in different directions seemingly not understanding us speak the international language - loudly and slowly!

"Screw it, I don't even want to go to the islands anymore!" I moan dropping my bags. "It's too hot, we can just stay here!"

"Wait here, I'll figure it out," Zack replies, walking off.

I slump on top of the bags in the tiny bit of shade that I manage to find.

"Louise, this way! Grab the bags!" Zack shouts, running after a guy.

He cannot be serious; he wants me to carry all of this by myself? As I can no longer see him, I assume that he is! Come on, Louise, you got this! I put one backpack on my back and the other on my front, with Zack's kite surfing bag in one hand and my wheelie case in the other. Ready, steady, go… I try to steady myself but the weight of all the bags pulls me backwards, resulting in me falling ungraciously onto my back with my legs flailing around in the air like an upside-down turtle! Just to make matters worse the toothless men find this beyond hilarious and stand pointing and laughing rather than offering to help me up.

Winging myself from side to side, desperately trying to flip over, I could hear Zack in the distance. "Louise, where are you?"

"Down here!" I shout, with a mouth full of backpack.

"What happened?" Zack says looking down over me.

"The weight pulled me down, and now I can't get up. Old gummy bears over there were no help!" I turn my head to see them wiping laughter tears from their eyes.

Zack peels each bag off me and throws them into a small fishing boat, our personal transport to the island.

We sailed for approximately an hour across the beautifully clear ocean, when eventually we could see some land in the distance. As we got closer I could make out a row of wooden huts, iron barbecues on the beach and a selection of random bean bags and beach chairs scattered throughout.

It was a tropical paradise; the front layer of the island was beach, with forest covering the centre.

The manager ran out to greet us. "Hello, many welcomes! You are Mr and Mrs Dalby, yes?"

"Er, we're not married." Zack laughs awkwardly.

"Oh, sorry!" he replied , throwing his hands to his face. "My mistake. Follow me; I take you to your room."

We follow him along the beach to our room (which was, in fact, a shed) where he opens the door elaborately to show us a mattress on the floor with a mozzie net haphazardly thrown around it.

"What do you think?" he turns to us and asks proudly.

"It's… erm, minimalist! ," replied Zack looking at me with wide eyes.

"And covered in ants!" I add. There was that many it looked as though they were devising a plan to scarper away with the mattress on their backs. "I'm sorry to be rude, but there is no way I can sleep on that. Do you have anything else?"

"I am so sorry, this is totally unacceptable," he said, looking genuinely upset and desperately trying to stamp out the ants. "I give you free upgrade! Follow me."

We trail behind him to another shack where he proudly announces that this one comes complete with an en suite. On further inspection, it looks as though the 'en suite' is in fact a hole in the floor! It was ant-free though, so we took it.

"Hot water on island for two hours a day; you must hurry to showers between five and seven p.m. if you want hot shower. Fresh food is served on the beach daily, straight from the ocean. We hope you enjoy your stay, please come to reception if you have any issues."

"I must say, I feel pretty fancy with this en suite!" I laugh.

"Don't say we don't live the high life!" Zack replied, laughing.

We jump onto the bed, happy to be somewhere cool and semi-comfortable after fifteen hours of travelling. We both quickly start to nod off, when the whole shack rattles, shaking us out of our slumber.

"What the hell was that?" I scream jumping up from the bed.

"Earthquake?" Zack asks .

"It didn't feel like an earthquake." As we were trying to figure out what the hell it was, the floor of the shack started to move slat by slat, like something out of a horror film.

Zack ran outside to investigate.

He slowly reversed back inside and gently closed the door. As he turned to face me, the colour had completely drained from his face.

"What is it?" although, judging from his face, I have a feeling that I really don't want to know.

"It was… the tail… scaly… massive…" he mumbled, shaking his head as though he was trying to un-see what he had just seen.

"Zack, what are you talking about? You're scaring me!" As I asked, the floor started to move again. Zack opens the door and stares silently. I creep past him to see what had made him so shell shocked.

"Jesus Christ!" Zack instantly plasters his hand across my mouth and drags me back inside.

"Shush! We don't know what it can do!" he whispers, visibly shaking.

"The tail! It was about two metres long! What attaches to something that long? Was it an alligator?" I ask, trying to rationalise what I have seen rather than seeking an answer.

"Whatever it is, we need to get the hell out of here!" Zack says.

We freeze for what feels like eternity, waiting for the sound to pass, then when the coast is clear, bolt towards the reception.

"There's some sort of, *thing*, living underneath our hut!" Zack shouts at the man. "What the hell is it?"

"Ah, you have met our neighbour the Komodo dragon," he replied calmly.

"You have a dragon as a neighbour?" I ask incredulously.

"He has lived on the island for many years; he passes under your hut to get to the forest," he explained.

"Then we want to move!" Zack replies.

"Not possible I am afraid, I upgraded you to the last hut," he says, checking his paperwork.

"Is it dangerous?" I ask.

"Not if you don't provoke it!" he said with a smile.

"And how would we provoke it?" I ask, starting to panic.

"Don't make any loud noises or hasty movements whilst he travels underneath you. If you remain calm around him, you should be fine."

"*Should* be fine? Zack said, pacing up and down. "How do we know we'll be safe?"

"He has lived on this island for ten years and has never hurt a living soul. I would be very surprised if he started now. Can I help you with anything else?" he asked, as if we were taking up his precious time with our ridiculous questions.

"This is ridiculous. We can't stay here!" Zack said, stomping back to the hut.

"What can we do? There's only one boat per day and it just left! Look, if this thing hasn't hurt anyone for ten years, then as the guy said, I doubt he'll start now. We just need to be conscious of our movements in the hut,"

"I'm blocking that 'en suite' hole, that's for sure!" he said, stomping off.

I'm so tired and dehydrated, I can hardly keep my eyes open. Dragon or no dragon, I need a nap.

I'm not sure how long I was asleep for when a knock at the door abruptly wakes me.

"Zack? It's unlocked, just push the door."

It banged again. "For God's sake!" I clamber up off the bed and stamp over and swing the door open… only to be met face to face with the Komodo dragon! Oh my god! What do I do? I freeze with fear, not even daring to take a breath. I must have disturbed it by stomping across the floor. All ten feet of it is perfectly still, staring at me, psyching me out.

The man said that if we didn't disturb it then it wouldn't hurt us. I just need to gently close the door and slowly make my way back inside. As I push the door, the rusty old hinges made a massive creaking sound – all that was missing from this picture was a fricking Chucky doll coming to life. The noise startles the dragon and he starts to move towards the hut (I'm assuming it's a he, a woman would never be this terrifying).

I weigh up my options. I wasn't about to test how quickly this thing could move. I glance behind me and see an open window at the back of the hut. If I slam the door shut, I reckon it will take me between three and five seconds to run across the room, jump through the window and pelt it out the other end.

He takes another step closer.

OK, it's now or never Louise. I slam the door shut, pull down the chain and race to the back hut. I quickly glance behind me; no dragon, I push myself through the window and run as fast as my legs will carry me, smacking straight into Zack.

"The dragon, it was coming into the hut!" I scream clutching onto him.

"What? What happened?" he asked with wide eyes.

"I jumped out of the window!" I pant, holding onto my knees for breath.

"Is it in the hut?" he asked in a panic.

"I didn't stick around to find out! I look down to see that Zack is holding a fishing net, beach towels and masking tape. "What's that for?"

"Dragon hole plug!" he replies seriously, looking past me and eying up the hut.

"Well, there's no sign of damage," Zack says, feeling his way around the hut door. "Unless he walked up to the door, removed the chain and shut the door behind him, I think we can safely say that he's not inside!"

"You go first, just in case," I said, pushing him from behind.

"Why me?" he asks.

"Harder to chew!" I reply, giving him another shove with my foot.

Zack leaps inside, shouting "Ah ha!" as though he was expecting to bust the dragon sitting with a cuppa and reading the paper.

"Clear!" he shouts in military mode.

I slowly walk in behind him, scoping out the perimeter. "Zack, I'm never going to sleep now that I've seen him. He's got at least four foot on us, he'll eat us alive!"

"That's why I have this kit!" he says, on his knees by the 'en suite'. "He'll never get through by the time I'm finished."

The only barrier between me and a ten foot reptile with razor sharp teeth is towels and a net. Perfect!

He stuffed the hole with towels, placed the net over the top and sealed it with masking tape.

"There!" he announced proudly. "Feel better?"

"Oh yeah, much!" I replied sarcastically. He clearly took this as appreciation and kissed my head.

I can't stay inside the hut any longer, it's giving me the willies so we walk over to the local café. The owner tells us that he is expecting a fresh batch of fish in the next ten minutes or so; their hunters were currently knee deep in the ocean, holding spears. They stand perfectly still with a spear poised above their heads, then, when the time is right, they launch with perfect speed and agility, catching the fish and bringing them back to the beach where they throw them onto a barbeque. You don't get much fresher than that!

"So, what do you want to do for your birthday tomorrow?" Zack asked. "I can put my birthday suit on for you?"

"I'm scared that the dragon will turn up in his birthday suit!" I reply, laughing.

"That is a slightly terrifying thought." He shakes his head. "I do have an idea if you're happy to just go with it?"

"Depends. What's the idea?" I ask sceptically.

"You'll have to wait and see!" He winked.

Hmm, not sure I like the sound of this!

Full of seafood, we stagger back to the hut, forgetting our fears, and pretty much pass out straight away. I fell asleep, clutching my hair spray, and Zack had his flip flop; that dragon had better watch his step!

Chapter Fifty-Three
Fooling Around in the Sack

"Morning, birthday girl! How did you sleep?" Zack asked, pulling me into him.

"Really well, actually. I didn't hear the dragon, did you?" I ask, stretching.

"No, but I had a word, told him it was your birthday today. He understood, said he'd give us the day off!" he replied cheekily.

"Hope you have that in writing!"

"It's a verbal agreement, we're all good!" He laughed.

Sitting outside the café, staring out to sea, lost in the beauty of the island, I hear singing from behind me. I turn to see the staff singing happy birthday to me, with one of them playing an accordion. They hand me a plate of birthday pancakes with candles scattered across them.

"Make special birthday wish!" a lady shouts.

I blow the candles out and make my wish that Zack will come back to the UK with me.

They cheer and even gave me my pancakes on the house.

"Why don't you go for a quick shower and I'll meet you back at the beach in half an hour for your surprise?" Zack says putting his knife and fork back onto his plate.

Nothing like a freezing cold shower to kickstart your day! Jesus. Even in the forty degree heat, it takes your breath away. I have no idea what Zack is planning; therefore, I have no clue what to wear. I'm assuming that the only option for an island is a boat tour. I'll wear my bikini with a beach dress, oversized sunglasses, big hat and a statement necklace. Very beach glam. I want some great pics of us out on the (I'm assuming) yacht for my birthday. I add a bit of lip gloss to finish it off - perfect!

I stroll across the beach to meet Zack, who is standing next to a row of cones and sacks. "What's all this?" I ask, desperately trying to figure out what all of this has to do with a yacht.

"Beach Olympics!" he replies, full of excitement.

"Beach Olympics?" Not quite the elegant day I had imagined.

"I've rounded up all of these people!" He points to about twenty people behind him, who look as confused by my outfit as I am by Zack's choice of birthday surprise.

"We have the sack race, egg and spoon race, cones for sprints, and sticks for dizzy bat," he exclaims looking really proud of himself.

"Dizzy bat?" What fresh hell is that?

"It's where you put your head on the stick, and spin round and round," he said, clearly very excited about all of this.

"Wow, you... shouldn't have!" I manage to say, forcing a smile.

"Anything for you, you know that!" He replied with his killer smile. "Oh, did I mention that you'll be doing all of this whilst downing shots?"

"Shots? It's eleven in the morning!"

"We're on holiday! It's not a problem if you drink early on holiday," he explained seriously.

It is very sweet of him to arrange this for me. I need to get into the spirit and embrace it. I pull off my hat, dress and necklace, and strip down to my bikini. Definitely no glam required for this surprise!

"Not what you were expecting, hey?" a girl next to me asked.

"Er, not quite." I laugh. "The shots should definitely help get me through it, though!"

"I'm Amanda," she introduced herself. "We've been here for a few days. What about you?"

"Louise. We got here yesterday. It's been amazing, apart from the giant lizard that's living under our hut!"

"We've seen that! It's humongous! How did you sleep with that thing underneath you?" she asked, shaking her head.

"Zack filled up the hole with towels and masking tape – don't ask!" I laugh.

"Come on girls, less chitter chatter, let's do this!" Zack shouts.

Organised fun, my favourite!

Zack splits us into two teams: the red team (my team) and the blue team. Even people who weren't involved came over to cheer us on. The restaurant owner had brought a table onto the beach with cocktails and the DJ had woken up early to provide music. I must admit, Zack has pulled this out of the bag.

First up was the egg and spoon race. Needless to say, I was horrendous. I ended up with egg between my toes and a tequila shot. Zack was a tough task master; he was screaming at everyone to be 'on top of their game!' He was less than impressed that I stepped out to wash the egg from between my toes in the sea.

"Louise, get back here! There's no time to be a pansy!" he shrieked.

Next was the sack race. The whistle blew and we were off. I am actually doing pretty well; I'm much quicker than I thought I'd be. I'm overtaking on the inside, climbing towards first place; I just have one guy in my way, there's no way I am letting him win on my birthday! I run along next to him and bump him out of the way. My team are jumping up and down cheering as I sore through the finish line! Although my victory is short-lived as Zack makes us all do a penalty shots for cheating. I pleaded for a pass as it's my birthday, but he's having none of it.

We had relay races, swimming races, even a weird version of tag. Zack had us all run ragged and slightly wobbly.

"OK, folks, final event of the day: dizzy stick!" he announces proudly. "You start the game by taking a shot from the table, you then run to the stick and place your hand firmly over one end." He motions for us all to copy him. "Bend down and put your forehead onto the back of your hand. This is very important! Do not put your head directly onto the stick or you could poke your eye out! Next, you spin around the stick five times, drop the stick and run between the cones to the end. Tag your teammate to start their turn. The team that completes the challenge first is the winner. All clear?"

"Yes, sir!" everyone jokingly shouted.

"DJ ready?"

The DJ counts us down. "Five, four, three, two, one, let the games commence!" he shouts into the mic.

I was first. I knock my shot back and run into the centre. OK, hand on the stick, head on hand, go! My team is counting down my spins, on my last spin I run towards the cones, or at least I tried to... my legs however have their own agenda and pull me in the opposite direction dragging me towards the ocean. I'm so dizzy, I fall hard onto the sand. "Come on Louise!" my team are screaming. I pull myself up, feeling like a phoenix rising from the ashes and stumble back towards the cones, desperately trying to pick up the pace, zigzagging towards my team.

I tag the next person in. "Did I beat them?" I ask, still seeing circles.

"Only just, it was tight!" Amanda replies. "We seriously need to pick up the pace."

My whole team have turned into Olympic coaches.

We're down to the last three. It's was neck and neck, the pressure is on.

"Come on, you reds!" I was screaming at the top of my lungs.

We have a man down: Amanda had thrown up all down her front. Maybe drinking from eleven a.m. isn't such a great idea!

"Get up!" everyone is screaming at her. All credit to her, she pulls herself up and drags herself through to the end. But it was too late, that was all the advantage the blue team needed to win. We have lost! The blue team was crowned heroes and received bags of sweets from the local shop.

It suddenly dawns on me that Zack has managed to avoid all of the boozing and is stone cold sober. I'm not having that! I stagger up to the DJ booth and grab the mic.

"Hi, guys! Birthday girl Louise here!" Everybody screams in response ; I feel like Beyoncé! It was all I could do not to spring into a dance routine. "It has just come to my attention that our slave driving taskmaster has walked away from this scot free! He hasn't had one sip of tequila!"

"Ooooohhh!" everybody gasped.

"I think we should rectify this situation, what do you think?" I held my mic out to screams. "The crowd has spoken Zack; get your ass up here!"

Laughing, he made his way to the stage. "OK, what's my punishment?"

"Well, we did six events, so I think you should do six shots of tequila followed by your little stick game! What do you all think?" The crowd screamed. "I think that's a yes, let's set it up!"

We cleared a space for Zack. The restaurant lined up six shots of tequila whilst the team set up the cones.

"OK, Zack, let's see what you can do!" the DJ said. "Three, two, one, go!"

Zack knocks back the shots one at a time. His face is a picture. He runs to the stick and does his five spins. By the fifth spin, he lands on the floor and is crawling to the cones.

"Now is not the time to be a pansy, Zack!" I shout into the mic.

I can see him laughing. He gets up and staggers his way through the cones, collapsing at the other end to loud cheers.

"OK, now we can party!" I shout to the crowd.

The DJ cranked up the music and the beach came alive.

I pushed through the crowd to get to Zack.

"Thanks for an amazing birthday," I say, kissing him. "It wasn't quite what I was expecting, but I'll never forget it!"

"I look forward to many more!" he said, kissing me back. "Fancy a walk?"

We strolled along the beach, hand in hand, with our feet in the water. I was doing everything I could to catalogue this image; I needed to hold onto this very moment.

"Let's sit," Zack said, pulling me down. "After six shots of tequila, I think I'm brave enough to have this conversation."

Oh God, I'm not sure if I'm brave enough to hear it.

"Louise, I had never planned to go back to the UK," he said, looking at me intently.

The bombshell had dropped. There it is, he said it. This is the end. I tried to choke back my tears.

"Until I met you," he finished.

I turned to look at him.

"Louise, if you can't stay in Australia, then I'll come back with you," he said, looking at my hands.

It took me a minute to gather my thoughts.

"But is this what you want? In a few years' time, will you look back and resent me for bringing you home?" I asked.

He sat for a minute, looking out to the water.

"I never planned on going back to the UK because there was nothing there for me. If you're there, then that's where I want to be," he said, looking into my eyes. "Louise, I love you."

I took a sharp inhalation of breath. Oh my God, he said it! He actually said it! I'm not a crazy person, he feels it too.

"Oh Zack, I love you too!" I grabbed him and kissed him.

I couldn't help it; tears were streaming down my face.

"Hey, why are you crying?" he asked, wiping my tears away.

"I'm just so happy!" I said, blubbering.

I am overwhelmed with emotion; I could scream at the top of my lungs and burst with happiness. But I had a niggle. I needed to know that this was really what he wanted and not the tequila talking.

"Seriously, Zack, I want this to work more than anything in the whole entire world, but I need you to be a hundred percent sure that you want to come back with me. To real life. No more sunshine, or tans, or aimlessly travelling; it will be real, gritty life. Are you sure that's what you want?"

He paused for a moment, really mulling this over. "I'm all in, Louise. I want you, I want us. I want to be wherever you are, forever."

My heart exploded.

"So the next thing we need to decide is, where's the first stop? London or Manchester?" he asked.

"You're coming to the UK for me; I can come to London for you," I said, kissing him.

"Really? Are you sure?" he asked, with that killer smile.

"A hundred percent!"

As we started to walk back, I stopped him and stood in front of him.

"I've played this moment over and over in my head a thousand times! To make sure this actually just happened and I'm not totally losing my mind, will you say it again?" I asked coyly.

"Say what again?" he asked cheekily.

I gave him my 'don't mess with me' look.

"Louise Johnson, I love you. I love your laugh, your smile, your sense of humour. Although it is completely ridiculous, I love the face you make when you smell something bad, I love your little strops that you throw when things don't go your way. I love the bones off you! Is that enough?"

That was more than enough. It was everything.

Chapter Fifty-Four
We're Coming Home!

Now that the decision had been made, I need to tell my parents. I have to handle this carefully as I need to drop the bombshell that not only am I coming back with Zack in tow, I am also moving to London. This should be interesting!

The phone signal is hit and miss; even the payphones rarely stay connected. I could either wait until we were on the mainland a day prior to flying home, or I could email them now. This is not the kind of thing that I wanted to tell them over email, but it was the best chance that I had to tell them the full story without getting cut off by the phone or their mad ramblings.

I logged on in the internet café and saw that I already had an email from Mum:

Hi Louise, it's your mum.

Hope you still have your head intact after your trip across the pirate sea! (LAUGH OUT LOUD).

You won't BELIEVE what has been going on here. You remember that lady I told you about (brown hair, big sunglasses, looking mysterious in the parked car). Well, the day after she sped off down the road, there was a knock at the door. I shouted to your father that I would get it (as he was on the loo). I opened the door and there she was, clear as day! I thought she had come to put 'a hit on me' as I had 'made her'.

"What do you want?" I ask. "I know you're sleeping with my husband," she says. Can you believe it? "Unless your husband is doing his business in my toilet upstairs, I very much doubt it," I said. "Don't lie to me!" she says. Just then your father comes out of the loo. "Come here, Frank," I shout. He walks down the stairs doing his flies up and says, "Who's this?" "Your wife is having an affair with my husband," says the woman. Well, your father creases up laughing! He was slapping his thighs, tears rolling down his face, belly laughing. Silly fool!

When he finally comes round, he says, "I think you've got the wrong house, love." She says her 'intel' told her it was this house! (Intel! I ask you, who the hell does she think she is?) "Well, your intel has gone to shite," I tell her! I was just about to send her packing when your father invites her in for choccie biscuits! (Choccie biscuits, I ask you!) I said that no one would be eating choccie biscuits in this house today, including your father, and shut the door.

I'm going to put your father on a rations diet for laughing at me. Silly sod, I could have an affair if I wanted. The man in the local shop always gives me a free chocolate bar with the Sunday paper.

Anyway, hope you are still having fun with Hot Boomerang Guy. Make sure you give us notice for when you are coming home.

Love, Mum

I quickly type a reply:

Hi Mum,

Of course you could have an affair if you wanted to, sounds like Dad should watch out for the guy from the corner shop. Free chocolate bars are saucy stuff!

Anyway, I have some news. Zack and I are flying back to Heathrow in a few days. That's right, we're coming back together! I'm so excited, Mum, I can't wait for you and Dad to meet him! Ideally, I didn't want to tell you this over email, but we're on an island and the phone reception is pretty shoddy, so here goes: we're moving to London! I know it seems like a big step, but Zack is coming back to the UK for me and the least I can do is move to the area that he wants to live in. You and Dad both love London, so it will give you an excuse to come and visit all the time!

We'll come and see you when we come back. We arrive at Heathrow on Thursday and then we were thinking of driving up to you on the Saturday. Is that OK? You can do the 'surprise' party on Saturday night. I promise to act shocked!

Love you, and see you soon.

Upon returning to our 'luxury' hut, Zack asks, "So, how did it go? Did you tell them?"

"The phone reception is terrible so I told them over email. Not ideal, but it'll give them time to freak out and then come back with a positive response!" I laugh. "Did you ask your parents about picking us up from the airport?"

"Yep, emailed as well. I'm sure it will be fine," he said, hugging me.

"Zack, I'm so nervous, we're meeting each other's parents!"

"I know! We've got to come out of our bubble and let other people in; not sure how I feel about this!" He laughed.

"Me neither! Better make the most of it while we can!"

We spent our last day on the island soaking up the sun, the fresh food and each other. I'd had such an amazing trip; I really didn't want it to come to an end.

However, the lack of funds in the old bank account was making it pretty impossible to stay. Maybe we could stay here and sell coconuts? I'd checked with the hostel and that was out of the question, apparently the coconut trees had that niche covered. I floated the idea of sunbed cash collectors, fishermen and waiters, but apparently they were all set. You can't blame a girl for trying!

We fell asleep one last time in our bubble of bliss, before the chaos of Kuala Lumpur and real life smacked us in the face. We'd gotten to know everyone on the beach so well after my birthday Beach Olympics that it had turned into Little House on the Prairie in the evening, with each hut shouting goodnight to each other. The dragon even popped in to say his goodbyes. We weren't scared anymore; we had built a connection.

"Goodnight, beautiful island!" Zack sighed as he fell asleep.

Chapter Fifty-Five
Malaysia on Speed

We rose nice and early to catch the once a day boat back to the mainland, which meant that we had to have an ice cold shower first thing in the morning. "My boys are shrinking!" I heard Zack shout from the men's. Yep, it was cold.

We thanked the staff for being an absolute pleasure and chucked our bags onto the little speedboat. As we sped off, tears were prickling my eyes. I caught Zack quickly wiping his eyes too.

Back at the port in Kuala Besut, the old toothless men were exactly where we had left them. I wonder if they ever go home? We had to walk for forty minutes back to the main station to hop on a train to Kuala Lumpur. There were no signs in English and the staff could only understand very few words. I found myself doing that really awkward 'Brit speaking to a foreigner thing', aka speaking loudly and slowly. We ended up with two tickets to somewhere; I'm just praying that it was Kuala Lumpur.

Luckily, the ticket inspector on the train spoke a little English and confirmed that we were in fact on the correct train for Kuala Lumpur. He even kindly said that he would come and let us know when we needed to get off. I'm really going to miss the Asian hospitality!

We didn't manage to get two seats next to each other, so had to sit separately. Zack was under a broken air vent spraying out freezing cold air and I was shoved into the centre of six sweaty people with no air con. Every time we switched seats, people seemed to huddle into us to get closer to our cool skin.

There was a little girl sitting in front of the broken air con. She couldn't speak English, but was desperate to try. Every time we said something she repeated it. I taught her how to say 'my name is' with a space for her to tell me her name. She clearly didn't understand so I completed the sentence 'my name is Louise', pointing to myself. It didn't quite work out; there is now a little Malaysian girl introducing herself to everyone on the train as Louise.

Four hours later, we arrive in the central business district of Kuala Lumpur. As we had come straight from an island, it was safe to say that we stuck out like a sore thumb. On the plus side, it made it easier to spot each other. Every time I lost Zack, I would look through a sea of black suits and spot his pink vest and bright yellow shorts.

As it was our last night as official nomads, we treated ourselves to a luxury hotel. After the shack, anything would have looked good, but this really was exquisite. I actually felt guilty arriving sweaty and covered in sand. We asked at reception for a recommendation on the best way to spend our one day in Kuala Lumpur. She advised us to eat. We were in luck; this was something at which we were already very accomplished.

After a quick shower, we were out the door, although I'm not sure why we bothered as Kuala Lumpur has really thick humidity. Coupled with the fumes from the bumper to bumper traffic, it made you feel like you couldn't breathe and my hair was back to the 80s frizz.

At one point, I was actually contemplating buying brightly coloured leggings, a leotard and a sweatband, and styling it out.

We decided to go to a different restaurant for every course to make as much of an occasion of this as possible in the few hours that we had. Our starter was at an Asian fusion restaurant for an exotic take on sushi. Our main course was from a Malaysian palace-style restaurant; it was traditional Thai food with a Malaysian twist. Finally, dessert was from a street vendor in the market, a slice of chocolaty heaven!

After living on fresh fish and fruit picked straight from the trees in the Perhentian islands, my stomach was ready to burst. We were staggering back to the hotel with a stomach full of grub when Zack spots a karaoke bar.

"Come on, Louise, we have to! It's our last night in Asia, we have to do it in style!" Zack begged.

"Style I agree with, not sure where a karaoke bar features in that!" I laughed.

"Come on! Please!" he said with that smile which he knows I can't resist.

"OK, two songs max!" I said laying down the law.

"Five!" he bartered. "And I'll book us a couple of massages at the hotel before we leave tomorrow morning."

"Deal!"

We shook on it.

Needless to say, at around four a.m., swaying around to 'I Got You, Babe', we went a little over five songs. We took a quick detour to the market to stock up on dessert and stumbled back to the hotel.

"Tonight has been the best night ever! I love karaoke!" Zack slurred as we flopped into bed. "Louise, I love you so much! We are going to be together forever!"

He managed to hiccup just before he passed out with a plate of waffles on his chest. I carefully moved the waffles, tucked him into bed, and set my alarm for four hours' time. Ugh, this was going to hurt tomorrow!

Chapter Fifty-Five
Welcome Back to the UK

My alarm screamed at us at nine a.m., rattling around the contents of my brain. I shrieked and Zack fell out of bed. It was going to be a long day.

"What day is it?" Zack asked.

"Monday, we're flying home today," I said, hiding my face in the pillow.

"Nooooooooo!"

My sentiments exactly.

We had to quickly check our emails to make sure that both sets of parents had got our messages. Zack checked first whilst I was in the shower. Halfway through, he came racing in.

"What's wrong? What happened?" I asked.

He bolted straight past the shower and chucked up, just about making it to the loo.

"Ugh, beautiful!" I moaned.

"Hey, you can't say anything! I have dealt with disaster after disaster with your foof and toilet issues," he replied.

Touché!

"This flight is going to be disgusting," Zack said wiping his mouth.

"So, are your parents OK to pick us up?" I asked, once he'd stopped throwing up.

"Yep, all sorted!"

Zack jumped into the shower as I was getting out.

"Are you sure you can't stay in for a bit?" he said, going in for a kiss.

"As hot as it was watching you chuck up next to me, I'm strangely not in the mood!" I laughed.

I jumped onto the bed and checked my emails. I'd had a reply from my mum.

Hi Louise, it's your mum.

We're glad that Hot Potato Man is coming back with you. I showed a picture of him to Auntie Cathy, she said she wanted two tickets to the gun show, whatever that means! Your nan is back to making a cake, so don't worry, it will be ready for the 'surprise' party on Saturday. I have hired the local village hall; everyone is talking about it. I'm not inviting all of the curtain twitchers, though. I'll see who offers to make cake and invite them on a food by food basis.

We understand about you moving to London. (Hi, Louise, it's Dad. I don't understand.) Ignore him, silly sod! We have to accept that you are with Hot Shot Man and you need to make your own decisions. Just don't forget little old us when you are in the Big Smoke.

Have a safe flight home, don't forget your aspirin and flight socks for deep vein thrombosis, it's a silent killer!

Love, Mum.

PS – It's minus three degrees here and snowing! Hope they sell woolly jumpers in Kuala Lumpur (Hashtag LAUGH OUT LOUD).

The cab arrived to take us to the airport. I really wished that there was some way we could stay, but scraping together our funds just about got us back onto British soil. As I was the reason that we were having to go back, I felt really guilty about feeling sad. Every time I thought that I was going to cry, I tried to disguise it as a yawn and twisted my face into some weird contortionist position. I was pretty sure that Zack hadn't noticed though, so it was OK.

"What's up with your face?"

Or not.

"Nothing, just yawning. Looking forward to going home!" I announced in a ridiculous overly chipper voice. "The good old British countryside and… country air and… cows." I trailed off.

"Louise, are you OK?" he asked, looking like he may have to call the men in white coats.

"Me?" I exclaimed. "I'm fine! In fact, I'm great! It's you I'm worried about, I'm over here excited about our future and you're over there being Mr Negative, being grumbly and… stuff." He'll never see through this, my emotions are locked down like Fort Knox.

"OK, what's really going on?" he asked, staring me out. "Are you freaking out about going home?"

"No," I said, picking at a piece of fluff and refusing to meet his gaze. "I'll take that as a firm yes!" He laughed. "Louise, look. It is going to feel weird at first, but we'll soon settle into it. We have each other and that's all that matters," he said, squeezing my hand. "At least we're going back in April and not winter! Can you imagine how depressing it would be to land in the freezing bloody cold!"

It was too much; I could no longer hold my steely façade. Blubbering, I broke down and whined, "It's minus three degrees!"

"Minus three degrees? Don't be daft!" Zack laughed, pulling me into him. "Louise, look at me. You're hyperventilating and being ridiculous, there is no way that it is minus three degrees in April!"

I silently nodded at him.

"Oh God, is it really?" he sighed. "OK, well, it's still fine, I'm sure they will sell jumpers at the airport."

I wiped my snotty nose and paid the cabby, I bet he was happy that he couldn't speak English, so he didn't have to deal with my crap! We checked in and went through to the shops. Operation sort out hangover and buy something warm was in motion.

"Louise, look!" Zack pointed.

I turned to see a sign saying 'Fried English Food' in all of its glory. Hallelujah, we are saved!

We bolted in and ordered everything fried on the menu with our last bit of Malaysian ringgit.

"This is going to be the best thing we have ever eaten!" said Zack, loosening his boardies in preparation.

The food arrived and it was, well, I guess it could have been fried English food, if the food was Alsatian and pigeon.

"Ugh, this is gross!" I said, subtly spitting it out into my napkin.

"What the hell is it?" Zack said, poking the flat processed meat on his plate.

"I really don't think we should eat any more to find out!" I said, lifting up something that looked like corn beef hash but smelled like mouldy cheese. "I can't contend with a hangover and food poisoning on a fifteen hour flight!"

"Yeah, you're right, let's grab something to eat on the plane and try and find some warm clothes."

Nobody, and I mean nobody, sells warm clothes in Kuala Lumpur airport.

"We're going to have to get something, we'll freeze!" said Zack.

"Can't we ask your parents to bring big coats and come into the airport?" I asked.

"Good shout, I'll jump online and email them now."

We rushed around the shops and grabbed an airplane friendly meal of chicken fried rice, M&M's and copious amounts of water. Thankfully, the plane wasn't that busy, so we had three seats and dumped all of our crap in the middle section. As the plane set off, I reached over and held Zack's hand and reflected on how far I had come during my time away. I boarded the plane to Australia alone and terrified, met some of my best friends, and now I am flying home with the man of my dreams.

Four in flight movies, five games of twenty questions, one attempt at the mile-high club (well, we opened the toilet door and realised that we'd never both fit in there), and two sleeps later, we had finally made it back onto British soil. It was two a.m. local time and, fudge me, it was cold!

As soon as the cabin door opened, the blast of cold air made everyone stand to attention. All of the super organised people were pulling their winter coats out of their in-flight bags, whilst we stood shivering in our shorts and vests.

We ran through passport control, jiggling from one foot to the other, to the luggage collection. I grabbed Zack's hand as we walked out to a sea of people in arrivals. I hadn't even seen a picture of Zack's parents so I didn't know what to look for. I'm so nervous, what if they hate me? What if I'm nothing like they expected!

Plastering on a big smile on my face, I clutch onto Zack's hand and crazy smile at everyone who walks past me.

"Where are they?" I ask Zack as the crowd starts to thin.

"They must be parking the car," Zack said. "I'll give them a quick call...

Hmm, that's strange, it went straight to voicemail."

"Maybe there's no signal in the car park?" I suggested.

"Yeah, maybe, I'm sure they'll be here soon."

A quarter of an hour passed and there was still no sign of them.

"Try the landline," I suggest.

"Straight to voicemail again," Zack said, looking concerned.

"You definitely told them the right date, didn't you?" I asked.

"Of course I did, I'm not a moron!" he scoffed.

"Just quickly check the email on your phone," I said violently shaking, feeling like pneumonia was taking over my body.

"Shit," Zack said, rubbing his head.

"What? Don't tell me it's the wrong date?" I can't take it!

"I told them two a.m. on the eighth. It would have been the eighth in Asian time when I calculated how long the flight was, but I forgot about the time difference; it's the seventh," he said, slumping down onto a bench.

"Try calling them again!" I said desperately.

He called and called, but there was no answer.

"OK, it's two a.m.; all of the shops are closed so we can't even buy any warm clothes. What are our options?" I asked, ripping my case open and throwing every item of clothing on that crossed my path. My lips were turning an on-trend shade of blue.

"We need to see if we can get enough cash together for a hotel," he said, calling and calling his parents.

I tried all of my cards; I had about twenty pounds in total.

"Give me yours; I'll try while you're on the phone."

Nothing.

"What about your parents? Could you call them and ask them to transfer some cash?" Zack asked.

"They don't do online banking; Dad says it's a gateway for terrorists! Transport doesn't start to run until six thirty a.m. We're stranded!" I can't believe this is happening. We pulled everything slightly warm out of our cases, including beach towels, and snuggled up like a couple of tramps on the airport floor.

"Well, I've left my parents approximately a billion messages; we'll just have to wait until they wake up and check their phones tomorrow. I'm so sorry, babe," he said, pulling me into him.

The situation was so dire that there was nothing else to do but laugh. I started with a little giggle that rippled through my body. As I looked at Zack, his shoulders started to shudder. Before we knew it, we were in an absolute heap, crying with laughter on the airport floor.

"It's not exactly what I had in mind, but welcome back to the UK!" I said, with tears running down my face.

"If I had to sleep on the airport floor with anyone, I'm glad it was you!" he said, pulling my chin up to kiss me.

"I love you, Hot Breakfast Guy!"

"And I love you, Louise Johnson!"